Edenhope

Louise Le Nay studied dramatic art at NIDA, and has worked as an actor in films, TV and theatre, and as a TV writer and script editor. She has also taught professional writing and editing at various tertiary institutions. She lives with her husband in western Victoria.

Louise
Le Nay
Edenhope

TEXT PUBLISHING MELBOURNE AUSTRALIA

The Text Publishing Company acknowledges the Traditional Owners of the country on which we work, the Wurundjeri people of the Kulin Nation, and pays respect to their Elders past and present.

textpublishing.com.au

The Text Publishing Company
Wurundjeri Country, Level 6, Royal Bank Chambers, 287 Collins Street, Melbourne Victoria 3000 Australia

Published by The Text Publishing Company, 2024

Book design by Imogen Stubbs
Cover photograph by Matthew Spaulding/Stocksy
Typeset by J&M Typesetting

Printed and bound in Australia by Griffin Press, a member of the Opus Group. The Opus Group is ISO/NZS 14001:2004 Environmental Management System certified.

ISBN: 9781923058071 (paperback)
ISBN: 9781923059078 (ebook)

A catalogue record for this book is available from the National Library of Australia.

To my sister, Marie-Hélène Turnbull

JANUARY 1977

When she was eighteen, Marnie met a man in a bizarre way.

She used to tell the story at parties in her twenties and thirties. How a total stranger stopped her one day and told her not to kill herself. She even built it up a bit, allowing a hint of sexual tension to creep in. How did you feel, people said. Stunned, she told them. It was a word that was in daily use back then. Everyone was always being stunned about something.

Truthfully, at the time of the meeting she didn't think or feel anything much. Perhaps embarrassed for a second because she thought it was a mistake. And, yes, wasn't there a flutter in the tips of her fingers and her insteps, a faint warning? Marnie was middle-aged before she even considered the mechanics of that meeting. She looked up the word 'bizarre' to see if it fitted. It did.

The important thing was—and this was not part of the story she told—meeting Heath Woolley changed her. At eighteen there is no part of your barely developed sense of self that believes a chance event will count for something. By sixty, though, Marnie could see the meeting in context with the roadmap of her life. And it was crucial. It was a junction. It was where possibilities branched, mingled and propelled into the void.

Pity, she thought, that she never recognised it at the time.

1

JANUARY 2022

Marnie's new job was at Treen's. It was a discount shop: officially Treen's Bargain Variety Store. The window display was a garish mess of rubber gloves and dusters, stuffed toys, candlesticks, picture frames and fake flowers. It had been Marnie's plan to look for office work but she was passing Treen's and she clocked the A4 sign—as well as, let's face it, the explosion of colour—and went inside without hesitating. The shop was three narrow aisles jammed with random goods and an underlying scent of mothballs. The woman behind the counter was Treen, actually spelled Trinh, Marnie discovered, who was the grandmother of the owner. She said, 'My granddaughter will phone you about police check but better start now. I have to get the kids back from holiday program at four. After, I'll come back, show you how to reconcile the till. When you're okay with it, you can close up for me every weekday.'

A ratification of the offer was required. Marnie figured

on-the-spot employment was not something she could count on at her age, so she said yes. She hadn't even unpacked yet but what the hell, she could do that after work. It also assuaged the feeling that had been sitting like an undigested sandwich behind her sternum: a nagging guilt about lying to her new landlord regarding her employment status. Oh God, was she getting weak? Anyway, here was a fix for it. She put her bag behind the counter and stood beside Trinh for the rest of the day, learning the ropes. When she left the shop, she had a box of face masks out of the Going-Going-Gone display, a notebook and biro, and a housewarming gift from Trinh—a small muscular ox with a nodding head from the previous Chinese New Year. 'No one wants it,' Trinh said. 'All tigers now.'

The ceramic ox, red and gold, stood beside three photographs of Marnie's grandchildren on the windowsill above the sink in her new flat. They had advertised it as a granny flat in the real-estate office, suitable for *one* occupant only, *no* pets. 'Don't expect too much,' they might have added, but didn't. The girl behind the desk had teal hair extensions and regarded Marnie with a look that meant: 'Yeah, that fits.'

The granny flat was in the backyard of a weatherboard house, the type that extruded like mushrooms in the fifties when this part of Melbourne was the backblocks on the edge of the Keilor plains. When Marnie walked up the driveway on her first (only) inspection, she saw a twisted plum tree with craggy limbs and light green leaves in front of a wall of mismatched windows.

The landlord explained as she signed the lease that it had been a sleepout for his older brothers. He was courteous, commenting that he felt pretty upbeat about the arrangement. She said, 'That's good,' and added: 'Me too,' which was her second lie, as she had already by this stage lied about the job, and was relying on him being too courteous to ask for proof. He was a neat dresser, boyish in manner despite being only ten years or so younger than her. He didn't seem to have a wife or partner. He had grown up in the house with his two brothers and sister. Took a tram to the city every morning to work, went to the footy on the weekends and coached under-tens cricket over summer. She thought she might come to dislike him but didn't know why.

Originally, the sleepout had been a single room with bunks, separated from the laundry and outside toilet. Now the buildings were joined together, so that at one end of the room there was a small bathroom and toilet behind a thin wall, and at the other end was a sink and a stove connected by a bench topped with brown-flecked Formica, possibly put by when the kitchen in the main house was renovated in the seventies—the mission-brown phase. In a corner of the kitchen area was a new all-purpose cupboard. It had a wall of sliding wire shelves that the landlord demonstrated to her with barely concealed pride. It would not take heavy things, he cautioned, but you could see everything at a glance. The floor, also new, was vinyl styled as floorboards. Butted up to a front window was a small preloved Ikea table and three chairs. Against the back wall was a cheap two-seater beneath a split-system wall heater and further along the same wall, looking straight out through

5

the windows, was a double bed (old) with a new mattress, still wrapped in plastic.

'No dishwasher,' he said.

'That's fine.'

'When I researched, it said it would put people off.'

'A dishwasher?'

'Not having one.'

He seemed to be after reassurance. She said, 'It isn't a problem.' Then she added, because she sensed he needed more, 'I love the light, it's a light place. I like that.'

He explained about the windows. His father had been a concreter, always around demolition sites and new builds. He brought piles of stuff home, beautiful light fittings, fretwork from old verandas, these windows. Back in the sixties, no one wanted old stuff. The landlord made a point of singling out the high centre window. It depicted a galleon in full sail.

He asked about her family and she disclosed appropriate details. That she was divorced, had one daughter and three grandchildren, all interstate.

He answered, as if suddenly remembering, 'There's no TV. My sister said you'd watch on your iPad.'

She said she was fine without a TV. She was fine—she'd said it how many times? It was his neediness, she realised, that she might come to dislike, and resolved to be careful with his feelings: never offhand or impatient. She made a mental note, too, to be ready for the sister who clearly looked out for him.

They shook hands. She said, 'Thank you, Mr Russo,' and he said, 'Call me Vincent.' Then she was alone in her new flat with sun slanting through the leaves of the plum tree, spearing colours out of the four mismatched windows and making them jig on the floor.

She already loved the windows. Of course she had seen the galleon from the driveway as she approached, and it buoyed her. She did not tell the landlord this, because she guessed rightly that he would enjoy pointing it out to her. In those twenty steps from the street, she had noticed much more—a tabby cat with white paws asleep in the afternoon shade on the lid of a compost bin at the end of the drive, right where the kitchen window looked out; variegated ivy snaking in from the house behind and executing a death-grip around a broken birdbath. Also, the remains of a vegetable garden on the other side of the yard. There was a Hills hoist, probably as old as the house, set like a war memorial in a square of concrete with a weather-beaten garden gnome at its foot. She mentioned none of it. She visualised her mother and tried to emulate her. A self-contained woman with neat hair and a discreet smile, all of which said 'trustworthy, slightly austere' to the observer. It was a quality that prompted people to open doors for her mother, and yes, Marnie's childhood memories were from a time when doors were customarily opened, but more than that, Joan Guest always conveyed dignity. She looked like someone who could only know desolation in the abstract.

So, a home. She unpacked that first evening. There wasn't much. She had things stored under Rhiannon's house and she would retrieve them when she was ready. Anyway, there were three bags, a cardboard box and a suitcase, and she was glad to bring them from the car, which she would take to the carwash after her first pay. Only then would she park it in the driveway as the landlord had invited her to do. She jotted down a list in her new notebook as things occurred to her. She would need somewhere to hang her clothes (the landlord had not noticed this glaring omission), a kettle, a doormat, a caddy for the shower recess. Down the track, an ironing board, bedside table and bedside lamp. Her wish-list included an iPad.

In bed that first night she realised she needed, as a matter of some urgency, a screen to go around her bed. The beautiful windows were curtainless and her bed overlooked the back windows of the main house, which was an open kitchen–living area where she could see Vincent doing his dishes. And of course he could see her. She snapped off her light and crept across to the bed in darkness. She reassured herself that he was not deliberately looking out at her; this was a period of adjustment for him as well. Perhaps they were both grasping the inconvenience at the same time. Perhaps he was having second thoughts. Why on earth had he gone to all the trouble of doing up the sleepout, and then renting it out? It was barely adequate, he couldn't charge much, it interfered with his privacy. Now he was making a phone call, his back to her as he sat on the couch. She could see *Midsomer Murders* on the wall screen in front of him. Calling his sister, probably—for God's sake get me out of this, it was a terrible idea!

That first night, she didn't sleep. It was quiet, some distant traffic noise but only enough to be comforting. The house smelled unfamiliar but fresh. The mattress was fine, no excuse really. It was her brain that was the problem. She tried to slow her breathing, let her limbs relax, all the old tricks. She pictured herself with the sun on her, feet sunk in buffalo grass. Back when she was eighteen. The day she met Heath.

New Year's Day, that's why she remembered it. Down at the river. All her life her mother said, don't go down there, there could be weirdos. But Marnie was too old for that now, she could go where she wanted. Not that it was much of place to hang out. Back then, stormwater drains disgorged rafts of trash into the river. At the water's edge it was all aniseed, opalescent slicks of oil, sometimes dead fish. Overhead, Canary Island palms bestowed oblique shadows. Impressive specimens, out of place and yet intrinsic—why on earth had they ever been planted there? Whose grand vision was it? Behind her was the road that went nowhere and beyond that were paddocks of dock and capeweed. Further up the hill the houses began. They were double-fronted brick veneer, orange-coloured. They had white railings around verandas, TV antennae, sprinklers running on lawns. One of them was hers, indistinguishable from its neighbours, front windows blinded by morning sun, anonymous, stupefied-looking. On this particular morning, she had her back to all that. She was looking down at the water.

A man's voice said: 'Hey! You doin' all right there?'

Marnie didn't think anyone was speaking to her. She ignored it.

The voice said: 'It's never as bad as you think.'

She turned slightly so as not to seem curious. There was a man climbing out of a van, looking directly at her.

He was old-looking—over forty anyhow. He wore Stubbies, thongs, a T-shirt with a picture on it. He was heavy in the face and looked the type who would run hot. His legs were bowed. His arms sprouted a forest of pinkish hair. He had a belly.

She said, 'Pardon?' or 'Sorry, are you speaking to me?' Something polite, not intending to engage.

He told her his name—Heath—but didn't ask hers. He said he would stay right where he was, by the van, so she didn't need to get nervous. He told her he drove along the river every morning before work.

He said: 'Plenty of lonely people around, you got no idea.'

He said: 'Things always change, up or down, the bouncing ball keeps bouncing.'

He said: 'You're in the driver's seat, it's a big world out there, plenty to look at before you park the ute.'

('Oh my God, the platitudes!' people said when she was recounting this.)

So, he seemed to think she was planning to jump in. Crazy idea. Couldn't he see how foul the water was? She didn't want to embarrass him by telling him he was wrong, but wasn't sure if she could keep up a charade either.

He said: 'In a hurry?' and sat down cross-legged on the grass by the van's passenger door and rolled a cigarette. He chatted about the cost of diesel, and last night's fireworks up the back of the old munitions factory, which he could see from his place. Eventually she sat too and accepted a smoke, which he rolled for her and chucked across to her along with his lighter.

He said: 'Don't get used to it. Smoking's for mugs,' indicating himself, which was when she saw the illustration on his T-shirt clearly. Fozzie Bear.

She found herself telling him she had finished school, achieved a middling pass, and now didn't know what to do with it. Her mother wanted her to take a studentship but she was not thrilled about teaching.

'Thrilled?' he said.

'You mean confident?' he said.

He asked her if she had a part-time job. She told him she'd never worked, not even at the Royal Show where all the girls in her class sold showbags, every year since they were fourteen. She was surprised her mother had never encouraged her to apply because her mother approved of working, of getting by on your mettle. She told him about the Alsatian five doors down when she was twelve who barked at everyone who passed the gate. How she spoke to it on her way past each day until it stopped barking at her. After that, it knew when she was coming and listened for her voice. Then one day it got out and came down to her house and stood staring in through the flywire. She said that her mother was nervous, but Marnie went out to it and just walked it home and it pressed its side to her all the way. She wanted so badly to keep it, but she knew her mother wouldn't agree, and the men in the house where Sheba lived were too scary to ask. Then they went, and Sheba went and she often thought about the dog because she felt that Sheba wanted to be with her, and she should have been brave enough to ask.

Heath said: 'Never hurts to ask. But it takes self-esteem.'

She also told Heath that she had two weeks left to finalise her preferences, two months until uni started, so now for the first time she really would have to find a job. She didn't know what she would be good at.

Heath, returning his lighter and his tobacco to a pocket in his Stubbies, said: 'I can give you a job.'

When Marnie walked home that morning, she told her mother she wasn't going to uni straight away. She was going to work for a man who had lived four streets away from them for thirty years. He ran a removal business, and he needed someone to do his books because his wife was in a nursing home. He said he knew her mother from the chemist shop and if her mother wanted she could call around and meet him first, and learn for herself that he was ridgy-didge.

Marnie started working at Woolley Removals five days a week and stayed on for several years. She learned bookkeeping, payroll, how to liaise with parole-board officers. She attained a driver's licence, then a truck licence. Sometimes, when they were caught short, she did a shift on the truck. The boys who worked with Heath called him Wokka. For years, whenever Marnie saw Fozzie Bear, she thought of him. Lately, it seemed to be happening more often. A song on the radio might bring an image of Heath into her head; the smell of Drum tobacco. Or at night, like now, when her brain was shuffling through memories and she couldn't sleep.

2

Her job at Treen's was five afternoons, three until six. She made it a habit to arrive early so that Trinh could get herself lunch in the tiny kitchen down the back. During the first two weeks, Trinh heated up noodles, made a pot of tea and brought them back to the counter. After a while, when they were familiar with each other, Trinh did noodles for Marnie, too, and brought two cups for the tea.

That first week Trinh ate rapidly and left the shop at 3.45, returning from the holiday program half an hour later with her two great-grandchildren, Grace and Ben, who folded themselves into a complex and impossibly small unit in a corner behind the counter and gazed at Reading Eggs on their notebook while the till was done. Occasionally Marnie heard grunts and saw them elbowing each other for a turn, but they were quiet mostly.

Their mother, Tom, blew in at odd times, always in a hurry. She ran a travel agency with her husband. There was no mention of the missing family member—Trinh's daughter, Tom's mother.

Life assumed a pattern of home and work repeated so often that it became a comfort, then automatic, then invisible. Marnie made a to-do list—report to Centrelink, find a cheap dentist, a hairdresser—and tried to follow it up in the mornings before work.

She came to love her mornings. She discovered a cane screen in a second-hand store around the corner from Treen's that cleaned up well and afforded her a small area of privacy. She bought an old metal hanging rack on wheels. Vincent was encouraging when she brightly suggested she would enjoy digging over the vegetable patch, a suggestion she felt herself regretting as soon as she made it. It was an impulse blurted out to fill a few seconds of awkward silence when they crossed paths at the letterbox, made worse by the arrival on her doorstep of a pile of ancient garden tools—his father's tools—about which she felt compelled to look pleased. She dug over the garden bed every day for a week, generating a mountain of weeds and roots that she did not know what to do with, and then left it alone.

Vincent's sister paid a visit, as Marnie had expected, after four weeks, a thin woman in a narrow skirt. She had protuberant eyes, perfect legs and an impeccable short haircut, and she arrived at Marnie's door proffering cake. Today was Vincent's birthday and the whole family was gathered at the house, so she thought it was an opportune time since Covid restrictions had been eased etc, etc.

'No, no,' she said when Marnie invited her in. 'I just want

14

to introduce myself—Sylvie.' Her eyes darted around; she couldn't resist looking over Marnie's shoulder. 'Vinny said you like gardening.'

'Well…'

'Yeah, I thought he might be exaggerating, I feel the same. Dad gardened, but whatever gene it was, I didn't get it. Black Forest,' she indicated the cake. 'Store-bought. It mushed up a bit when I cut it.' Sylvie didn't look the nervous type, but Marnie felt she was talking in hyperdrive.

'Are you sure you won't come in?'

'No, no, I'm rude enough just lobbing. I wanted to say, if there's anything wrong with the place, now's the time to speak up. My brothers are here with their kids—that's the noise— Joe's the builder, he did the reno. He never comes when you need him, absolutely never, so I thought while we've got him captive down at the house—'

Marnie assured her that everything was good, excellent. She loved the windows.

'We all do,' said Sylvie. 'I used to be really jealous of my brothers having that ship. It was only the boys allowed in the sleepout.'

Sylvie handed over the cake, shook hands and waved as she walked away. Marnie felt optimistic. She imagined Sylvie reporting back to the family—She's good, tidy. And she's way old. You know, steady.

Later, during another of her brief exchanges with Vincent, she learned Sylvie was a teacher, wanting to retire but scared, because she didn't know what she would do with herself. She also learned that the cat belonged to

Vincent's deceased mother. It was eleven years old; its name was—unfortunately—Darling. Vincent admitted he felt embarrassed calling it, but it showed up at mealtimes without summons. His eldest brother Joe had no patience and said Vincent should get rid of it, but Vincent said what harm did it do, and anyway it reminded him of his mum. Marnie liked Vincent in that moment. He told her his mother's dementia had advanced fast, within a year of diagnosis she was forgetting the names of her children. But she always remembered Darling. His sister said that Joe had an oldest child's sense of entitlement and probably resented the cat, while the others just shrugged it off. He said, 'Sorry, I wasn't trying to be mean or anything—are you the oldest in your family?'

She said, 'Worse. An only.' She added, 'My daughter is an only, too. I guess that makes me a lost cause.'

And he gave a short laugh, a fraction too loud. This was one of their few lengthy conversations. For the most part Vincent kept out of her way.

A lost cause. Why did she say that? She stewed over the remark in bed, where it became not nonchalant, but dishonest. All her life, she'd said things she didn't believe, like the idiotic gardening comment. She had certainly longed for brothers and sisters when she was a child, but it was a phase that passed. She was secure enough without siblings and without a father, since she'd never known him, in that orange-brick home where she grew up. She passed her childhood watching Saturday-afternoon movies that maintained a warped post-war world view—deserts and cowboys, heroism and austerity. A world where women were generally pathetic but nonetheless aspirational. She collected cards of pop groups from bubblegum packages, played tennis sometimes, Scrabble with Joan on rainy days. She even made up a four for Solo afternoons at the church hall when someone called in sick. Girl Guides every week and church on Sundays. A muted kind of living, she decided, looking back.

Change came into her life like a gentle nudge applied lightly at first. Marnie remembered a summer morning when she was eleven, eating breakfast with her mother. They were listening to Germaine Greer on the radio, being interviewed about her book. And Joan put her toast down and said, 'You know, that woman is making so much sense!' Joan borrowed the book from the library, and Marnie gazed at the baffling cover and felt proud to have a mother who read *The Female Eunuch*. Her schoolfriends were dismissive, their mothers didn't approve of Germaine. Marnie asked her mother what she thought of the book, but Joan only said, after thinking for a moment, that it was 'hard going'.

The first real change was ushered into Marnie's life the day Heath climbed out of his van and said, 'I can give you a job.' She lived a life of newness after that, and really believed that this was the world she had been waiting for.

The next change was when Eleanor was born. That was like being poleaxed. Not change so much as transformation. Now she thought: how was I never alive before? Had Marnie altered her mother's life, the way Eleanor altered hers? It didn't seem so, but how could she know?

Anyway, she would be glad of it all. She would be grateful.

Marnie turned over in bed and looked out through her windows at the plum tree in the moonlight. Three months in her flat and the tree was threadbare. Its life cycle was cranking on, just like hers. She must always remember she wasn't done yet. Change was behind her and before her—paths still branching off into the mist. Someone, possibly Rhiannon, said once, 'Embrace Change, it might be Glorious'.

Glorious—that was a hyperbolic word, maybe even dishonest. A word to promote a false sense of hope and occasionally incite crazy actions. Marnie did not expect anything to be glorious; she would certainly resist crazy. But she would embrace hope. There was no other option.

Step one. Here we are again.

3

Eventually, after nearly four months, Eleanor arrived at Treen's one afternoon looking for her.

Marnie was serving, there was a small rush on, customers lined up at the counter. She could only acknowledge her daughter and mouth the word 'wait'. It was mildly distressing to see Eleanor nod, then slope down an aisle and out of sight. Marnie continued to serve, glancing at the camera monitor at her elbow, watching her daughter prowling, stopping, lifting things up. She didn't look too bad. Eleanor's thin hair was very black with blue streaks through it, which was a pleasing change from mouse. She was wearing grey trackpants and a limp hoodie. Marnie kept checking the door for the others. When the final customer was gone, Eleanor appeared at her elbow with two rainbow-coloured teddy bears. Close up, her skin was spotty, her blue eyes vivid.

'Hi, Mum.'

'Baby. Where are the children?' She hugged her.

'In the car with Bray, I wasn't going to wake them up and get them out.'

'No, sure, it's so good to see you. I've rung a few times.'

'My phone got stolen.'

Of course. 'I thought maybe something like that had happened. Are you okay?'

'I rang Dad, he didn't know where you were.'

'I haven't told him yet, I've only been here a little while. How are the children?'

'How do you expect them to be?'

This was one of those make-or-break moments. Marnie said, 'Bigger, I guess. I'm dying to see them. Are you going to have dinner with me? See the place?'

'When do you finish?'

'I close at five-thirty and then there's stuff I have to do, so I don't get out of here until six, just after.'

'Well, okay, give me your key and the address, is it close?'

'Two streets—'

'I need to get them inside. Koa starts coughing and I need to get meds into him. Can I have these?' The teddies.

'Sure, let me scan them—'

'Can't I just have them?'

'They're not mine, don't worry, I'll pay for them.'

'Okay. My mum the shopkeeper.'

'Shopgirl. Get it right.'

They both laughed, and Marnie handed over her key and scribbled her address on a post-it, then Eleanor was gone, teddies under her arm with their paws extended, as if begging to be saved.

Marnie sat down between customers, planning. There was another hour and a half to go, Vincent would be home at 6.45, she needed to avoid him. What would her place be like by then? She would have to buy something for dinner, or there would be the usual mess-around and she'd be out getting takeaway which she definitely could not afford, which anyway the children would pick at and then refuse. Bananas, yoghurt for the children...sausage rolls? Did they eat baby food, surely the little one did? Should she cook vegetables? She had forgotten to ask if they still had that dog. Please God, no. She felt her pulse quicken—all as familiar and as exciting as Christmas.

This is how it begins, she thought, walking past a clapped-out Fairlane in her driveway. All the lights in her place were on, the galleon luminous in the gathering dusk. She could hear children. She felt a clutch inside and then she was among them, smiling and hugging and lifting Frankie into her arms while the baby pulled back from her in alarm and tried to climb up Eleanor's legs until Eleanor was forced to lift him.

Marnie hugged her daughter properly, reaching around to include the baby, to just feel his roundness and be close to the flushed cheeks and the dark ringlets. He resisted her and Frankie told him bossily, 'No, no, bubby. Ganny—see?' She patted Marnie's face and kissed her.

Eleanor said drily, 'He's a Covid baby, it's been so much fun.' She swung him into Marnie's free arm and he went rigid, then shrieked.

She tried not to say simpering things, she tried to smile

and laugh. She did not ask where the dog was, was relieved not to see it. She said how well they all looked, what a big girl Frankie was, while the baby continued to wail and struggle, finally succeeding in getting to the floor and bear-walking to Eleanor who said, 'No, Ko. No up. Mummy's tired.' So he crawled under the table and sat with his teddy up to his face, sobbing heartbroken into its fur.

'Holy shit, Mum,' Eleanor said, an appeal for solidarity.

'I'll get some dinner,' Marnie said. 'He'll come around to me. You sit down.'

'I can't, he'll just want to climb on me. He's so clingy!'

Marnie put Frankie onto the bench while she unpacked groceries. Frankie pulled packages out helpfully and named them.

'Where's Brayden?'

'Chemist.'

'For Koa's cough?'

She nodded. 'Plus Bray has this sore back, don't get me wrong he's great, but it's all about him, you know?'

So maybe the dog was with Brayden?

'Dinofaur agetti,' said Frankie, holding up a packet.

'Show it to Koa,' said her mother, and Marnie helped Frankie down off the bench. She went over to the table and joined the baby underneath it. He stopped crying and examined the packet of pasta with her.

'See? Brayden says it's all put on.'

Marnie felt a little chill. Brayden the early-childhood expert.

'Can we stay tonight? It's been a shit time, Mum, I didn't

know how to get on to you. Dad was useless, I even phoned TJ. We had to get out of the house, the landlord was a pedo, always wanting to know about the kids. It was weird, I really felt unsafe, you know?'

'Darling, that's terrible.'

'So here's me, freaking out, and Bray says he'll leave me if I don't get it under control.' She started to cry and Marnie put her arms around her daughter and said comforting things which included that yes, of course they could stay.

If only Brayden the toothless wonder weren't part of the package, she thought.

'Oopsie,' said Frankie, followed by a patter of pasta dinosaurs and a chortle of delight from the baby.

'Oh fuck!' said Eleanor.

Marnie plunged into peacemaker mode, down on her knees retrieving spilled pasta, reassuring everyone. Koa permitted her to pull him out and stand him up at the window, where the cat was looking in at them. Both children were happy with the cat for a few minutes, enough time to get a saucepan of water on and pasta sauce poured into another saucepan. No time for a proper bolognese, she could have predicted that. She had two cold sausages; she'd cut them up and throw them in.

'Brayden's gluten-free now,' said Eleanor. 'Want a drink?' Eleanor opened the fridge, which contained an assortment of bottles and jars that hadn't been there when Marnie left for work, including a tin of toddler formula, thank the good lord. There were, as well, some cans of Scotch and cola, which was possibly Marnie's least favourite drink, but she accepted the proffered can and they clanked them together.

'Love you, Mum,' said Eleanor. It almost made it worth it.

Eleanor said, 'The flat's crazy small, but it's nice.' Then, 'Why the frig haven't you got a TV?'

They were two drinks in when Brayden arrived. He entered the place with that air of jaunty magnanimity he always conveyed, even though in the year he had been on the scene he had never to Marnie's knowledge had a job, always wore trackpants with something gothic and unreadable printed up one leg and, on one memorable occasion, had given them all headlice. He was missing three teeth, two top and one bottom. Inexplicably, he seemed to believe his smile was seductive. With a haircut and a full set of teeth, he might have passed for a very dodgy salesman, but as it stood, there were honestly no words to do him justice.

'It's good for Lenny to see you, she's been really missing you,' he said, hugging Marnie. 'Hey, I see you found the drinks. Way to go, Mum. I've brung chips.'

The smell had preceded him into the room. He put down a flat white parcel on the table, pushing aside the children's half-eaten bowls of pasta and pulled back a couple of chairs, a real gent. 'Dig in, girls. Grab us a tinnie, Len.'

The children clamoured for chips. Marnie gritted her teeth and put her drink down, retiring to the sofa to finish her pasta. From here, she watched Eleanor on Brayden's knee, slotting hot chips adoringly into him while he drank and told her about his trip to the chemist. This had involved, apparently, misunderstandings with dickwad salesgirls, having to explain his problem to people who didn't speak English, and a prescription that restricted the quantity of drug that he required, which was—it goes without saying although he said it anyway, more than once—a total cock-up. And finally, when he decided to cut his losses and supplement it all with a few packets of over-the-counter painkillers, they had tried to give him a lecture about not mixing paracetamol with his prescription drugs.

'And I go, hold it *right there*, I think you'll find I know my own fucking medical condition,' he glanced over his shoulder at Marnie. 'Sorry, but sometimes you just gotta say it, don't you?' That smile. 'Hey, who's the guy in the front? Gave me a greasy when I come up here, perving out his window.'

'The landlord,' Marnie said, heart sinking.

'Mum said we can stay the night,' said Lenny in a little-girl voice she reserved for Brayden, especially when she wanted to change the subject. In her other voice she said sharply: 'Koa! No! No touching Ganny's bag! No!'

'No Koa!' echoed Frankie, with startling ferocity.

The baby, both hands in the depths of Marnie's bag, went scarlet and dissolved into shuddering floods. 'Oh Jesus fuck,' said Eleanor.

Marnie gathered him up and rubbed his back. Brayden got to his feet, long-suffering, and explained to Marnie that it didn't work to be all soft about things, that made them think you were weak. Children only understood things that were simple. No and Yes. He demonstrated by putting his face close to Koa's and saying 'NO! Got that, Koa? NO!' Marnie felt the baby flinch in her arms.

25

Frankie echoed: 'Got that, Koa?' then added, 'It's oorwite, bubby. It's oorwite.'

Marnie said, 'I think they're just tired. How are we going to do this? There's only one bed.'

Eleanor said, 'They can sleep with you, Mum, that'd be easiest. We'll take the pull-out bed.'

She started to say there isn't one, but Eleanor was already chucking cushions off the sofa and unfolding the seat, so Marnie shut up and kept her annoyance quiet—annoyance that was mostly at herself, because she had lived there nearly four months and hadn't known that the sofa was also a bed, while they had worked it out in minutes, opening and shutting things, stowing their garbage in her cupboards and her refrigerator, combing through the whole place while she was at work.

They brought in sour-smelling blankets and towels from the Fairlane. They expressed dissatisfaction with the size of the bathroom and the absence of a washing machine, then showered and changed while steam fogged up the wall of windows and slowly condensed. Marnie scrubbed out sippie cups and a bottle and teat, and mixed formula into them. She was relieved to get the children into bed beside her, Koa on the wall side since he was still shy of her, Frankie in the middle. She moved the screen to create a barrier between her bed and the sofa and sang nursery rhymes to the children while they drank their milk and Koa coughed. Brayden had apparently been unable to find suitable medication for the baby; he denied forgetting it completely, it was the pharmacy that was hopeless—no, criminally neglectful. From the other side of the screen Marnie heard Eleanor and Brayden clinking things in and out of the refrigerator, going outside to smoke in the darkness, sneaking back in again, whispering together. 'Now, now *Ella-noor*,' she heard Brayden mimicking her, followed by snorting and shushing.

Koa dropped into a deep sleep with the bottle still plugged into his mouth. Marnie reached over and uncoupled it gently. In the dimness, she felt Frankie's fingers tapping her wrist.

'Ganny.'

'Yes, honey-kitten?'

'I tickle-wing you.'

'You're such a tricker!'

'Ganny—will you be here omm-owo?'

She laid her head by the child's and whispered to her that in the morning she would take them to a park. She described the swings and slides that were there. Frankie repeated the words in a whisper—fwins, fwide, park.

Much later: 'Mum, you awake?' Eleanor's voice, quiet in the darkness.

'Yes.'

'Thanks, I mean it.'

'It's okay.'

'I should have said it before.'

'It's okay, hon. Brayden asleep?'

'Out to it. It's the meds.'

And the alcohol and whatever the hell else he'd pushed into his face or his arm or his eyeballs in the hours he'd been absent, Marnie thought. She knew she was making excuses for her daughter, though. Easier to blame the toothless wonder.

'How did you find me in the end?' she said.

'I remembered that annoying hippie chick, Rhiannon, with the fishpond and that butt-ugly dog. She had some of your stuff under her house.'

Rhi would never have given out Marnie's address, though.

'She couldn't remember the street, but she told me where you were working. Do you like that job?'

'It pays the rent.' Beat. 'It's okay.'

'Christ, Mum.' The derision in Eleanor's voice rankled.

Marnie waited a few minutes before speaking again. 'What happened when you called TJ?'

'He couldn't tell me anything.'

'I haven't spoken to him in ages. Did you ask about Michael?'

'What do you think?'

'How is he?'

'Eleven, nearly.' She was silent, then she said, 'TJ spoke to me like I was dirt.'

'It was probably just surprise, hearing from you.'

'You always take his side!'

She started to protest, but there was no point, Eleanor ranted for a moment in a barely controlled whisper about TJ's arrogance, and her innocence, and how she hated them all.

Marnie said, when silence returned, 'I'm sorry, baby.'

'He's learning piano,' Eleanor replied.

'Michael is?'

'It shits me,' she said. 'I don't even know why, it just does.'

'He'll be back in your life when he's older.'

'He won't. I've lost him, Mum, you might as well accept

28

it. He's not even on my new Medicare card. Just Frankie and Ko.' Then she said, 'Stop talking. I don't want to talk about it.'

Marnie was relieved, she wanted the silence, the dim shape of the galleon breasting the waves up there near the ceiling and the breathing of the children in her bed. She went to sleep trying to picture Michael playing piano. She saw him at a grand piano, brown hair, blond cowlick, and his feet swinging in gym shoes because they didn't reach the floor.

She knew that was wrong. It was the way she remembered him when he was five.

4

It was her plan to lie low and avoid Vincent in the morning, but she had forgotten how early children wake. They were rollicking around her on the bed by six, so she rummaged through Eleanor's bags to find clothes for them. There seemed to be no socks. She laced Frankie, sockless, into damp canvas shoes, fed them both bananas and oatmeal and was on the street by seven, balancing a bag of laundry on the back of the stroller, her handbag slung across her front, Frankie beside her, talking non-stop.

Vincent was collecting his paper from the front lawn. His habits were regular and slightly anachronistic, fitting more into the behaviours of last century than this one. His papers were delivered each day; he wore a woollen dressing-gown and scuffs with Nike printed across the top. The cat was weaving through his legs, making a racket, and he was saying. 'Okay, okay, give me a break,' and it seemed to Marnie that they were both having a similar start to the day.

He said, 'Oh—uh,' when he saw her passing.

'Grandchildren,' she smiled and shrugged, attempting insouciance.

'I saw the car,' he said.

A rush of explanation. 'They're passing through, I said they could stay a night. Well, I think it'll be two, it gives me a chance to catch up, I haven't seen them for a while, this is Frankie, say hi Frankie, and this is the baby.'

She took a breath. The children stared at Vincent, he gave a vague wave.

'Yeah, the car,' he said.

'I'll tell Brayden to move it, he just drove in while I was at work—'

'It's the tyre—'

'They're incredibly stressed at the moment—'

'He may not know—'

She stopped, confused.

Vincent said, 'The back tyre needs air, probably a slow leak. If he drives on it, it'll ruin the rim, he may not have even noticed yet which is possible, believe it or not, because the steering's stable in Fairlanes. Good cars, I mean, that one needs work, but they go and go. He'll be kicking himself if he does the rim.'

'Thanks, you're right, I'll tell him.'

Vincent who, she had already observed, did not maintain eye-contact easily, tapped his rolled newspaper and added, 'All bad news, don't know why I bother. Warnie's gone. Pakistan's a dead wicket. Putin's gone crazy.'

'Yes, terrible,' she said, aware that she was perhaps not

31

offering adequate sympathy.

Vincent nodded and headed back to his house, followed by the chirruping cat.

Marnie started walking again. The children made cat sounds all along the street.

The laundromat was not yet open. She bought hot chocolates at the petrol station and took the children into the park which offered a clear view of the shops opposite. The play equipment was wet, the sun not yet on it. But it was a fenced area, and that meant she could relax a little. She wiped the slide down with the baby's grubby blanket and let them explore, only getting up from her seat at intervals to fish tanbark out of Koa's mouth. He was uncomfortable crawling through the woodchips, so stood up when he could and walked around hanging on to poles and ropes in his gro-suit feet.

When she saw Trinh opening the shop, Marnie gathered up children, laundry and stroller into an unsteady jumble and dodged through the morning traffic to get there. Trinh made a fuss of the children while Marnie grabbed socks and leggings from a random assortment of clothing on racks in aisle three. Trinh put knitted hats on their heads. 'Cold mornings now,' she said. 'My treat.' She also gave them a packet of pop-tarts. 'Are you good to come in this afternoon?' she said, bouncing Koa on her knee.

'Of course. I told my daughter I work afternoons.'

'Daughters can make demands.'

The look Trinh gave her was enigmatic. Marnie wasn't sure if it was understanding or critical, but there was something that could have been a share, if she could interpret it right. It only occurred to her then that she did not want to let Trinh down, and she might have to assert herself with Eleanor—something she was historically not good at.

They moved along to the laundromat where Marnie did two loads of washing and two loads of drying, flicking through fuzzy-edged magazines showing pictures of movie stars with 'baby bumps', and dogs with neckerchiefs catching frisbees hurled by a Hemsworth. Koa became irritable and tore several pages in his frustration. But he was asleep when they walked home, curled like a hedgehog in the stroller underneath the bag of clean laundry. Frankie walked along holding Marnie's hand and described road rules in a dramatic voice. Her pronunciation slid randomly on a moving scale between perfect and hilarious. 'If you go onda woad, Ganny, you det stwashed. I say "no, no Koa" when he does go onda woad. Because, if he det stwashed, my mum will twy.'

'She sure would. Ganny too.'

'And Bay.'

Brayden? Well...

'And kitty-cat?'

'How do kitty-cats cry?'

They reprised cat sounds until they reached home and Frankie greeted the Fairlane with the now obviously flat tyre. 'Bay's car.'

The cat was on the doormat, the windows fogged up again. Inside, Eleanor and Brayden were in varying stages of dressing and eating breakfast, the pull-out bed strewn with stuff. Brayden was the least dressed, possibly on purpose, displaying an entire sleeve of tattoos, a dripping dagger on his shoulder blade and a neckband which pronounced *Every Saint has a Past, Every Sinner has a Future*. She wondered what had made him choose that. It would have been cheaper and less time-consuming to opt for *Such is Life*, which she read regularly on the tattooed necks of customers at Treen's. Perhaps it said something optimistic about Brayden.

'Had the kids all to yourself, hey, Ganny? Bet you loved that!' said Brayden, shovelling her precious muesli into his mouth steeped in milk and what looked like jam. He flashed her his repellent smile. The place reeked of old toast, so this must be at least their second breakfast.

All goodwill towards Brayden evaporated and she wanted to thump him instead. But Eleanor was picking up Frankie and swinging her around, 'Did you have a good time with Ganny? Aren't you a lucky bunny?' A smile to Marnie. 'Thanks so much, Mum, I can't remember the last time we got to sleep in.'

'Koey as-eep,' said Frankie, pointing at the bag of laundry.

'Do you think I can transfer him?' Marnie said, putting the laundry bag on the floor. She lifted Koa's sweaty body into her arms and moved him to her bed where he frowned and commenced a creaking protest, until his dummy was unearthed and plugged in.

'Hey, Ganny, you're a natural, you really are,' praised Brayden. At what? Putting dummies in? Marnie didn't say this. Instead, she told him the news about the back tyre of his car, and Vincent's advice.

'You might thank him, if you see him,' she suggested.

Brayden's mood completely changed. 'That's a fucking pisser,' he said to Eleanor. She indicated to him that he should calm down, a pressing down of her hands in his direction.

'We have to go to Centrelink,' she told Marnie, which explained the slew of paperwork on the pull-out mattress. 'We're just trying to find all our stuff—they have to see everything, even stuff they've already got, they're bastards.' To Brayden: 'We can take the tram in.'

'Jesus,' he muttered. He glanced at Marnie but said nothing.

'My car doesn't have seats for the children,' she said. 'And, no, I'm sorry, but I can't mind them, I have to work.'

They both protested, that wasn't what they wanted, they weren't even thinking it. 'Shit no,' said Brayden. 'It's better taking the kids, we get seen quicker. It's just that my Myki's got pinched.'

She took her own Myki from her wallet and handed it to him. 'I need it back.'

'Hey, what do you take me for?' he hugged her around the shoulders. 'Your mum's a pistol, Lenny, isn't she? I mean you really are, Marnie, how old are you?'

'Sixty-three.'

'Je*SUS*, you're a pistol.'

Marnie tried to move the conversation on. 'You know how to change a tyre?' she said. 'I mean, is there a problem? I can help you.'

'When did you learn how to change tyres?'

Was that amused disbelief she could detect in his voice? 'Somewhere between my eighteenth birthday and now.'

'Thing is, it got wrecked,' he said, shrugging.

'Isn't there a spare?'

Eleanor butted in. 'He just told you it got wrecked, so no, there's no spare. Don't be annoying, Mum.'

'So, what, the car just stays there?' The voice in her head saying, shut up.

'You weren't parked there. You could have parked there, but you weren't.'

'I don't always park there.' Where was the point in explaining that every morning she drank her tea looking down the driveway, across the street, over rooftops, at a new sky, and saw the airbus making its descent into Tullamarine—and she liked it that way.

'So, it was free for us, right?'

'Not to dump your car there!'

'It's not dumped, it will get fixed. Fuck, Mum, you're not even being logical. We need to get to Centrelink to sort our payments out, and when the money comes in, we get the tyre fixed. How hard is it to understand?'

Marnie noticed Frankie climbing quietly onto the bed and curling around the baby.

'Yes.' She listened to her breaths, slowed herself. 'I'm only trying to help. Sorry.'

'You always do this!'

'My landlord lives right in the front.'

'Who cares about the frigging landlord? You pay the rent, that's all he cares about. You're just being unreasonable on purpose.' To Brayden: 'She always does this.'

And Brayden: 'Hey, ladies, that's enough.' He extended

his arms around them both; Marnie found her face way too close to his bare skin and his tatts, the nest of pimples in his chin stubble. 'I don't want my number-one girl and her number-one mum fighting, okay?'

That was where it ended. Brayden looked smug about the docility that followed. Eleanor dressed herself and packed the children in the stroller again. They trooped off to the tram stop, Koa awake and grizzling, while Marnie stood at the kitchen bench and ironed a shirt for work.

The silence that settled around her in the empty flat was not comforting, but she got on with her morning, washed the dishes, wiped down the sink and made it to work in perfect time, her customary half-hour early. Trinh fetched tea for the two of them while Marnie bashed leaves from the front of the shop with a straw broom, driving them into the gutter. When she came back inside, Trinh offered her a bowl of caramel snows, and she ate one and felt the buttery, burnt flavour seep into her. She washed the sweetness down with tea. Trinh put a caramel in her own mouth and said, 'Sometimes these are better than Valium.'

That night in bed, with the children on either side of her— Koa had decided to trust her—Marnie slept badly, waking several times from lucid dreams. One of them was about changing tyres. Heath was there, and it was the front wheel of the truck, and she couldn't get the wheel nuts off because someone had already jacked the side up. Heath said, 'Some things take longer, kiddo.' But she knew it was hopeless because the sequence was already messed up.

5

The start of another day and another trip to the laundromat. It was her decision, so she knew she had no right to feel hard done by. The stale blankets and rancid towels out of the Fairlane had permeated the flat to a point of indecency. Marnie packed them around the baby in the stroller along with a grotty doona. This she had found in the boot of the Fairlane when she was having a surreptitious look for the spare tyre which was, as Brayden had explained to her several times, gone. She found the dog's collar there, though.

When they reached the park she made a phone call to Rhiannon, who told her what she already knew—it was not a good idea to fork out for a retread.

'I don't know how long I've got before the landlord kicks up, Rhi.'

'You have to tell them to go.'

'How, without a tyre?'

'They need to get it patched themselves. They're

grown-ups, they know what to do but they want you to do it for them because it makes their lives—'

'Easier. I know. They don't have anywhere to go.'

'Friends.'

'And the children—I don't even know where they've been living.'

'You have no power over that, it sucks, but that's how it is. If you like that place—'

'It's not a matter of like. I'm lucky to have it, it's near my job and it's affordable.'

But she did like it. While she was protesting to Rhi she could hear the truth in the back of her head. That stern other voice that so often said 'Lie!' to her now said 'You love it.'

She ended the call with vague promises, and pocketed her phone, hating Rhiannon for making sense. She remembered what Eleanor had said, Eleanor's small superpower in life being that she could sum people up entertainingly in a couple of sentences. Rhi was an annoying hippie, and the details of the ugly dog and the fishpond somehow succeeded in nailing an instant judgment. Amusing but, as always, reductive.

Marnie should ring Rhi back and apologise for not being open to her advice. She didn't.

Arriving home three hours later with clean washing and tired children, she found Eleanor on the doorstep navigating a new phone.

'Bray's dad sent us some money,' she said. 'I'm trying to get it working, they keep telling us to do everything online at Centrelink but it takes eons and Bray loses his shit. So, we have to go in again.'

'Is it still the old number?'

'No, Mum.' That long-suffering tone. 'All of it's new—I told you mine got stolen.'

'Sorry, yes, I just need a number, that's all.'

'I'll write it on a bit of paper for you.'

She got up and went into the flat, yelling for Bray. 'They're back. Let's go.' Over her shoulder to Marnie, 'We need your Myki again.'

'He's still got it.'

'Okay, we'll bring back dinner. Can you get nappies? We're running out. There's cheap ones at your shop, isn't there?'

Then a commotion of packing and setting off, followed by silence. Marnie couldn't face tidying today, toast crusts, coffee cups, wet towels on the bathroom floor, assorted heaps and spillages. She piled the clean laundry onto her bed and made herself a cup of tea which she drank, sitting on the step in a patch of sunlight, the cat at her feet. 'Hey there, Darling, good girl, Darling,' she said, and thought about Vincent's mother, who had probably said the same thing and then she thought about the brother who had wanted the cat put down.

At work that afternoon, the till wouldn't balance. It wasn't significant but it was unsettling. She ran the sequence three times. Ten dollars under, that's all. She should leave a note for Trinh. But she didn't. She added ten dollars from her purse and stapled the balance sheet to the activity sheet with a smiley face on it—all shipshape.

*

40

When she got home, the flat was lit up. Eleanor and Brayden were hoeing into fish and chips at the table. They also had a bottle of vodka and a king-sized bottle of home-brand lemonade. Koa was under the table with a bowl of chips, smooshing them doggedly into the face of his teddy.

'Where's Frankie?'

'In the poo,' said Eleanor, topping up her glass. 'Have a drink, Mum, don't interfere.'

Frankie was on the floor between the bed and the screen. She gave Marnie a furtive, blotched look and held up a bandaged hand.

'Look at the wall! Don't you dare get up,' Brayden's raised voice was threatening. He switched to his pontificating tone for Marnie: 'She knows what she did wrong, don't you Frankie?' Raised voice again: 'Don't go looking at Ganny for help.'

'What on earth?'

'Ganny thinks you're a naughty girl, too,' he continued.

'I don't! Don't say what I think, I don't even know what's going on.'

'It's discipline, Mum, you have to be a united front or you end up confusing them,' said Eleanor. 'Brayden knows what he's doing, she broke a glass after he told her not to pick it up.'

'Is she okay?'

'Yes! A tiny cut, it's nothing. She's in time out.'

'She's three!'

'That's not too young,' said Brayden. 'Now, I know you're Ganny, but you need to let Lenny and me do what we have to do.'

'And back us up,' added Eleanor. 'It's five minutes, and she's already had more than half the time, hasn't she, Bray? Sit down and have a drink, Mum.'

Eleanor poured more vodka. 'You'll have to share my glass because the other one's gone. I told Frankie how upset you'd be, they're your best glasses.'

'They're not.' But Eleanor glared at her, so she sat down, seething. Koa climbed onto her knee smelling of dirty nappy and chip oil.

When two more excruciating minutes were through, they made a show of hugging the hiccupping child while continuing to preach at her. 'Now, you know what you did wrong? You won't do that again? You know what happens when you don't do what you're told?'

Like kicking a dog, thought Marnie. She said suddenly, 'What happened to that dog you had, Rastus?'

Eleanor said, 'That fucking landlord, that pedo, Bray saw him letting Raz out. He took off, Bray went after him but we never found him.'

Marnie met Brayden's brazen look.

'Time for Ganny gib you cuddle,' said Bray, cute-voicing now, with a wink to Marnie. He allowed Frankie to be lifted into Marnie's arms. She carried both children into the bathroom and turned on the shower.

6

There was a new person being trained at Treen's next afternoon. 'Two mornings a week,' said Trinh after she sent the woman out of the shop to sweep the leaves away. 'She can learn the till with you today.' She added quietly: 'I'm not sure about her yet,' but this intimacy was not enough to offset the plummet in Marnie's gut.

Patsy was a few years younger than Marnie, koala-faced, with meticulous makeup. When Trinh was gone, Patsy took on a hush-hush tone between customers, keen to tell Marnie the story of her life. She had always lived in the area: been christened up the road, married a local boy, raised four children. She had worked in a furniture store—'You would not believe what that game is like!'—her eyebrows intimating scandalous misdoings. She had been a caterer for a while, stupendously successful. Everyone thought she was crazy to chuck it in, but she was done with cutting pineapple, she said. She'd also run the college tuckshop at the Catholic school.

They'd given her a magnificent send-off and were begging her to come back after only a few months because the whole place had gone to pieces. But it was too much stress, and she'd been completely honest with them about it. 'It's my nature to be generous, that's my downfall,' she said. 'I told them what my doctor said—You need to be selfish, Patsy, you need to put you first.' They'd thanked her sincerely for her feedback.

'You're not from around here,' she accused Marnie with a shimmering smile. 'That colour suits you,' pointing to her shirt. 'You're an autumn person. I've done colours,' she continued. 'I'm telling you, darling, it makes all the difference.'

Patsy spoke loudly to customers, many of whom she knew by name. She chiacked them as she packed their bags, upselling all the while.

'How much do you think the business makes?' she asked Marnie in a lull. Marnie didn't know, but suggested that the shop wouldn't be here if it didn't make a profit.

'They know money,' Patsy assured her, the pronoun layered with judgment as she swabbed the till with a Pine-O-Cleen wet wipe. 'They all do. Have you met the other one?'

'Tom?'

'I've heard it's a front for her travel business.'

'Front?'

'Money laundering.'

And of course, there is no real answer to a claim like that unless you understand money laundering, which Marnie did not, even though she had watched most of *Breaking Bad*. Patsy's opinions did not stand up to scrutiny, but scrutiny was not something she allowed time for anyway, releasing pronouncements in relentless waves.

They did the till together, Patsy refusing assistance. The count and print-out were wrong again, this time fifteen dollars and a few cents in excess. 'Bugger,' said Marnie.

'No, that's our little tip,' said Patsy, snatching out a couple of notes. 'Believe me, it's easier than going through the numbers again. Over's a bonus! We can share it.'

'I don't feel comfortable…' She could not possibly explain that some of it at least was her own ten dollars from the previous day.

'Don't worry, we girls gotta stick together. I'll buy us coffees tomorrow on my way in.'

That's how you become an accomplice, thought Marnie: that easily. She refused Patsy's offer of a lift and walked home.

First thing she noticed was that her car wasn't there.

It had been parked opposite the house. She was used to seeing it each morning, each evening; now its absence was glaring. Her Subaru. She was not a car person, it had not been a new car, she had hardly used it since moving in. But owning it was important. Several times in the last few days she wished she had parked it in the driveway so that Brayden could never have put the Fairlane there. But no point regretting that. Mistakes happen. Choices are made for good reasons that turn out to be lousy ones, and vice versa.

The flat was in darkness. She called out as she went in, but she knew there would be no answer. Their clothes were there, the usual agglomerates, children's cups and bottles in the sink. Someone, Eleanor, had made Marnie's bed, and tidied the pull-out bed. In the bathroom the towels were hanging up. She knew what that meant; Eleanor was feeling guilty. She looked in the back of the cutlery drawer and saw that her spare key was gone. She went outside and looked through the windows of the Fairlane. The children's car seats were also gone.

So, the two of them, Lenny and Bray, had wrestled the car seats from one vehicle to another, gone through the rigma-role of transferring, shortening, lengthening straps, locking everything into a new car—oh, God, she hoped they had done it properly—and to go where?

Certainly not Centrelink which was what, a few stops away by tram? No, this was something else. It was familiar enough, there was no reason to be crushed by it, nor even surprised. She looked for a message on her phone. There would be one eventually, if everything went to plan. *Sorry, Mum, absolute emergency…no choice…back soon…* She regret-ted the nearly full tank of petrol, considering the price of fuel right now. There was also the chance that they were gone for good—would they have left all their stuff? Perhaps, with enough incentive. She would have to consider that. But not yet.

Marnie looked around the flat for clues. The vodka bottle was on the sink, empty, the replacement sixpack of Scotch and cola empty, flattened cans in the bin. That was a pity and a blessing, but it also suggested that whoever was behind the wheel—probably Brayden, with his conviction that his sex gave him priority in the driver's seat—was not fully in charge of his faculties.

This led to unwelcome thoughts about consequences. She could lose the car in a collision, her insurance would not buy her another one as good; possibly there would be no payout anyway, depending on the kind of accident and the condition of the driver. She could lose her daughter and Brayden. She could lose them all. She could lose only the children, and Lenny and Bray survive. This last notion made her lean her head on the door jamb and bang it hard. She would not allow fantasies. The only thing she would allow herself to list were the immediate actions that she might now take. These were:

a) *stay home and wait*

b) *phone Rhi*

c) *phone the police*

d) *start screaming*

She wanted a) and d), they were the two options, done together, that would feel the best. But she had tried them in the past, more than once, and knew they didn't work.

She had done b), a seemingly simple task, a few times. Right at this moment Marnie could not face the conversation she would have to have, the level of calm she would be exhorted to reach.

She had carried out c) and wrecked her relationship with her daughter once before. That rift had never repaired.

Lenny was in remand for weeks, bail refused because of a previous no-show at the Magistrates Court, and Michael was given into Marnie's care. Marnie's abiding memory of that period was Eleanor spitting across the table at her—actually spitting in her mother's face, so filled with rage that she couldn't form words—there in the visitors' dining room in

Dame Phyllis Frost. People all around them at other tables, talking quietly in that bland room, prison guards watching. Less than a year later, the 7-Eleven debacle that resulted in a custodial sentence, all Lenny's bridges burnt.

After that, the custody claim for Michael, who was given to his father, a boy Marnie judged to be as hopeless as Eleanor, maybe worse. But TJ had risen to the task, moved back to his family in New South Wales, parents and grandparents, aunts and uncles, whole generations living on one property. They had taken TJ and Michael in and taught their prodigal boy how to be a father and a man. Over the phone, the mother had said to Marnie, 'I'm sorry, but we're so glad to have Tim away from Lenny. So glad.' The repetition was the worst bit.

Tim. Marnie had never known his name. Not TJ, Tim. She said, 'My daughter's name is Eleanor,' because she wanted to tell that unknown woman with the trembling voice, farmer from an unimaginable world, for some dumb moment in her head, she thought it counted. Not Lenny, Eleanor.

TJ's mother said, 'I honestly don't care.'

Now, on the doorstep of her flat, she felt that every organ inside her was swelling up. She would not resort to d), it did not work. It did not work.

She woke late after a disturbed night, felt stillness around her, saw colours from the windows swaying ever so slightly on the wall in pale bands of sunlight. She did not want the day to begin. Finally, she sat up, took her phone and her reading glasses from the floor and looked at her messages. She knew there was nothing. She would never have missed an alert.

She drank black tea on her doorstep because the milk was gone. She watched the airbus make its stately descent over rooftops and idly fancied letting the Fairlane's handbrake off, allowing it to bumble backwards on its three good tyres and one flat one, down to the road where she would set a fire underneath it.

Vincent left his house. He glanced over his shoulder from the letterbox, straight up the driveway and almost made eye contact with her, before shouldering his backpack and walking swiftly away. Marnie wondered when there would be a letter under her door. Sylvie would write it for him, it would be firm and reasonable, it would brook no argument.

She showered, squeezed water and soap out of Koa's teddy which was lying sodden on the floor of the shower recess, scrubbed the muck from its fur, rinsed it and squeezed it out again, as if it mattered. She dressed, tidied the flat the way she liked it, folding up the sofa bed, wiping the bench and table, mopping the bathroom properly. She cleaned spilled yoghurt from the door of the fridge. She took a long time over everything. She thought, whatever happens, I need my bond back.

On her way to work, she pegged Koa's teddy on the Hills hoist by one rainbow-coloured ear and gave the line a push so that it juddered in a grudging half-circle before coming to a halt. The clothesline had probably been swung on by rowdy children for years, carried a lifetime of washing. It had done its duty.

7

At work, Trinh brought noodles and takeaway coffee to the counter. She said, 'Patsy left you a coffee. I microwaved for you. I found Ukraine flags online—little ones. The last lot sold out quick. They might arrive today.' Marnie sipped stale coffee obediently. Trinh added, 'I forgot to tell you, I took ten dollars from the till the day before yesterday, I put it back later.'

Marnie said, 'Oh. Yes.'

'Patsy said she worked it all out for you. You were confused, she said.'

Patsy would always be the self-appointed hero of any situation. The realisation that Marnie had been cast in the role of Fool was galling.

'Is she in today again?'

'Finished at eleven. She talks too much,' said Trinh. 'But I need time at home for a while.'

'Customers like her.'

'Maybe some,' said Trinh, non-committal.

That was heartening. After Trinh was gone, Marnie found some energy. She tidied the counter, unpacked Easter eggs. She blended winter scarves in complementary colours and hung them in a cascading display. She bought one for herself, knotting it around her neck. The evenings were getting cool, daylight saving pretty well done for another year. The till balanced.

She bought half a roast chicken and a salad and walked home in the gloom, watching streetlights come on. Friday night, football season. Vincent would be watching a game, she would be able to see the screen from her flat, but it felt weird looking in on him. She definitely needed a TV if she stayed, just a small one. And someone to tow away the Fairlane. People bought cars for scrap. She would have to cancel her car insurance, that would be a big saving. Recalling suddenly that it might all be too late and staying here might not be possible now blanked her thoughts.

When she rounded the corner, she saw her car parked in its usual spot.

Walking up the driveway she looked for signs of life, but the flat was still, although the bathroom light was on.

She opened the door and the cat shot out, startling her. It disappeared under the Fairlane and out the front of it, heading for the house. There were McDonald's wrappers and bags on the table, bottles of flavoured milk and a smell of alcohol. There were clothes on the floor, the pull-out bed was still folded, and the children were lying in a nest of blankets on the floor in the semi-dark. They were awake, but quiet, dressed in soiled nappies and T-shirts—Brayden's T-shirts by the look of them.

'Ganny,' said Frankie and Koa made an echoing sound—almost a word. She bent down and held them. She wanted to weep.

'Well, hey there, little lambies.'

She looked around the side of the screen and saw two shapes stretched out on her bed.

'Are you awake?' she said but there was no answer. She made sure they were both breathing. They were.

'Eleanor,' she said. Then she said, 'Lenny.'

From the depths of the blankets a movement. 'Mum?'

'Hi, I just got home.'

'I stuffed up, Mum.' Her voice was slow.

'I guess.'

'Kids there?'

'They're fine. I'm home now.'

A long pause. Then: 'Thanks, thanks Mum. Thanks.'

'Sleep it off.'

A sound, not words, then silence.

Marnie found the children's clothes where she'd stacked them, folded, on the floor by her bed. She collected the few remaining nappies from the bathroom where she'd put them when she'd tidied. Eleanor would have found them if they'd been left lying around. It occurred to Marnie that that was why Eleanor lived in chaos. Everything had to be at her fingertips.

The children needed food. They needed nappies, nappy-rash cream. She needed to check her bank account to see if her pay was in. She bundled the children up, could find no shoes for Frankie, and carried them both down the driveway. Koa saw his teddy on the line and began to cry, so Marnie made a detour across the yard where she unpegged it and was surprised to find it dry and soft—the sinister miracle of synthetic fur.

On her way past the back windows of the main house, the whole place suddenly lit up and she found herself face to face with Vincent, who had just arrived home. He was still in his suit, his tie loosened. A moment of stillness passed between them before he put his backpack on the kitchen bench and nodded at her.

'Are you—all right?' he said, his voice muffled through the glass.

She made a rapid analysis of possible replies. 'No,' she said and shook her head in case he hadn't heard her. 'But it will be…' She nearly said 'okay' but, oh God, how could she say that?

'I don't know,' she said and shrugged, feeling the need to mime her answer in this absurd circumstance, in the diminishing light. She said, 'Sorry, I have to…' pointing to the driveway.

He nodded and she turned away, feeling Frankie slipping down her hip.

Frankie said, 'Oopsie,' in an unsurprised way, and Marnie put her down, hitched her bag up on her shoulder and the baby up on her left hip, then she lifted Frankie high onto her right side. 'Gotcha,' she said.

*

The children were awake now, squirmy in their car seats. Marnie drove onto the freeway because it was the way the car was pointing. Oncoming headlights dazzled her, overhead the blinking of planes, seemingly in convoy. She drifted left until she was on the Sydenham turnoff and driving down a long straight boulevard lined with gargantuan hardware emporiums and reception centres—even a circus, big top and sideshows, lights glittering from a Ferris wheel. She pulled into a carpark, unloaded the children and took them into a shopping mall.

She needed to walk around shops with the children safely in a trolley. She needed to be stultified by background music, which, sign of her age, was so often muted versions of songs from her girlhood. This evening it was Mary Hopkin's ethereal, childish voice, singing 'Those Were the Days', a song that Marnie's mother had particularly loved.

What kind of nostalgic longing did it generate in Joan back then? She told Marnie once, as they did dishes together, that modern songs were more truthful than the songs of her youth. But music was never truthful, Marnie felt. It was a sop for fear, but it sopped up happiness too. It messed with reality.

Heath was the worst, he was a sucker for nostalgic stuff; sometimes he'd shed a tear right there in the truck. Well, it was understandable, considering his wife. 'Listen to this, this is bee-ootiful,' he would say twisting the knob on the dangling transistor. It might be that song about an old man taking a daisy up to his wife's grave. The boys in the truck would grin and wink at Marnie. 'I saw that!' Heath would say, and they would laugh, because Heath never really took offence. He would nearly drive the truck off the road in ecstasy if Dean Martin came on, which was a frequent enough occurrence since the trannie was rusted on to Easylistening.

'Dean, the fuck, who?' one of the boys said once, and Heath had threatened to put him out onto the road then and there.

'I'm surrounded by Philistines!' he bellowed.

'Who're you callin' Phyllis?' Marko, who didn't speak a word for the first two weeks on the job, turned out to be the funny one.

'Button up! Dino's singin'!'

The faces of the boys, usually hidden under shaggy hanks of hair, shone with hilarity.

Now, Mary Hopkin had given way to Captain and Tennille. Marnie was holding a box of Vita-Brits. There were raised voices in the supermarket aisle ahead of her. She slowed down, intending to reverse away from trouble. But disturbances, especially domestic ones, always draw onlookers, and she couldn't get her trolley by.

A skeletal woman with hair down to her waist was holding on to a trolley and a boy was putting grocery items into it while keeping up what sounded like a pep talk. There was another boy, much younger, running up and down the aisles pulling packets off shelves. The mother was pleading with the older boy.

'It's going to shit, I can feel it,' the mother said, her voice surprisingly deep.

'We need baked beans, sausages—' He made a grab for the younger child as it ducked away.

'Home I said, now.'

'Cheese. Hey, come on, you can help, can't you?' He succeeded second time around in grabbing the younger boy, who kicked at him. The older boy didn't react, he held the younger one at arm's length. 'What kind of juice we gettin', Clint? You choose—go get it.'

The child dashed off. 'I'm at the end of my rope,' the mother said. Marnie could see her hand trembling as she pushed hair from her face. It was an ancient face, Fucked-up Ice Queen, Eleanor would say, not appreciating the irony. Lenny could be condescending because she did not favour ice. She preferred heroin and oxy, although there were times when ice had been a tolerable-enough port in a storm. She'd even had a go at manufacturing it, in company with a previous boyfriend, now dead.

Thank God, Marnie thought, then felt guilty because it was likely that Zac the meth cooker was Frankie's father. His death had pushed Eleanor into rehab for a third time, under a court order, and kept her pretty well clean until after Frankie was born. Thank God for *that*, at least.

This wizened woman was probably not more than thirty. Younger than Eleanor. And that child, apparently uncontrollable, would that be Koa in a few years?

'Nearly done. Just bread, cheese...' Reciting his list, the boy pulled the trolley and the woman trotted behind it like a toddler with a walker. Clint reappeared lugging dogfood cans and laughing. 'Juice, I told you!' his brother said and the child dropped the cans and watched them roll away, then accelerated out of reach again.

'You got no idea how my head is…' The woman raised her voice.

The boy held up fingers and said, 'Five more things—bread, cheese, baked beans, peanut butter, Vegemite.'

'I hate Vegemite,' her voice peevish now.

'It's for Clint.'

'He gets no treats; he's being a shit. Jesus, where is he?'

A series of yells and a crash reported his whereabouts to everyone in the store.

Marnie pulled her trolley away, carving a path out. At the checkout a man ahead of her said, 'They've called for backup.' Then: 'Always like this on pension day. I don't know why I come.'

Marnie did not tell him that pension day was three days past, and that what she had seen was a desperate effort by a responsible child to get the last of the money spent on food before it disappeared. She could have told him, too, that her own daughter was home right now, bombed out of her brain. She smiled sympathetically and unloaded groceries.

They sat in the car in the shopping-centre carpark, and she fed pieces of cooled-down roast chicken to the children with a single bamboo fork, followed by mandarin segments and a tube each of apple and blackcurrant puree. Because her pay was in, $345.17, she had a coffee from McDonald's. She cleaned rubbish from the floor of the car, empty cans of ultra-sugared ultra-caffeinated energy drink and old bottles of water, gathered up children's knitted hats and Eleanor's black hoodie. She unearthed Frankie's shoes and socks and teddy bear, wet leggings and a half-empty bag of snakes, which the children grabbed at. She gave them one each to shut them up and jammed the rest in the car door pocket. Finally, she made a phone call.

'Do you want to come here?' said Rhiannon.

'No, I still have a home, I'm on the pull-out sofa now.'

'Demoted.'

'It was always going to happen.'

'Have you told them to go?'

'What's the point, they're non compos.'

'They'll be coming out of it.'

Marnie pictured Lenny and Bray fumbling around the flat. She didn't want to be there for that grotesque routine, the slurring excuses. Or they might be past that stage, in defensive mode, ready to turn on her if she looked sideways at either of them.

She said, 'I don't trust how I'll be. I'll make it worse.'

'You know where to go.'

'The kids are with me.'

'Okay, but that's an excuse.'

She was silent in the face of Rhiannon's logic.

Rhi continued, 'You need to be careful not to buy into the drama. It makes you feel alive, I get that, but it'll drag you under.'

'Sorry, Rhi, I have to go.' Marnie heard her voice break and ended the call. Rhi would not call back. She knew the way it went.

'Fucking hippie,' Marnie said to the steering wheel.

'Fucking pippie,' Frankie enunciated perfectly.

*

The children were asleep when she parked the car. She left them while she crept past the Fairlane to the flat. The Friday-night game was on in the main house, washing green light through the family room and out into the yard. Vincent was glued to the last quarter; the cat was perched on the arm of the couch beside him. Marnie's flat was in darkness.

She went inside and listened. The wall heater was pumping out heat, the air solid with it. She looked for the remote control to turn it off but couldn't find it. Eleanor and Brayden were still on her bed, but there was evidence they'd been up and about. McDonald's wrappers had been pushed aside. Cereal boxes were out on the table, Eleanor's bag sat in a pool of milk. Their new mobile, supposedly bought with money from Brayden's dad, was buzzing. Marnie picked it up: No Caller ID. She put the phone down. 'Lenny,' she said quietly, but there was no answer from the bed. She listened for breathing, then continued past the bed to the bathroom where she gathered up toothbrush, toothpaste, brushes, hairdryer. She pulled a bag from under the bed and stuffed it with her hanging clothes. From the kitchen she added some bowls, cups and spoons. The three photographs on the windowsill. She quietly removed a folder of paperwork from a box beside the bed, then she upturned Eleanor's bag, picked out her wallet and removed the Medicare card. Eleanor's name was 'Lenny' on the card, followed by the two children, Frankie L and Koa I. No Michael. She wrote the numbers on her hand.

'Hey, Mum,' not Eleanor's voice. This was Brayden getting up for a piss, pausing unsteadily to speak to her. As if speaking and walking were a bridge too far. 'How're you doing?'

'Fine. You?' Neutral voice.

'Hey…cruisin'. You're a fucken pistol, Marnie. I mean that.'

'Thanks.'

He staggered into the bathroom. She followed him. She said, 'I'm taking the kids away for a while, looks like you guys need a rest.'

'Yeah, sure.' He leaned one hand on the wall while he pissed, gazing with hooded eyes at a stream of tea-coloured urine.

'I spoke about it to Lenny before, she thought it was a good idea.'

A pause. It took a long time for him to process information. Then: 'Shit yeah. Ace.'

'I'm writing a note with the address on it, okay? It's here on the table. Tell her to phone me tomorrow. Or, I'll phone you guys.'

Another pause. 'Sure thing.' He took time tucking his dick back in his shorts, absorbed by the task.

'Okay, the flat's paid up until the end of the month.'

'Sweet.'

He was moving again, swaying like a sleepwalker in the direction of the bed.

She retrieved the mobile from Eleanor's bag and walked out the door.

8

When she had passed the irregular boxes of outer-suburban housing developments, sailed down through a gorge and past the chess-board fruit trees outside Bacchus Marsh, when bald, black hills seemed to fold mutely around her, Marnie began to feel herself unclench. Legs, arms, spine; finally the muscles in her face.

The children slept on; the car engine buzzed tranquilly over sound bitumen. Other vehicles on other trajectories swept past her. Gargantuan B-doubles, sometimes three at a time, rode king tides of air that thwacked the wall of her car. She kept her sights on the outer white line of the carriageway, all that was visible now. She did not make a list. For a while she did not think.

Frankie woke needing a toilet when they were climbing the hill out of Pike's. They pulled into a fuel stop lit up like a mediaeval castle on the highest point of land, banners proclaiming fuel and food. She lifted Frankie out, carried

Koa in her arms. Inside, it was a cavern lit with white light, a cornucopia of food and gadgets, music playing, the smell of burnt coffee, a wall screen flashing images of American football. The toilets were, mercifully, clean. The children clung to her, pale with tiredness. Walking back to the car in the dark, she felt in the pocket of her coat for Lenny's phone and dropped it into the bushes edging the parking bays. After she had strapped the children in, she felt a wave of guilt. She retrieved the mobile and stowed it under her seat.

She drove past the exits to Ballarat, through Beaufort and on and on, past more exits that enticed her with unusual names, but she stayed with the highway, and so into Ararat. The streets were wide here. Pubs were lit up but everything else was dark. The children were sleeping again, so where was the point in stopping? But she was flagging, aware of a drag under her ribcage that told her she wanted to lie down. North of the town, a mob of kangaroos broke from bushes and burst across the road in front of her and she braked, blood jumping in her chest.

Koa protested in his sleep. She pulled into a roadside stop and stepped out of the car.

She was only metres off the highway, but it was dark here—country dark, not the penumbra of city dark. Here was a cloudy night with no visible moon. The air was sharp. She squatted to pee with one hand on the passenger door. She thought for the first time, 'What am I doing?' but it seemed that the question had surfaced too late.

She corrected herself: it was not too late. If she drove home now, she'd be back by one or two in the morning and they probably wouldn't even know she'd been gone. There they'd all be, full house, she on the sofa bed with the children. The unfolding of another day, Vincent watching through his kitchen window to see what they were up to, the children prising her eyes open with damp fingers, asking for breakfast. Lenny and Bray might drowse until Saturday afternoon. At some point she would have to say: you can't have my car again, I won't let you. That would lead to a fight in which accusations would be hurled like knives, but eventually they would make up. Lenny and Bray would never allow you to get to the point of no return, they would say whatever it took to bring about rapprochement if there was a risk of them being disadvantaged. KFC would be bought to celebrate, loyalty and commitment would be reiterated. She could hear Bray patronising her: 'You're a pistol, Marnie.' Another bottle of vodka would be produced, maybe something cheaper, depending on how much money was left, how much they could persuade her to give them to make up a shortfall.

And so on. Whatever they'd taken, there would be more of it, tonight, tomorrow, whenever it could be got. They'd established a supply line. Their money would be gone, soon they would be in debt. Marnie's money would go, too, feeding them all and putting nappies on the children. Maybe when there was absolutely no money to be had, they'd leave. They would get a retread with money from a payday lender, using her name, and then just go. As they'd done before. Maybe they would leave behind the children, be glad to, not give it a second thought. Even then, she would be up the creek. She wouldn't be able to work. The unemployment benefit wouldn't pay the rent and keep them.

Marnie climbed back into the driver's seat and realised the car had cooled rapidly with the engine turned off. She put Lenny's hoodie, her own jacket and her new scarf around the children. She needed food and she needed to sleep. She would have to find somewhere less isolated to pull over. She was not far enough off the road to feel safe here, but would she feel safe anyway in all that shadowy bush? She opened the glove box looking for jelly snakes and found, instead, a roll of twenty-dollar notes and a purchase statement from a pawn shop in Dandenong. She counted eleven notes, there had been more, she could tell from the looseness of the roll. Well. Could she call this a bonus and not feel guilty about it? She switched on the internal light and read the statement. It described a diamond ring, circa 1952, the year her mother married. The ring had been Glad-wrapped, along with her mother's garnet pendant, and hidden at the back of the kitchen drawer from where Lenny and Bray had extracted her car key. She should have guessed. Lenny would have told Bray the ring was meant for her, which it was: it had always been promised to her. So far Marnie had managed to hold it back.

Marnie looked at the money in her lap. Lenny and Bray had three weeks' free accommodation if Vincent didn't turf them out, and she had two hundred and twenty dollars. She was still the loser, but holding cash in her hands made her feel less doomed. She made two new headings in her notebook:

Things To Do   Things To Get

She remembered the packet of jelly snakes in the door pocket and ate the last three. Then she pulled out onto the highway.

9

Marnie drove into Stawell around midnight, across a rail line and along a main street with darkened shopfronts. She located supermarkets, discount stores and a bakery, took some random turns and chanced on an aquatic centre. It had a carpark, so she pulled in there and dozed until the children woke her in the early morning. They were hungry and restless but not thrown by their night in the car. She drove back along the main street until she came to a park with a toilet block. She combed hair, wiped faces with wet toilet paper, cleaned teeth, tried to make them all look, if not respectable, at least unremarkable. Then to a supermarket with her list—quick oats, fruit, liquid soap, little cartons of long-life milk, a hot-water flask, a quick scan in the baby section for specials on tube food and formula—oh, dear lord, the cost of formula. Next, she drove to a petrol station for fuel, coffee (a celebratory coffee, bought with her windfall money) and to beg hot water from the petrol station for her flask. Then back to the gardens, where she mixed up quick oats and fed the children while they wrestled with rocking ducks and swings, spooning gloop into Koa while he walked determinedly upright, clutching structural rails to keep himself steady. Marnie couldn't remember Koa's actual birthday, which bothered her, but she knew it was May and he was almost one. He might soon walk independently. She needed another list, she thought.

Important but Can Wait

a) Shoes for Ko

It was a damp morning under a pale sky. Older children played on a nearby oval, shouting to one another. Dogs erupted from parked cars for their morning runs. When breakfast was done and the children could be persuaded back into the car, Marnie circled around the main shopping street. She was searching for the aquatic centre but became disorientated. She took some turns, tried to locate the rail line and came instead to a street of light industry and a second-hand place, which was opening up. She pulled in.

It was called Barney's Barn. It was mostly yard junk, old gates and window frames. The wrong kind of shop, she knew as soon as they walked in. But there were pink gumboots, in good order, just right for Frankie to replace the canvas lace-ups that were already soaked from the park. At the counter, the serving girl kept her phone jammed to her ear, talking, while she turned the boots upside-down and shook them vigorously, then felt down to the toes of each one. Marnie started to say, 'Is there a problem?' but stopped herself. The girl wasn't looking at her. The price came up on the till and the server waited without speaking.

Marnie wasn't sure why she was offended. Because she felt invisible? Was that also why she wanted to walk out?

But there was Frankie reaching up to carry the boots, so Marnie paid and ushered the children out. After that she found the railway line and the road out of town. The highway stretched out like an old friend now, quickly grown familiar. She turned north, sparse bush on one side of her, desiccated pastures on the other. Three brown dogs in the back of a ute stared as they sailed past.

The next major town was Horsham, streets laid out in parallels, intersections built for road trains. Here, the dominant feature was sky. Everything human seemed bundled and slipshod at the base of a vast sky canvas. There was an op shop on the outskirts with balloons out the front, also a narrow flag on the footpath, swaying in the almost-still air, with the words *Opportunity Knocks* down the centre of it. Marnie pulled up and unloaded the children. Inside, there seemed to be a party going on. The women running the place were eating slices of buttered Boston bun and calling out to one another. One was ironing clothes behind the counter. Another gave the children a piece of bun each and took them to the toy baskets in a corner. She said to Marnie, 'There're some wealthy young mums in this town. When they do a drop-off the quality of the clothes goes sky-high.' She pointed to racks. 'I've already rung my daughter-in-law, but you're here first.' She handed Marnie a wrinkly plastic shopping bag. 'Fill it up,' she said, 'five dollars a bag.'

Marnie picked up jumpers, trousers, overalls. 'Does everything go in the bag—if it's not clothing?' she said.

'Separate bag,' said the woman. She frowned for a moment, long enough to make Marnie's pulse race, embarrassed that she might be judged as an opportunist. 'But there's a discount on a second bag, isn't there, Kath?'

Kath, who was behind the counter modelling necklaces for the ironing woman, looked up. 'Well...three dollars?'

'And third bag's free,' confided the first woman with her mouth full of bun. 'We're overstocked. You're doing us a favour.'

Unexpectedly, Marnie felt her throat tighten. She bent to examine the rack of clothes. There was a hollow sort of silence in the air around her. Then the woman beside her said, 'Singlets?'

Marnie nodded, and the woman riffled through a shelf, bringing out singlets, socks, pyjamas and a Bluey dressing-gown. 'There's still tags on this,' the woman shoved the dressing-gown in a third bag. She added, 'Some people have more money than sense. But that's a lucky break for us. Do you live here?'

'Passing through.'

'Pity, we can always use volunteers.'

'I've got my grandkids.' Her voice would not work beyond that sentence.

The women looked at the children, whose entire bodies were almost in the toy basket by now.

'Actually,' the ironing woman called out, 'do they like Octonauts?'

When Marnie left the op shop, she had three bags of clothes for eight dollars, a single bed doona and two towels for five dollars and a bucket of Octonauts for two dollars. Marnie handed a twenty-dollar note to the ironing women, accepted her change and left feeling that she had not thanked them properly, or smiled enough. She felt terrible about it, and weirdly bereft. She drove into the town centre, found clean toilets at the mall and put *Frozen* swimmers on Frankie and cotton shorts on the baby. She pulled bike shorts on herself and pulled her jeans back over them. They asked directions and drove to the swim centre just off the main road, paid entry and stayed in the toddler pool for two hours. Frankie floated Octonauts and Koa scooped them up and sucked them. Marnie lay on her stomach in the shallow, warm water, settling disputes when needed and being crawled on by Koa. The children splashed, jumped, fell down and shot up again coughing and laughing. Their skin shone.

When they were getting fractious, she wooed them into a shower cubicle and washed them properly. Then she showered herself, keeping up a running commentary while she dragged her clothes back on, to distract them before they made a break for the pool again.

Afterwards, outside in the car, bottle and sippie cup were distributed and they were driving again. Koa was asleep within minutes. It was not late, but Marnie felt herself sagging. She would have to find somewhere for them to spend the night.

'Ganny, is this the beach?' said Frankie.

'No, it's the country.'

'Does it have a house?'

'There are houses, look.' There weren't many houses. They

were passing paddocks, sparse roadside trees bent by a lifelong battle with elements.

'Does it have our house?'

Marnie didn't answer at once. She said finally, 'It might have. We're having a holiday. We're looking around.'

'Will we go at the pool?'

'We'll go to the pool again, of course we will.'

'But not unda da water.'

'If you went under, Ganny would pick you up.'

'I don't like barfers,' said Frankie. 'Bay make you go unda in barfers and I cwy for Mummy.'

'In baths,' a faint effervescence in Marnie's chest.

Frankie said, 'I ony want sowers, not hot just warm.'

'Okay, we'll only have showers at our house, and we'll go to the pool to play sometimes.'

'With Ganny.'

'With Ganny, yes.'

'And Mummy.'

'Yes. Look, cows. What do cows say?'

Frankie did not answer.

10

Marnie drove north on a road straight as a ruler, the whole world bathed by the setting sun in post-apocalyptic umber. There were signs indicating towns ahead—the car swept past a school road, a church road—but they continued many kilometres before she realised there was no town at all nearby, just flat land, expanses of bare dirt, lines of silos. She pulled in at the first structure they reached which, from a distance, promised some sort of settlement but turned out to be a speed-way. A high circular fence spattered with advertising, lights along the bleachers, a large central field of gravel, all locked up behind cyclone wire. Behind this, the more familiar array of green grass and goalposts, bitumen netball courts, a fenced-off playground. There was a shuttered kiosk but no barbecue. Marnie had bought a packet of sausages which she now found she couldn't cook. She opened baked beans and pulled out slices of bread which she buttered with her bamboo fork—gently, so it would not break. Frankie stomped around in her new boots eating bread and butter while Marnie put pieces into Koa's hands. He shuttled them diligently but inaccurately towards his mouth, and Marnie caught them when they dropped. Then there were tubes of apple puree, Tiny Teddies and a bottle and sippie cup of formula, which she hoped would plug nutritional gaps. The toilets were locked, so she changed Koa on the ground and put a night nappy on Frankie.

Trucks rushed through the dusk, illuminated all over as if they were something wondrous—which, she supposed, in their way they were, thundering northwards, southwards, rocketing past each other. In periods of quiet she could hear wind. They all looked up when a squadron of whooping corellas passed overhead, heading south for the mountains. Then darkness came, then, finally, silence.

The speedway buildings, bleak enough by daylight, loomed eerily in the gloom. Marnie drove further north and stopped at a corrugated-iron shed just off the road with spindly trees beside it and a brick toilet block behind. The sign above the front entrance said Sailors' Home Hall 1923. It was locked up and so unfortunately were the toilets, but there was something comforting about the building, a relic, settled into the landscape to witness passing juggernauts and further away, a meticulous plantation of wind towers, their vast faces all turned to the southwest. The windows of the Sailors' Home Hall were dark, but one of them sported a lace curtain. She parked close in to it.

She unloaded bags and boxes from the back and stowed them in the passenger seat and footwell, and now there was room for the children in the luggage space, under the newly acquired doona. She rolled it around and under them for warmth. Frankie sang *Twinkle Twinkle* to an Octonaut in each hand. Koa grizzled, dummy in and out of his mouth, and said, 'Mum, Mum,' crossly to himself a few times. Then they were both asleep.

It would be the driver's seat again for Marnie. Now, at eight o'clock on a Saturday night, there was nothing for her to do except sleep. She lowered the seatback as far as she could, dragged her coat over her chest, towels around her legs. She lay still and waited for her feelings to surface, which they inevitably did, hauling up from her subconscious like the undead. She thought, 'What am I doing?' and 'How is this going to end?' She got out her notebook and wrote by the light from her phone:

a) *Centrelink*
b) *Texts x 2*
c) *Salvation Army(?)*

To this, she eventually added *d) Rhiannon*, then crossed it out and changed item b) to *Texts x 3*. She experimented in her head with wording for the texts and when this became too difficult, she scrolled through photographs, rather poor ones. Pictures of Michael over a range of ages—birth, in his highchair, dressed as Harry Potter. Pictures of Frankie newborn, transparent hair over a yellow skull criss-crossed with blue veins, a disappointed look on her colourless face.

The infant welfare nurses never said anything, but they paid visits—more than the usual rush-in-rush-out kind in the first weeks after Frankie's birth—giving Marnie bland smiles while they watched the baby nursing, weighed her before and after, wrote things down. They couldn't fault Eleanor, though. She fed diligently, she spoke to the baby and held her close. She drank tonics to build up her milk supply, whatever was suggested to her: vegetable juice, bone broth, oatmeal and stewed apple, all prepared by Marnie. They didn't know, it was none of their business, that Eleanor was fourteen months out of prison, eight weeks out of rehab, her newest boyfriend was dead from an overdose and she was grieving for the child who had been taken away. Presumably she was grieving— if Marnie so much as mentioned Michael's name, or TJ's, Eleanor would fly into a rage. It was easier to talk about Zac. He was an idiot, Eleanor said, he deserved to die.

When the infant welfare nurses decided it would be wise to supplement Eleanor's breastmilk with formula, Marnie took over the night feeds so Eleanor could sleep. Then she took over morning feeds and daytime feeds. The baby began to look less feeble; her skin turned peach-coloured; she began to smile and kick her feet in the bath. It seemed so logical to help, the transition was so smooth. It was all for the baby, Marnie told herself, what else could she have done? But she never knew if she'd prefigured what was coming or whether she enabled it. Because by the time Eleanor attended her six-week check-up, she was using again.

Cold settled on the car like a weight. Marnie overturned bags, unearthed the children's beanies and went around to the back to cover their heads. While she was outside the car, she found the whole world had changed. She was under an icy sky glinting with stars. The paddocks were alive—those bleak expanses she had seen in daylight were now full of massive tractors pulling air-seeders. Far, far away she could see lights moving in steady procession, she could hear the baritone of engines. She wanted to be absorbed into it; stood there against the car until it was too cold, and she had to climb inside again.

She was sorry she hadn't bought a book at the op shop. They'd had boxes of them, but she was thinking of other things. She hadn't started out a reader, but she'd become one in her twenties because of Heath's wife, Lorna. Before that, she read the set books for school but nothing for pleasure other than magazines. Her mother read sporadically: people gave Joan books over the counter at the chemist shop, old customers handed her Jean Plaidy novels wrapped in coloured cellophane, along with talc or chocolates at Christmas. Apart from her short foray into Germaine Greer, Joan was an indifferent reader, preferring cards.

Lorna Woolley, on the other hand, was voracious. The Woolley house, when Marnie came to work there, was dusty and airless, reeking of nicotine. Neglect had settled over the place after Lorna was taken out of it—cracked lino, loose hinges on the kitchen cupboards, a briquette heater that smoked and smelled and yellowed the wallpaper. But the sitting room had a whole wall of books in it. 'Lorna's,' Heath said, waving his hand at them peremptorily as they passed through on her first visit. 'My wife is a terrier for books.'

Marnie put a warm hand over the end of her cold nose. She could hear the children breathing and rustling. She thought of the phone stashed under her seat. Of course, if Eleanor really needed to contact her, it was only a matter of getting on to Rhiannon. She thought she might call Rhiannon herself, but didn't. Rhiannon would say, 'Okay, this is your choice, but what is your intention? You need to be clear.' And there would be no answer, because what Marnie needed was time to decide. She peered at her phone screen for a while, at a map of the roads around her, pink lines snaking in a sea of white, but couldn't even decide which direction was best for them. She felt stiff, empty, cold. She wouldn't turn on the engine to get the heater going because of stories drilled into her about carbon monoxide poisoning, and there was also the matter of using up fuel. She thought, if I go north, it'll be warmer. It occurred to her that if she crossed the border she could visit Michael. The thought encouraged her.

She looked at the map for a while then, still sleepless, she composed text messages. The first to her landlord.

> *Vincent, Am sincerely sorry to leave without telling you. Hope you understand things were difficult. I regret not managing it better. Marnie*

Followed by: *Also I loved living there. Thanx.*
And to Trinh:

> *I'm sorry I am unable to come in Monday, and indefinitely. Personal issues at home and with family. I am sorry to leave like this, I know it will be difficult. Marnie*

This made her feel terrible. Neither text conveyed the right sentiment, but the one to Trinh was worse. She typed an addendum: *Thank you for everything. I mean it. You really helped me. Marnie*

76

Even that seemed too dismissive. She could not bring herself to press send on either message. She would. She would have to. But there was still all of Sunday. She could still drive home and be there at 2 p.m. Monday for work if she changed her mind, and Trinh would never know. Her flat was still there, she could offload the children and tell Lenny and Bray to get out, tyre or no tyre. She could be that person she always wanted to be, firm and resolved. Like Rhiannon, like Trinh, like Vincent's smart sister, Sylvie. How did people get like that? How did they know how to be, and draw on that knowledge at exactly the right moment?

She lay back and thought of Heath's wife, Lorna.

The work responsibilities Marnie signed up for when she was eighteen soon expanded. When Heath was going to be late back from a job he would call Marnie and she would go up to the nursing home to help Lorna with her meal. Nervously at first, because Lorna's condition affected her voice and she spoke in a garbled, underwater way. It made Marnie panicky, she hated saying, 'I'm sorry, I didn't quite catch that,' even once, and sometimes she had to say it three or four times, and worse—sometimes even after repetitions she still couldn't understand what Lorna was saying. But Lorna always smiled and nodded at her. Not ever, not even once, did Lorna express impatience. When Marnie arrived at her bedside, Lorna would reach up with a shaking hand to touch Marnie's face, with a look that said: You are exactly the person I was hoping to see.

The first word Marnie came to recognise, sometime in the

second week of nursing-home duty, was 'thank you'. After that it was like her ears simply opened. Soon Marnie understood Lorna perfectly. She understood when Lorna turned her face away and said 'No, it's awful,' about the dinner. Lorna hated the stew they sent up, but she liked sandwiches. Marnie cut them into small pieces and propped Lorna up on pillows so that she could eat them. Lorna still had some autonomy with finger food, and preferred it, although she tolerated being fed.

On Lorna's bedside table was a framed wedding photograph with rosary beads draped across it. In it, Lorna was like a magazine model, wearing a satin dress she had sewn for herself. Tiny buttons all down the bodice, and a low waist that hugged her slender hips dropping away in liquid folds to the floor. Standing alongside her was a younger, slimmer version of Heath. Even buttoned up in his wedding suit, the cleanest and neatest he may ever have been in his life, Heath managed to remain distinctly bear-like.

Beside the photograph, on Marnie's first visit, there was a stack of books: *Alice Through the Looking Glass*, *The Enchanted April*, *Dombey and Son* and two anthologies of poetry. Heath said to Marnie, 'She'll let you read for hours. You tell her— only two chapters. Plus maybe a poem. You probably won't get out without a poem, but that's okay, they're pretty good.'

'Is that what you do?'

'In sickness and in health, kiddo. Just a hint, keep her away from Dickens—they're creepy and there's a lot of words, I mean a *lot* of words.' He nodded conspiratorially. 'My Lorna loves books, the more words the better.' It was said with admiration. He added, 'She only decided to speak to me that first time we met because my name was out of a book.'

'Heath?'

Nodding, 'Heathcliff. Lucky I'd seen it at the flicks. I said to her, you don't really want me to be like that joker, do you? Because I'm telling you right now, I'm not trawling around cemeteries at night, calling up ghosts. Not even if you are the most beautiful woman I've ever laid eyes on.' He grinned. 'Which she was.' He added: 'Her name's out of a book, too.'

Of course, the first book Lorna pointed to with a bony finger was the Dickens. Marnie looked at the picture of a sad girl and a dog on the frontispiece and read the first line of *Dombey and Son* with trepidation. She still remembered it.

Dombey sat in the corner of the darkened room in the great arm-chair by the bedside, and Son lay tucked up warm in a little basket bedstead carefully disposed on a low settee immediately in front of the fire and close to it, as if his constitution were analogous to that of a muffin, and it was essential to toast him brown while he was very new.

It was like falling in love. In the months following *Dombey*, they read both Alices, *Death Comes for the Archbishop* and *The Path to Rome*. She romped through *Sense and Sensibility* and almost converted to Catholicism after *The End of the Affair*. She broached the subject with Heath as they were driving to a job together. 'Well, it probably needs more than a novel for you to make up your mind,' Heath cautioned her.

He was a convert himself, a former Presbyterian, it seemed there was nothing he wouldn't do for Lorna. 'And you're the next best thing, aren't you? C of E. Or maybe we're the next best thing to your lot. There's a lot of hoo-ha in the Holy Roman Church, that's my opinion and Lorna agrees, only she says Jesus is more important than the cardinals in Rome. You gotta think about your mum, too.'

Parked outside the Sailors' Home Hall, Marnie stared at the windscreen. Fronds of frost were beginning to form at the top of the glass and extend feelers in downward and sideways tendrils. Like Lorna, like Joan, like Florence Dombey, she thought: delicate but indomitable.

11

She sent her texts from Kerang on Sunday afternoon. She had been able to book into a caravan park at lunchtime: a one-room cabin without a bathroom, the cheapest they had. It had a kettle and a microwave, a tiny fridge, a squeeze bottle of hand sanitiser. It also had a small, powerful blow heater. She made up the double bed with her only sheet, and covered it with the doona, the Bluey dressing-gown and their coats. They showered at the brick toilet block, and she put a load of washing on in the adjoining laundry. Then she sat on the bed with a cup of tea and watched the children spreading out Octonauts over the floor.

'Is this our house?' asked Frankie.

'For tonight. Do you like it?'

'Will Mummy come here?'

'Probably not.'

When Marnie's mobile rang, Frankie looked up expectantly but didn't ask. Marnie considered declining the call but found herself picking up. 'Hi, Rhi.'

'Didn't hear from you yesterday. How's it going?'

'Just needed some space from everything.'

'No worries. Are you okay, though?'

'Has Eleanor contacted you?'

A beat. 'Should she have?'

'I just wondered,' Marnie said.

'Okay, so I'm trying to join the dots. They left finally?'

'I left.'

Silence. Marnie wanted to let the silence stand but found herself compelled to fill it. How was it that Rhiannon was stronger every time? Yes, yes, it was her role, she had all the experience. But just once, Marnie would have liked to be in charge. She said, 'I don't think they'll leave until they're made to. Or the rent's due, whichever comes first.' She added, 'How's the dog?' which was an obvious deflection, and Rhiannon would see through it in a second.

But Rhiannon said, with a break in her voice, 'Well, he died.'

'Oh gosh, Rhi. Sorry.'

'It's okay. Yesterday.'

'You didn't say anything when we spoke—'

'I didn't expect it. I mean, I took him to the vet because it just—suddenly—had to be done. One minute he was walking, staggering—you know—and the next it was time.'

'If I'd known, I would have rung.' She was filled with remorse. The dog had been important. It didn't matter that Eleanor loathed it, and it was unkind of Marnie to laugh when Eleanor mimicked Rhiannon tending the decrepit animal so devotedly, because she knew the whole story. Chase had been Josh's dog, and five years ago he had sat whimpering in the garage, pawing at Rhiannon's legs while she cut her son down.

Rhiannon said, 'All part of life's rich tapestry, huh?'

'Are you coping?'

'No choice.'

She thought of blurting out: 'He'd had a good life,' or 'You did everything you could,' or (much worse) 'Well, he's with Josh now,' but she shut up. She felt that it might be one of the few times in her life that she ticked the right option.

Rhiannon said, 'Are you up for a coffee or...where are you, exactly?'

Which is when Frankie yelled, 'No, Koa, *no!*' in her startling Brayden voice, and Koa squealed an escalating protest that morphed into roars of rage as the two children tussled over a plastic penguin in a diving suit.

Rhiannon said, 'The kids are there?'

'Just a minute. Sorry, Rhi, this isn't a good time. I'll call you, okay?' Marnie ended the call before Rhi could speak again and switched off the phone.

She separated the crying children and when they'd settled, she took them to the laundry block to transfer washing from machine to dryer. Frankie fed in coins and Koa pressed the button. The dryer whirred, laundry rolled, and the children pressed their hands to the glass to feel the vibrations.

That night, with the children curled up in bed beside her, she expected to be awake and agonising. But the room was warm, and being able to stretch out flat was completely blissful.

Oh God, how quickly our standards drop—she could hear herself sharing the irony with Eleanor, who always got the joke.

The next morning she turned on her phone, and three messages in-rushed with commanding bleeps. They were exactly the three she expected. She turned the phone off without reading them and walked the children to the shower block.

Toileted, washed and dressed, they strolled back to their cabin in sunshine, stopping to spend time at any distraction—a kookaburra on a fence, duck poo on the path, a leaf clinging to Frankie's sleeve.

They stayed another night in the caravan park, but with Easter only days away that was all they had and, truthfully, it was all Marnie felt she could afford. In the late afternoon of the second day, a large caravan eased into the area beside them. It was like a mothership, its fanciful name—*Wellaway*—was painted in windswept font along the side. Its owners, a well-dressed couple older than Marnie, she thought, set about opening, arranging, unfolding elaborate sections of wall, working together like a well-oiled machine, so that soon they had assembled an annexe with an eating area, barbecue, bar, table, chairs and an eye-popping outdoor mat. Also, inexplicably, a palm tree in a pot. Marnie felt herself shrinking from them, but the children stood on their tiny entrance porch and watched the process in awe. From inside the cabin, Marnie could hear Frankie conversing with them.

'I got this, see!' holding up an Octonaut.

'Well, well, aren't you lucky! What's your brother got?

Is he your brother?' A relevant question, considering how unalike the children were.

'He's Koa.' She had to repeat the name several times.

'And you are—'

'Fankie. What oor name?'

Their names were Nan and Pop. They were on holiday, just like Frankie. Where was her mummy and dad?

'Just fucked off,' replied Frankie, giving a shrug, both arms raised in a universal gesture of helplessness.

Marnie appeared at the door and explained that Frankie meant they were in a truck…heading…She couldn't spin the story rapidly enough. It didn't matter. The woman was laughing while the man, less amused, offered around a bowl of Easter eggs.

'One each,' said Marnie quickly.

Frankie took three and Koa took a handful, which he immediately dropped. He saw them roll away from him on the grass beneath the steps and had a meltdown.

They helped to collect scattered eggs and return them to the bowl, although Marnie noticed that a few found their way into Frankie's pockets. She was amazed that, at three, Frankie knew already how to be surreptitious. All the attention was on Koa at this moment, he would probably always garner the spotlight, she thought with a pang of loyalty for Frankie. Koa had long eyelashes and dense corkscrew curls. Lenny had never said anything about his father. Like Frankie's, his birth certificate said Father Unknown.

'There you go, Cody,' Pop tucked an egg into each of Koa's hands. His wailing stopped quite quickly. Marnie took a proffered egg, too, and asked polite questions. They were from Albury, they were here to spend Easter with old friends, a regular get-together in the years before Covid. Their own grandchildren lived in Western Australia. Where was she heading?

'Deniliquin,' she said. 'I have a grandson there.'

They were interested at once. They knew Deni, although to Marnie's relief, not that well. In town, out of town, they wanted to know?

'Out,' she said. 'It's a farm.'

Property name? She hesitated, making a play at recall, then said she couldn't remember. But she knew how to get there. Pop, whose name was in fact Bruce, fetched a satchel of maps and stretched one out on the table for Marnie to look at while Nan (Pauline) poured white wine and produced home-made cheese biscuits. Marnie looked casually at the roads that led to South Sligo and tried to memorise the main ones.

Later in the evening, when the children were sleeping, Marnie sat outside with a cup of tea and found Pauline outside too, smoking. The glow at the end of her cigarette was luminous in the semi-dark, seductive, like in an old movie.

'He's watching his shows,' Pauline explained, indicating the caravan with a movement of her shoulder. 'I like outside better. Little ones off?'

They gazed at the darkening sky together, shrinking waves of salmon, stippled green clouds, encroaching black.

Pauline said, 'Glory be to God for dappled things.'

And Marnie replied, 'For skies of couple-colour as a brinded cow.'

'Did you do him at school, too?' said Pauline.

'No, I used to read to someone in hospital. It was one of her favourites.'

'Funny how things stick.'

'Do you like caravanning?' Marnie asked.

'Bruce does. I'm here for him, and for the views. You have another half?'

'Divorced.'

'Long?'

'Ages.'

'No one else?'

'Not for a long time.' She was surprised, saying it. 'It's weird but I hardly remember my husband being part of my life. He's in Queensland. Not in good health, I don't think. No Christmas cards or anything.'

'Do the little ones know him?'

'Probably not. My daughter isn't sentimental, I guess. It's been twenty years, longer even. He wasn't in for the long haul.'

'I often wonder if connection stays.'

'I'm probably not the benchmark.'

'Sounds like you're well shot of him, anyway.'

Marnie said, 'Who knows?' and realised that it was not just an easy rejoinder but the truth.

Pauline finished her cigarette, and they sat in silence.

In the morning, Marnie packed her belongings into her car while caravans manoeuvred into spaces around her. Pauline and Bruce were greeting friends, the air full of voices, and did not look in her direction. Well, they were busy, she was not part of the big picture in these people's lives, it was ridiculous to expect that after two brief conversations she might be. She wouldn't like Bruce and Pauline anyway, most likely, and they wouldn't like her. They probably already had suspicions and would certainly shrink from her if they heard her story, not wanting to be tainted; as if addiction was something that could infect them. And actually she did not want their life either. Oh, the money would be okay, right now their caravan would be awesome, but she'd lived in the real world for too long to give up real for the comfort of ignorance.

She drove into town, angry inside, filled her car with petrol at a nerve-jangling price, bought a saucepan, a sharp knife, a pumpkin and some cooking oil, and drove north to the river.

12

It was school holidays, Easter weekend looming. Cars pulling boats belted past Marnie's Subaru. Loaded sheep trucks growled in low gear at the back of them. She felt surrounded by water, lakes, channels; finally the river. It looked flat, deceptively benign, the trees flanking it seeming to lean into the brown water. Branches hung limp, roots splayed on banks. Every conceivable space was taken up with campsites, tents, caravans; all the world out and about after lockdown.

Once Marnie had crossed the river, road traffic dwindled. Bushland became grassland, then pasture and paddocks of stubble. Passing a sign, Marnie realised that Deniliquin was closer than she expected. It startled her and she slowed, eventually turning off onto an unmade side road, driving along it for a distance and parking in a patch of shade. Deniliquin already. She needed time to think about her next move.

Ahead of her, the road seemed to recede into haze. She stared for a while, before realising she was looking at a mob of sheep moving, rag-tag, towards her. Those at the front grazing the roadside until those at the back caught up and the whole mob swarmed forward, before slowing and breaking apart again. A brown dog ran along a fenceline urging the groups together. Behind it all, a man on a quad bike.

Marnie unbuckled the children. She put them on the bonnet of the car and climbed up with them. Within minutes a murmuring sea of sheep surrounded them. Lambs called for lost mothers. Koa's hands tightened around Marnie's neck.

The quad bike came through the middle of the mob and drew alongside Marnie's car. The driver had a lamb draped across his knees, one large, blackened hand holding it steady. He said, 'You can drive through if you want.'

'It's okay, we're enjoying it.' Frankie seemed to be; Koa was strangling Marnie by now. She shifted his hands and reassured him. The mob poured around the car. Up ahead, the brown dog panted from the middle of the road, by an open gate, impelling the mob to swerve sideways and through it. Finally the quad bike drove into the paddock, slowing at the gate so the farmer could pull it shut.

Marnie lifted the children from the bonnet. 'Look, look, Koey!' Frankie pointed out little towers of droppings. Marnie leaned against the side of the car.

All right, think now. She couldn't just arrive at TJ's place. She didn't even know if the number she had for him was still the right one. Why had she thought he would want Michael to see her? And had she thought beyond that dubious meeting? She could guess his mother's attitude: *so glad to have Tim away from Lenny. So glad.* Was she ready to meet that woman?

It occurred to her that crossing the border might even constitute kidnapping. How did you find out what the law was? After she had changed Koa's nappy and cut some fruit up for both children, she packed them into the car again. She wouldn't risk it. She drove south to the river, back through the jumble of holiday-makers, then turned west. A sign said Swan Hill. She had never been there, but it was a nice name.

Swan Hill was a bigger town than she expected, also full to overflowing with trailers, boats, motor-homes. There was no chance of a cabin here, she knew it. She fuelled her car, went to the supermarket and drove away again, pulling over in a truck stop for the night. These stops, she was discovering, were randomly equipped with tables, bins, sometimes barbecues. The larger ones had toilet blocks, which meant taps. The downside of this last was that toilet facilities attracted a constant stream of visitors and were invariably putrid, as well as being a traffic hazard for children.

Over the next few days they drove southwest to Sealake, then north to Ouyen, then south again, Hopetoun.

The weather continued fair. Sunny days, cold nights. Koa, she noticed one morning, had two upper incisors poking through his gums. His cheeks were flushed, but he had pretty well cut teeth without complaint, although his nappies smelled bad. Was it possible her car smelled like a truck-stop toilet block, and she had become inured to it? She wound down her window.

At night she sought out the smaller variety of truck stop, without toilets, the ones set off from the road with space where the children could be outside. Her phone was out of credit, both a nuisance and a comfort. During the dark hours she could indulge lengthy fantasies about speaking to Eleanor, without having the means to do it, which seemed to keep guilt from overwhelming her. When the children were awake there was no time for existential torment. She preferred the days.

Most nights, her hips ached and pain stabbed through her right shoulder when she tried to adjust herself in her seat. She used up the painkillers in her toilet bag and missed them. That splendid ebbing of pain, the way you could anticipate it by the clock and allow yourself to ride it into sleep, even if only for an hour or two.

She had never asked Eleanor what was so good about heroin. It had been all shock and shame those first years, when she realised her child was taking drugs. A bit like drowning slowly, finding too late that she was unable to touch the bottom.

Eleanor's behaviour became Marnie's obsession. Trying to deal with it—ineffectually, as it turned out—took over her thoughts and influenced her actions for, oh God, how long? First there were suspensions from school, bongs under the bed, absences from home. Marnie tried discussing it with Gerald, much good that did, finally reaching the conclusion that Eleanor had got in with 'bad company', the implication being—she clutched at it eagerly—that it wasn't her fault. Gerald never believed it was his fault.

Later there were police calls in the night and expulsion from school. The bongs under the bed were joined by ice pipes, mysterious packets in the toes of her shoes or, when she wasn't being careful, her pockets. Money disappearing out of Marnie's purse. This led to hissing fights with Gerald, who was mainly focused on the way Eleanor's choices were ruining his life, and screaming fights with Lenny—which led to more absences from home, and more police visits. Marnie feeling all the time as if her head, her heart, the whole inside of her was raw. Even now, if she lingered in memory too much that hopelessness would emerge as real as ever. In the nights she tried blocking it with poems, writing down the ones she could remember, random lines mostly.

> *A light, she said, not of the sky*
> *Lives somewhere in the Orange Tree.*

As she set each word on paper, she felt seconds of fragile happiness. What was the rest of it? She remembered, quite easily, the opening of Lorna's absolute favourite poem.

> *I fled him down the nights and down the days*
> *I fled him down the arches of the years*
> *I fled him down the labyrinthine ways*
> *Of my own mind and in the mist of tears*
> *I hid from him…*

She stalled at that spot. How many times had she read that poem? It was long and difficult, but she got good at it. Lorna said it with her sometimes, her favourite bits anyway.

'It's an effing acid trip,' Marko said, the first time he heard her reading it. 'The Hound of what?'

'Heaven.'

'Hell more like it. Geez! She actually likes it?'

'It grows on you.'

'Like gangrene.'

Marko must have been at the nursing home the day they had that conversation. Waiting for her to give him a lift back to the house, probably. Marko, the funny one, Heath's favourite. He used to paint Lorna's nails for her, and the other boys teased him. Marko didn't care. That was the first of many things that was memorable about Marko.

Now, sometimes, she recited that half-stanza to herself in the dark, in the hope of jogging up the lines that came next. There was a thing about feet…but no.

Sometimes she dropped off to sleep, words in her head tangled up with images of cliffs and rocky paths, before waking disoriented, amazed that she had been sleeping at all. How long could you go without a good night's sleep? What were the long-term consequences of not sleeping? Madness? Well, she didn't feel mad, she felt drab. *Drab*—one of Joan's words. She needed a shower, they all did. Sometimes she pictured her little flat. The bed, the cane screen, the galleon window, Darling on the doormat. She wanted it back.

13

Driving on Easter Sunday evening, she noticed dense black clouds rising ahead of them and sombre shawls extending to the horizon in a few places, disappearing into bloody mist over mallee dirt.

'Raining up ahead, kids,' she said.

'Will it hurt?' said Frankie with interest.

'It'll give the car a good wash.'

'Gar,' said Koa unexpectedly.

'That's right! Good boy! Did you hear that, Frankie? Koa said car.'

'Goo-boy,' said Frankie. 'I can say car too.'

'You can say lots of words, but he's only a baby.'

'I'm fwee.'

'And Koa's not even one.'

Marnie considered Koa's possible birth dates. May the second. Or was it the fifth? The ninth? How could she not remember?

The storm came on them quickly, a few introductory splatters on the windscreen, a moment of nothing, then a deluge. Visibility was gone in an instant. Startling fissures shattered the darkness ahead of them and both children began to squeal. She slowed the car trying to see out, but it was all water and windscreen wipers and nothing beyond. She could not see the side of the road either, could not see if there was a deep channel or a shallow trench there which made it risky to pull over.

She said, 'We're okay, kittens, we're okay.'

Water pounded on the car's roof, then eased, then pounded again.

'Ganny!' Frankie cried, a thin, pleading wail, then: 'Mummy! Bay! Wastus!' and Koa bawled, 'Mum-mum-mum!'

A gate emerged out of the curtain of grey in her peripheral vision. In a few seconds of slowed rain, she swung the car towards it. Then she plunged out into the rain, leaving the engine on. There was a chance the gate wouldn't open and it would only take a moment to find out. She was soaked within seconds, water running down her face, down her neck, through her clothing. She felt for the gate clip and fumbled, trying to find the release, which turned out to need a powerful squeeze. After that, the gate opened inwards on its own as she ran back to the car, clay gumming her shoes. By the time she was back in the driver's seat, the children were inconsolable.

'I'm here, it's all right, I'm here,' she said and put the car into drive, taking it slowly through the gate in the renewed surge. Frankie was choking as well as wailing. Not because of the rain, Marnie knew, but because she had been left.

She could not deal with that now. She peered through the windscreen, talking to the children then singing to them, 'Rain rain go away, rain rain, go away...' faintly peeved that Frankie was calling for useless bloody Brayden. And the dog. Yes, and Lenny. Damn them all.

Ahead, to one side, was a dark structure that turned out to be a hay shed partially full of round bales offering protection on its west side. She drove the car straight in, feeling the tyres sink a little but not stick. The pummelling on the roof eased at once, the car stopped vibrating. She turned to the children and said, 'Here we are, see? We're safe now.' And hoped the shed roof would not fall in. It was an expanse on slender steel posts. She crawled through to the back seat and unclipped the children so that she could hold them against her while the rain drummed on. 'Ganny's here, Ganny's got you,' she said.

In grey first-light, Marnie unfolded herself with effort and sat up because Frankie was calling her.

'Toilet,' she was saying. 'Ganny, toilet.'

They were back in their seats wrapped in towels and coats. Koa was also awake with his hand on the window, patting at the underbellies of two large huntsman spiders side by side on the glass. Marnie took a deep breath and willed herself not to gasp. They were impressively large, but they were after all on the outside, and Koa seemed transfixed by them. He was saying 'Ahhh...' in a descending scale: soothing them.

She climbed from the car, her knees creaky, sending the spiders rushing abruptly across the roof and down the other side of the car. She heard Koa saying, 'Bar-bar' followed by 'Gone'.

More words in his lexicon. The world is a classroom after all, she thought, and could hear Eleanor snorting with laughter.

It was nearly seven, the sky lightening fuzzily at the horizon, shifting through gunmetal to dove grey. No sign of sunlight. Everything around her indistinct, the ground itself swollen-looking. In the distance, a small copse of trees seemed to be crouching low to the ground as if weighted. It was not as cold as previous mornings though; her fingers were not aching as they usually did. Marnie crouched beside Frankie and peed into the sodden hay floor. Back at the car she unpacked the last tubes of baby food and changed Koa, then brushed her hair and brushed her teeth and tried to brush the birds' nests out of Frankie's fine hair while the child squealed.

    a) *Hair ties*

    b) *Headband*

    c) *Conditioner*

she added to the list in her head.

When she tried to brush Koa's hair he said, 'No-Ko-No!' He wanted to get out of his seat and arched his back, pushing at her face, at the brush, at her hands. In the end, she unbuckled him and put him on the ground beside the car, while she hunted about on the floor for Frankie's dropped boots. While she was retrieving them, she heard an engine and saw a flash of headlights. She banged her head on the car-door arch when she swung around to locate Koa. A huge twin-cabin ute with bullbars was facing into the shed with Koa, on all fours, in the glare of its headlights.

She snatched him up and shielded her eyes. 'Can you turn them off? Please.'

The engine was cut and the lights dimmed. Frankie was crying again, standing by the car. How easily they cried. Was this new or had it always been like this?

Marnie went to Frankie, lowered Koa to the ground, which he objected to, and fitted Frankie's boots. She waited for the owner of the ute to speak first. The ute door slammed, a man's voice said, 'You okay there?'

'Yes.' She straightened. 'Thanks for asking. I guess I'm trespassing. I'm sorry, I couldn't see in the rain.'

'No, fair enough.'

Well, that was a relief, anyway. He came closer. A shortish man in several layers of clothing, the top layer waterproof. Rubber boots caked with mud and a football beanie that covered most of his face. The part not covered had spectacles on, and these were fogged up. Mr Magoo.

'Saw the lights last night, figured you were getting out of it. I come down to see the gate was shut.'

'I'm sorry, I didn't—'

'She's tricky.' The pronoun was confusing until she realised he was referring to the gate.

'The children were scared.'

'Yours—'

'My grandchildren. We needed shelter, I'm really sorry to impose.'

'No harm, what else could you do.' He was walking away from her to the gate, which he closed, then walked back. 'Got a mob of lambing ewes up there,' indicating somewhere to the back of him. 'Cross breeds got a sixth sense for open gates. Heading north?'

'Mildura,' she said randomly.

'More on the radar; mind you it could just buzz over the top, give us a light-and-sound show and nothin' else. I'm 'appy with seventy-eight points but I wouldn't say no to a follow-up.'

Now he was talking about rain, she realised, farmer talk. Somewhere in her memory she heard TJ waxing lyrical about a fall of rain, standing at the kitchen window with Michael in his arms, surprising them all with his enthusiasm. She said, 'Seventy-eight points—'

'That's old gauge. Twenty-eight mils, about. Sounds better in points.'

A mud-coloured dog staggered into view and sat at his feet. Both children shrieked.

'Holey-moley,' the man said. To the dog, 'They don't like you, Poll.'

'They're not frightened of dogs, come on guys,' she said to the children. 'The storm sort of freaked them out.'

'Wet dog,' said Frankie with distaste.

'No sense, no feeling,' the farmer said genially, and put his hand for a second on the old dog's head. Droplets of rain beaded the dog's grey muzzle. Its tail thumped in response.

'You right getting out, then?'

'Yes; yes thanks, is the nearest town far?'

'You after shops?'

'Yes.' Well, obviously.

'Local place only has a pub and petrol, oh they've got milk and bread, but they gotta do the mail run first, so they don't get open before eleven. Oh, hang on, no mail today anyhow, but there's still the paper run.'

'It's okay.' Another time she might have stood there and listened to the welter of random information, the comforting certainty of it all, but Koa was straining to get out of her arms again. He was saying 'go-go-go' angrily, which she took to mean 'down' or 'go'.

'Nhill's your best bet.'

'Nhill. Okay.' The name of a place in a made-up story, akin to Samarkand or Timbuctoo.

'Mind you, it's not your best path to Mildura.'

'Does it have petrol?'

'Only place that's likely open on Easter Monday. I'd send you the short way, but it's a dry-weather road. Just head south on the bitumen about ten mile, you'll see the sign.'

'It'll take me a minute to get the kids packed up,' she said, physically dragging them back to the car, trying to remember mile-to-kilometre conversion, not wanting to start another digression with him. She couldn't properly hear the man speaking over the wall of Koa's complaining anyway. She had to push his tummy down to get him into his seat. Her bonked head was starting to hurt.

The man shouted, 'I'll get on and do the ewes, c'mon Poll. Leave the gate if you can't do it, stick the chain through to hold it, I'll swing by on me way back. Ooroo.' She heard his engine rumble into action.

Marnie settled in her seat, focusing herself away from the children's crying, switched on the engine and drove forward. The front wheels dug in. She counted ten and selected reverse. There was a jerk backwards, the wheels spun and the engine revved hard. She cut it quickly. Said, 'Crap! Crap! Crap!' and climbed out, looking for the farmer, who was well gone on his way to that distant plantation.

A light was visible to one side of it now, a house. She unloaded the children and the stroller, and they walked through misting rain until the house came into proper view: a wartime weatherboard with a sheep-wire fence around it, leggy rose bushes dangling clusters of orange-coloured hips, a woodpile down one side of the house under a tarpaulin.

A woman came to the front door looking startled.

'I'm sorry, I was parked down near the gate—'

'Oh yes, did you see Jock?'

'I thought I'd be all right, but I'm bogged. I'm sorry. He'd already gone. My name is Marnie Odell,' she added, vaguely feeling it gave her more credibility to introduce herself. 'I'm travelling with my grandchildren.'

There was a hiatus while she was invited to remove her boots, and the woman helped Frankie do the same before ushering them inside. 'Shocking night,' she said. 'We saw your lights. Any ewes get out?'

'He thought not.'

'We're lambing,' she said. 'They'll be in the plantation. That's where he's gone. I'll try to get him on the radio.'

But in the end she couldn't reach him and so it was the woman, Helen, who got the tractor out and went down to the car. She found a towel for the children's hair first, then fed them toast and honey and filled a thermos with hot water for Marnie to take back to the car. She had an abrupt way of speaking, used to dealing in facts rather than speculations, it seemed to Marnie; she quick-fired questions but did not seem to be prying, just getting the picture right.

Marnie felt her shoulders softening. 'I'm a bit embarrassed,' she said, following Helen outside later. She couldn't think what else to say.

'No, I'm sorry, I probably looked surprised when you arrived. We don't use the front door much. Now, you'll have to walk back. Just stay to the side.' To the children: 'I'm bringing the big green tractor down. You wave to me when you see it.'

The whole passageway inside that door had had an untrafficked look about it, Marnie thought, closed doors all the way down to the kitchen. Maybe they were the good rooms. Did people still do that? Keep rooms for best? Oh God, the luxury.

This place was shabby but had seen bouts of refurbishment. The kitchen had a large central bench and she glimpsed a big-screen TV on the wall of an adjoining room, with pictures of racehorses hung in a line. It smelled of woodsmoke, toast and bacon. She regretted leaving it, wanted to stay, drink tea with Helen and watch the children play. But here she was, pushing the stroller down the road again, avoiding potholes.

The tractor passed them, amazing the children. When Marnie reached the shed, Helen was already on her back attaching straps underneath the car.

'Can I help?' Marnie said.

'Stick it in neutral, handbrake off, keep the kids back.'

They stood by and watched in some awe as the tractor grumbled forward and the car shifted gracefully backwards onto the roadway. Helen swung off the tractor seat and unhooked everything.

Marnie said. 'I have about twenty in cash, that'll cover fuel, at least.'

'Forget it. Jock charges, he calls it the idiot fee, but it's discretionary. You don't seem like an idiot.'

Marnie figured her age and the presence of the children helped with that appraisal, which was possibly incorrect. She transferred hot water into her flask from Helen's and handed it back. 'He said to go south about ten miles,' she said.

Helen pointed and Marnie was grateful because she really didn't know which direction she was facing anymore.

Helen said, 'Where've you come from, anyway?'

'Melbourne.'

'Going to?'

'Mildura, well…then Deniliquin.' She wondered if Helen noticed her hesitation.

'I have to say, this isn't the most direct route to either.'

'We were visiting people.'

'Both parents work?' indicating the children.

Marnie nodded. 'They needed a break, I wouldn't like them to know I'd gone and got us bogged.'

'Tell them nothing. They'll use it against you.' Helen had the tone of one who knows. 'They'll tell you how different everything is from when you were doing it, but it's not. More gadgets, that's about it. What's harder is the need for two incomes to pay for a *lifestyle*,' she exaggerated the word and laughed. 'Did you ever think you were having a lifestyle? Me neither. Anyway, in my opinion it's harder for kids.' She looked at the children. Koa was scarlet in the face, doing a poo, Frankie's nose was running. Neither looked inspiring.

Helen said, 'He's got a few spots,' she pointed to the side of Koa's face. 'Has he had his chicken pox vax?'

Marnie looked at the cluster of spots near Koa's right eye in some surprise. 'Of course,' she said, although she had no idea.

'Probably heat rash, then.'

'Where da dog?' said Frankie.

'Off with Jock,' said Helen. 'Checking the lambs. You look after your grandma, now.'

They waved the tractor off.

The remaining petrol got them to Nhill. It was sunny when they arrived, the rain had 'buzzed over the top' as predicted. The town was quiet. Full of empty shops, pretty buildings and elaborate leadlight windows in storefronts. She was familiar now with that sense of history, struggle, decline. Sometimes, rarely, you could see where good times, a new industry or a philanthropist had given hope to an old town, evidenced in a short stretch of modern shops or new houses. There were always closed-up hotels. Nowhere out here seemed able to sustain more than one or two pubs now, where once there might have been five.

In Nhill she found smart council offices, a newish police building, a bakery with tables and seats outside and a modern supermarket in the town centre where Marnie bought food, nappies and phone credit. She bought fleecy hooded capes, too, adult sizes, hideous colours, rejects at marked-down prices. They would keep the children warm. She found books for the children in a sale bin—a collection of four books called

Seasons in a little cardboard folder for Frankie, and a *Row, Row, Row Your Boat* book for Koa. She checked her bank balance at an ATM and saw how little was left—most of her money eaten up by fuel, nothing she could do about it, really. Holding that print-out in her hand she was aware of a lack of emotion. So, was she not facing up to reality? Or had she reached some weird emotional wasteland where she could no longer care?

Outside the town boundary there was a playground on the edge of a brown swamp. The swamp had raised walkways, and the playground had toilets and a barbecue. They parked there in the afternoon and the children built mounds with mulch while she boiled pasta, stirred through a can of tuna and regretted not buying herself a drink. Even a can of Brayden's shitty burnt-barbecue Scotch and cola would be all right at this moment. It was the effect she wanted, something to carry her through the night ahead. Bad luck, she told herself. She had nothing, not even tea, and it didn't matter. Her mother would never have looked for a drink. Mind you, her mother would never have been in this situation. Joan guarded herself, her home, her belongings, her job, her place in that little corner of the world she occupied. 'Interesting woman, your mother,' Heath once said to Marnie. 'Never looks over her own fence.'

While she watched over the children, picking them up at intervals and helping them on and off play equipment, Marnie finally became aware of an emotion. She felt glad at this actual moment that they seemed happy. Well—not to over-egg the moment—perhaps not happy, but content with what they were doing, digging and climbing and throwing. Her gladness was a modest sort of emotion, too, but it was truthful, she thought. The day grew gold-coloured, and then faded to fawn. Drab, Marnie thought. She read the children their books. She watched Frankie slide each book into its folder, out and in. She could feel Frankie's pleasure at fitting the books together so competently. Koa pointed to a dog in his book and said, 'Go-go-go,' which made her realise she had been misinterpreting him for a whole day and no doubt contributing to his rage and frustration. 'Dog,' she said. 'Sorry, baby, I get it now.'

During the night, too sore in her back and hips to settle, Marnie got her phone going again, and read the text messages that had been waiting for her for some days.

Rhi: *R U OK? Len came over. Call when U can*

Vincent: *I'm sory this has happened I understand things are hard. Cant allow your daugter to stay. Have notified agent. Please phone. V. Russo*

Trinh: *Hi this is Tom, my grmother is in hospital for an op. Will tell her later and can do afternoons for you in short term this is inconvenient I know my grmother would say not your fault but would have preferred notice*

Rhiannon, the most recent: *Give me a break! R U OK?? I feel forced to be complicit in a situation that I do not understand and which may be unethical. Send reply so I can stop worrying and maybe fob Lenny off. She is confused. Detachment difficult.*

Nothing comforting there. However, now Marnie had finally read the messages, they weren't so frightening either. But they stretched out grasping fingers to her, pulled her in, tying her to needs that she could not address.

She wanted, badly, to phone Trinh and find out what had happened. Trinh had complained of tiredness and put Patsy on because she needed—what did she say?—time at home. Vincent's text was formulated after advice from his sister; Marnie could almost hear the discussion that had preceded it. And worst, reading Rhiannon's texts, she could feel a familiar weight descending on her. Guilt, of course. It wasn't fair. It was too hard. Bugger them all. She pulled Lenny's hood down over her eyes.

After a while she sat up and typed a text to Rhiannon:

All OK. Giving E a break. Gave Bray details, typical if he has lost them! Will call E

She sent the text and had an immediate response:

You can't call Lenny. Phone lost. Next time she turns up, I will phone you. Send pic at least. Brayden says he wants to go up north for a job—ha ha. Can I call you right now?

Marnie replied: *No. Sorry. I'm grateful but this all not your problem. Thanks*

She attached a smiley face, which she recognised as both shallow and dishonest. Let's talk about dishonesty, the voice in her head suggested.

No, let's not.

14

A snarling engine woke Marnie sometime after midnight. Car headlights were blinding her through the driver's side window. Her first thought was it must be the police checking her out; in the back of her mind she'd been expecting that for days. She dismissed this when she heard laughter. She pushed on the door lock instinctively, to make sure they were all secure, then realised she had unwittingly unlocked all the doors. She slammed the lock on again, completely awake now, pulse accelerating.

'Hey! Lady!' said a voice. A boy's voice, not even a man's. A broad hand slapped the window.

There were other voices behind this one. 'Who is it?' 'Is she awake?' 'Some old slag.' The car bounced a little.

'Hey, lady!' the voice taunting, a thump on the bonnet and a body rolled across the front of the car and disappeared onto the ground on the other side, followed by an eruption of laughter, several voices. There seemed to be people on all sides.

The children were in the luggage space. She could not get to them. They were wrapped up in their new hooded capes, swaddled in their doona. Miraculously still asleep. The car bounced again.

She lowered her window slightly. 'Could you not do that?' she said. 'It'll wreck my suspension.'

There was a sound of hilarious fear. *Ooh-ooh.* A voice said, 'Hey, what's your name?'

'Marnie.'

'Arnie?' More laughter, the word bounced around the group like an echo. There were four of them. Five maybe? One of them said, 'I'll be beck,' in the Arnie voice. It was oddly comforting to know that he watched old movies, it placed him at a young age, maybe not even eighteen—a boy who still watched TV with his parents. Still washed up after dinner.

'What's yours?' she said, recognising too late a doomed attempt at what? Conviviality?

'Chopper, baby.' More laughter. Conviviality was always going to sound fake; they sensed their power; she could feel it. They were moving all the time, springy like colts, the way young men were when they had no purpose, full of hormones, energy, stimulants. Not men. Boys, she reminded herself. She knew about boys—hadn't she ridden in the furniture truck with them, Heath at the wheel, settling them down when they got out of hand, pulling their focus back onto hating Dean Martin when it could have spiralled in any other direction? He usually never took more than two boys at a time. She understood why. Even Heath took precautions with those damaged kids. Right now, she recognised that bullshit bravado. Don't get near me, it said. And sometimes it said worse.

A body landed on the bonnet again and rolled off. A voice said, 'Arsewipe! Quit it!'

Laughter. Incoherent calls.

Marnie said. 'Listen, I'm stuffed if you wreck my car, I don't have enough money to get it fixed. Give me a break, okay?'

Chopper, she thought it was Chopper, said, 'Calm down, we're not doin' anythin'.'

'Yes, you are.'

'What? What are we doin'?' She could hear the challenge.

An abrupt tussle, protests, and Chopper was forced to one side. A face pushed up against the driver's side window, startling her. Cheeks and nose smooshed on glass, inches from her, a gaping mouth with a fuzz of whiskers around it, crooked teeth, a smell of sweet alcohol and weed through the tiny crack of open window. Then the whole apparition slid sideways, leaving a trail of spit on the glass. She knew it was a game—scare the old lady—but knowing didn't stop her chest tightening.

'Get out of the car, bitch.'

'Sorry. Not happening.'

The car rocked. A voice said, 'Push it over the bank.' The car rocked again. There were voices of protest, voices of encouragement. More rocking.

Then Frankie screamed. Everything stopped momentarily. She said, 'I've got kids here. Okay?'

There was a slight hesitation, they could hear Frankie. She was screaming loudly, no words. Marnie said, 'I'm here, I'm here, baby,' while suppressing the urge to scream herself, although it also occurred to her that it might startle the boys again, perhaps sufficiently to stop them. She started her engine, revved it, her headlights illuminated a ute parked right across her path, and another car at her side. On her other side was the grassy bank. She couldn't see well enough through the rear window, but her brake lights showed movement.

'Give us your money,' said a voice. Not Chopper, she thought.

'I've got hardly any. Look, you're scaring my kid.'

'That's not your fucken kid.'

'She's my granddaughter.' She tried a stern voice. Heath's stern tone could have stopped a lava flow. She said, 'Just settle down and watch your language—why would you want to scare a little kid?'

Frankie was saying words now, 'Ganny! Ganny! Ganny!'

The request for money was repeated. Marnie got her purse out and showed them its contents. Two ten-dollar notes and some coins which she fed through the crack in the window.

'Card, too.'

'I'm only going to cancel it.'

'Hand it over, bitch.'

She slid her ATM card through the gap. 'That's it,' she said. 'You've got everything, now piss off or I'm calling the police!'

There was confusion, different opinions being expressed, so many expletives that everything was jumbled. She heard,

'Come on, come *on*!' Advice to retreat from someone with a conscience, maybe? Then, 'Give us your phone,' from another voice close to the window crack. The demand was repeated. The insistence scared her. It was her threat about the police that had done it. Frankie was squealing and gasping now.

She dropped her mobile on the floor beneath her feet, made a play at fetching it back, saying, 'All right, all right.' Her fingers scrabbled around and located the other mobile. She lowered the window a little more and fed Lenny's phone through it. 'It's flat,' she said. But it was a good one, brand new and shiny in Lenny's hands that day on the doorstep. Maybe it would appease them.

The person at the window was yanked away by someone else, but he resisted with an explosion of invective, then lowered his mouth to the gap, letting fly a gob of mucus that hit Marnie's cheek.

He said, quite calmly: 'Fucken die you fucken old cunt,' and then he was yanked again by an invisible arm and dragged to the ute. She could see him momentarily in the lights: drunk, jeans hanging loose down his skinny arse, just a kid off his face, she told herself. Bad skin and a shitful childhood. He was a boy, that's all, with a need to shout louder than the rest, to be more offensive. One day soon he would commit some crazy act out of his desperate need to be noticed and finish up in juvie. After that, maybe some other Heath would single him out to work on a truck and give him some time and some skills so he could grow up and calm down and just survive. It worked for some of them—Marko, Sheenie. Not all.

She said, 'It's all right baby, they're going, they're just silly, they're going now. Ganny's here.' Repeating each sentence two or three times, automatically. A spotlight on the roof of the ute lit the area abruptly. Revving engines, the smell of fuel, vehicles wheeled around her, showering her car with dirt and mulch before bumping over garden beds and finally spinning onto the highway. Minutes later, the only remaining sound was Frankie.

No choice: she needed the police now. They drove slowly back into town, Koa still asleep in the luggage space, Frankie curled up against her chest—a dangerous and crazy thing to do, but she couldn't work out how to do it any other way and her failure clanged inside her like a bell. Wasn't this what she was trying to save them from? Wasn't she thinking all along that she could do it better, offer a better chance at safety and security than they ever had with Lenny? This was a mess and it was her doing. She had nothing to offer them, nothing at all.

The police station was dark. There was a sign at the front listing emergency numbers that she couldn't work out: couldn't decide which category she belonged in or whether it was even an emergency. What was an emergency? Murder? She parked outside the front entrance, even though it said *No Standing*. The one blessing was that Koa remained asleep. She cuddled Frankie, felt the child's thin chest heaving, the banging of her heart. Eventually, Frankie's breathing slowed, and she sat up and asked for a drink. When Marnie got out of the car to go around to the tailgate, Frankie became

114

agitated, so she lifted the child into her arms and took her along to fetch the remains of their orange juice. She felt the little knees digging in, the fingernails scratching for a hold around Marnie's throat. Frankie accepted the juice bottle but insisted they get back inside the car immediately.

'It's okay,' Marnie told her. 'Look at all the stars, honey-kitten, look at the Milky Way.' But Frankie ducked her head and shut her eyes. When they were back in the car, Marnie phoned her bank to cancel her card, navigating around a confusing jumble of menu options until finally she got through to a real voice. When it was done, she sat back and watched the sky slowly lighten, her arms numb from holding Frankie in her arms.

15

The police officer took her statement with professional detachment, but she noticed his demeanour soften as he watched Koa explore the waiting room, walking from chair to chair, saying 'Ooh,' in three ascending notes whenever he paused to look at something—a poster, a water cooler, a waste bin. Koa, well rested, full of apple custard, was at his most charming. He pointed out every feature in the blonde-wood room. Frankie sat on Marnie's knee watching him, her head against Marnie's chest.

'She woke up while they were pushing the car around,' Marnie said.

The police officer had no difficulty with her story—he had a fair idea who the boys were, plus someone had already reported the vandalism of the flower beds in the park and texted a helpful picture of burnt rubber on the road leading away from it.

'Not sure what they think we can do, go around town

matching up wrecked tyres with rubber tracks.' He went on to say that the same citizen had sent through a description of a car that had left the park in the small hours. Marnie verified that this was her. She admitted she hadn't even known there was a house nearby, had seen no lights. She told him she'd parked outside the police station because she didn't know where else to go. He nodded.

He might have been thirty-five, a square-chested man with a face mask dangling from one ear, and a hesitant delivery in his speech that suggested self-consciousness. He said, 'I'm really sorry this happened. It's not a bad town. My wife teaches at the high school. These kids—this is worse than their usual—which, unfortunately, that's the way it goes a lot of the time.'

She said she did know. She added, 'It's probably not worth pursuing.'

'It's robbery,' he said, and looked at her for the first time with something like curiosity. He asked her where she was heading, and she said probably back to Melbourne and regretted the 'probably' at once; it felt like a red flag. She said that right now she needed to sort out money at the bank because of her card being cancelled, as well as get to a Centrelink. She hoped she sounded organised and clear-headed enough to cover her gaffe.

'You taking the little girl to a doctor?'

'Yes, I should.' She hadn't thought of that, and her omission seemed at once reprehensible. The 'should' seemed to put up another flag. She noticed him studying Frankie, who closed her eyes and turned away.

Aidan, she could see it on his name badge, made her a cup of tea and brought it out to her on a tray, along with paper cups of Milo for the children. There were packages of biscuits. 'Bit sub-standard,' he warned her. 'I wouldn't bother. Kids might like them, though.' He explained that he needed to type up a statement and get her to sign it, so they would have to stay for a while yet. She remembered the procedure.

He added, 'Just to make it easy on me, any prior dealing with the police? I gotta check.'

She said, 'My daughter.'

He indicated the children. 'Their mum?'

'She served a custodial sentence.'

'Drugs.' Not even a question.

'Possession, dealing, armed robbery—7-Eleven. Failure to appear on bail. Contravening bail conditions. That's the main stuff.'

'Child Protection interventions?'

'Two formal ones. They're not current, I don't think.'

His face didn't change although she suspected he had an opinion. It was an impressive list, and she had recited it with ease. 'Anything recent?'

'I didn't see them for nearly a year, so I don't know. I saw him in the hospital,' pointing to Koa. 'Then they left town.'

'Do you know where they went?'

'Barossa. She said her boyfriend was doing grape pruning.' Marnie had never believed it. Brayden wasn't the type anyone employed. 'They were stuck over the border for a long time,' she said. 'I'm not sure where they were living. I got a couple of photos of the children.' She nearly added 'after six months',

118

but didn't. Instead, she looked at Koa on the floor. She didn't want the police officer to see her face and maybe read that surge that was sweeping up inside her, heaving some powerful resentments with it.

Rhiannon came into her head, abruptly. 'Deal in facts,' Rhiannon said. 'No one wants an editorial.'

Too late. She had already said too much, but the reminder helped her to compose herself.

The police officer went to his computer in an adjoining room. Marnie tried to drink her tea, which was shatteringly sweet and tepid. The quiet room, almost too hot, lulled her. Frankie drank Milo only if Marnie agreed to hold the cup for her. Frankie did not want to be a big girl today. On the other hand, Koa insisted on holding his own cup and immediately tipped it down his front.

After fifteen minutes, the police officer returned. He'd phoned the hospital and there was a doctor there right now, he'd already let them know she was coming. He added, casually, that a social worker would be there, too. He fetched a handful of paper towels for her to clean up all the spills and reassured her he had a toddler of his own. He added that coming to work sometimes felt like a guilty pleasure.

After that, they went through her statement and she signed it. The police officer suggested he could see her to the hospital, it was a short walk across the road. He pointed it out in case she hadn't noticed it: a modern edifice, benign, welcoming. The thought of arriving accompanied by a uniformed officer was intolerable, so she refused him, politely. He suggested she leave her car where it was. He'd keep an eye on it. He reminded her that they were expecting her and held the door so that she could get the stroller through.

But for the brook-no-argument offer of parking, and the fact that she had no debit card, she might have considered driving away as she left the police station. It was a bad idea, an impulse, and she didn't give in to it. But there was a definite sinking feeling.

At the hospital they had their temperatures scanned, Marnie was given a mask and they were shown into a consultation room, where a nurse took details. Koa continued his charm offensive, making eye contact and a range of conversational noises until the nurse was forced to smile at him, but his overweening confidence inspired him to grab a box of tongue depressors off a trolley and dump them out at his feet. The nurse had a smoker's laugh. She said, 'Finders keepers. No good to us now.' Which turned out to be for the best, as Koa sat on the floor playing with them in near silence.

The first real problem that emerged was, predictably, the lack of a Medicare card for the children. Marnie produced her notebook and showed the numbers, explained her relationship with the children, explained that they were travelling, that her daughter had the card. Both doctor and social worker arrived during this explanation. Introductions and repeated explanations muddied the flow of the consultation for a while after that. The doctor was Dr Ashika, the nurse was Roz, the social worker was Declan. Only their eyes were visible. Brown, hazel and blue. The blue ones, Declan's, working overtime to make connections in lieu of full-face expression. He came from Deniliquin, he told her. Declan from Deni, he said, and the nurse and doctor laughed heartily along with him, as if alliteration were the highest form of humour imaginable. By now, Marnie was on edge. She didn't trust the jaunty schtick and was relieved she hadn't mentioned Deniliquin in her story so far. She would keep clear of the topic because Declan, of indeterminate age behind his mask, could well have been at school with TJ. She was finally beginning to understand the flow of information in the country. It was like a river with inlets and outlets and pools of speculation and judgment, goodwill and, yes, ill-will.

The doctor said to Frankie while listening to her chest, 'Are you having fun with your grandmother, darling?'

Frankie looked confused. She searched Marnie's face.

'She calls me Ganny.'

'Oh, I understand.' To Frankie, 'And I call my grand-mother Daadee. Isn't that funny?'

No response from Frankie.

Doctor Ashika said, 'And, Frankie, is this your brother? My goodness, he has pretty curls! Can you tell me his name?'

No response. Marnie said, 'You can tell the doctor.' But she wouldn't. From the floor, Koa held up a fistful of tongue depressors and made his wondrous ascending 'Aah!' and they all turned to admire him.

Frankie pointed toward Koa's pile. 'Mine,' she said, her first word that day. Declan scooped up a few tongue depressors and gave them to her. She hugged them.

The doctor checked Frankie's ears. 'She has some spots on her face,' she remarked.

121

'Koa has too,' said Marnie. 'Actually, I only just noticed. I thought—I think they're vaccinated—but it's maybe possible it's chicken pox.'

The doctor changed gloves and looked at Koa's face crouching down to him on the floor. He beamed at her and gave her a tongue depressor.

'Thank you, little one. Impetigo,' she added, glancing up at the nurse.

Marnie knew the word. It had an old-fashioned ring, a word her mother might have used. She had a vague recollection that impetigo was something to do with poverty and felt her face flushing. She said, 'I'm sorry?'

Roz said, 'It's nothing, but doctor will want to treat it.'

'What is it?'

The doctor said, 'A bacterial skin infection, very common, please don't let this cause you concern. Children pick it up from one another. People in the best homes have had it.'

'School sores,' Roz offered.

'They're not at school. Or child care.'

The doctor discarded her gloves. 'Are you aware of any spots yourself—it's quite contagious. You may have picked it up from them.'

'No...I'm not sure—but where did they get it?' Marnie was aware of a panicky, bleating sound in her voice. She was suddenly on the edge of tears and even knew, quite firmly, that it wasn't necessary; but she couldn't seem to control it.

'I had it when I was about seven,' said Declan. 'No big deal.'

That was just irritating. If she had Ebola he'd probably

122

say the same thing. Marnie's opinion of Declan was going downhill by the second. There was a rising, bubbling mistrust inside her now. She really wanted to get out.

Roz bathed the children's spots and covered them in antibiotic cream. The doctor returned from checking a database and announced that there was no record of immunisations for Koa and Frankie's record showed only four—all of which Marnie could confirm, because she'd taken her for them. Koa was given his three-months vax and Frankie was given her eighteen-months booster, which made her turn white with shock although she did not make a sound. This was, of course, the signal for Koa to switch from charming to frightful. Marnie was given what remained of the cream, and a prescription, and they were finally ushered out. Frankie was sleeping quietly in the stroller now and Koa was roaring. Declan walked alongside her.

The Centrelink visit took ages. Frankie slept on, and eventually Koa crashed too, with his head over Marnie's shoulder and his ringlets wet against her ear. They continued to wait, until Declan decided they would all die of hunger and he left to find sandwiches. Marnie was relieved he wasn't with her when she was finally called to a desk. The Centrelink worker resembled an ageing bikie with a wild beard that stuck out all around his mask. His desk seemed too small for him but his sausage fingers moved across the computer keyboard like dancers nonetheless. He quickly found her online, then the children and everything connected with them.

'How are you enjoying your holiday with the kids?' he said, scrolling his monitor, reading while he spoke. A similar question to the doctor's. It made her uneasy.

'Look, I'll be honest. I took them away because I felt they were at risk.'

A glance in Marnie's direction then back at the monitor. 'Have you spoken to your daughter?'

'I told her. I told both of them. What I mean is, I agreed to take them. My daughter's partner was there, he was more compos at the time. They wanted a break and I said, great, not just for them, actually I don't care whether they get a break or not, their whole life is a break.' She stopped abruptly. No one wants an editorial.

'So where are the parents now?'

'Parent. The boyfriend is no relation.' And he's a waste of space, she nearly added. 'They were at my flat, I don't know if they still are. The rent was paid up to…the end of this week.'

'Are you continuing to pay rent? Do you intend maintaining your place of residence?'

She tried to say, 'I don't think I can.' Her voice left her; for a second she couldn't breathe.

There was a pause. The man behind the desk, who had introduced himself but she couldn't remember the name, picked up his phone and asked if the Daffodil Room was free. Then he ushered her into an empty room with a large table and windows that gave a view, through venetian blinds, into the street. Not a daffodil to be seen, but sunlight was streaming in, warm white lines on the carpet the length of the room. She had an urge to curl up there. Centrelink bikie guy gave her a glass of water and a box of tissues and helped her settle Koa on her jacket on the floor. While he powered up the computer on the table, he chatted about the footy. He played ruck for the Super Seniors, which was an ironic title, he said. 'Old Farts is the nickname.' He asked her if she was interested in sport.

She found it difficult to focus on the question. 'Guides,' she said, after a hesitation.

'Sorry?'

'I went to Girl Guides.'

'Oh yeah. Good?'

'You only did one thing in my day. Tennis, tap-dancing or, you know, Guides.' She laughed. 'I was a patrol leader.'

'Oh, right?'

'Kookaburras.'

'Sorry?'

'My patrol name.' She was wishing the conversation would end, this was way past an editorial, it was veering into sad-old-lady wittering. Where the hell had she dredged up Kookaburras from?

Declan came through the door with a cardboard box. 'Sorry, I should have knocked, no spare hand, had to open the door with my bum.' He unloaded brown paper bags and takeaway cups, adding, almost fretfully. 'I didn't know what you'd like. I got all vegetarian and a vanilla slice—my nan loves them. Is tea okay?'

She noticed him looking inquiringly at Centrelink guy while continuing to rabbit on about sandwich fillings, so she must look terrible, she thought. When you were young it was easier, you could be miserable and still command a kind of positive presence. Now, she guessed, her face was haggard, hair all over the place, eyes squinty and watery. These men would judge her as incompetent; worse, pitiable. That's what happened when you were older.

Declan's voice picked up pitch and pace as he distributed food, avoiding her eyes, confirming her suspicions. He wasn't very experienced, really. It wouldn't have occurred to him that buying her a vanilla slice because his nan loved them was a judgment. In spite of herself, she now felt a spark of tenderness for him.

Over sandwiches, she told the two men her story, more or less. She held back the editorial, although it played in her head like a soap opera as she spoke. Her history of receiving assistance was there in front of Centrelink guy anyway, the paperwork she'd submitted over the years amounting to a partial picture of her life. She only had to confirm the details.

There was the property division after her divorce, which amounted to a mortgage she could not pay and the immediate sale of the Ivanhoe house. Gerald had so wanted that bloody freezing pile in a posher suburb; they had sold her mother's perfectly good house in Maribyrnong for it and taken on a horrendous loan just so he could live on the Right Side of the Tracks. Then there was the house and land package in the thistly, wasted paddocks of the outer north. It was all she could manage after the bank got its money back, and she was grateful for it, too: relieved and full of hope. It turned out to be a cheerful-enough place in a curving street with tiny street trees and stone animals in everyone's front yard.

But Lenny unravelled there. She quit the education

system completely after two terms at her new high school, even though the school counsellors fell over themselves to help. Then there were the years of Marnie's work life, after she started needing help—bouncing from full-time to part-time to casual and back again, taking whatever she could get, bookkeeping in a real-estate office, a building firm, a school library, then assistant food prep at Nubbies Childcare, telemarketing, a couple of fast-food places along the path to Treen's, haemorrhaging money to keep Lenny out of squats and off the game.

Marnie was still at the Craigieburn house, Bree-Maree Avenue, when Michael was born. They were all together —Lenny and TJ had moved in with her when Lenny was six months pregnant, promising to help with the mortgage which they never did. They ate a lot of roast chicken and salad, compliments of Marnie's job at Canadian Rooster. She went with them to the hospital when the baby came; Lenny swearing at everyone and demanding pethidine, which she got, of course. The baby's shell-shocked little face examining Marnie's as she held him at close range. TJ out in the corridor with his mobile, sobbing the news to his parents. It was a turning point for him at least.

Back home, TJ and Marnie sat up at nights drinking hot chocolate and sharing the horror shift. They took turns pacing up and down the passage with that writhing, screaming infant. Marnie was relieved that TJ downright refused to call the baby Wolf-Rider, which Lenny wanted. He was firm about Michael, his granddad's name. He still smoked too much dope and took pills when he could get them, but at least he was guilty about it. This was more than Marnie could say of Eleanor.

'We can offer you emergency accommodation,' Declan said, and she was present again in the Daffodil Room, a cheese and pickle sandwich in her hand.

'I'd take it, if I were you,' said Centrelink guy, making a poor job of cutting the vanilla slice in two with a bamboo knife. 'Major housing crisis everywhere. You've probably seen it in the news.'

She said, 'Am I an emergency?' And the two men went silent for a second.

Declan said, 'You've been living in your car, isn't that what you said?'

'Well, yes, but—' She nearly said 'by choice' and stopped herself.

'And you're not able to pay rent at your last place.' Centrelink Guy.

'That's, yes, it's the way it worked out.'

Silence again.

She tried to rally her thoughts. She said, 'Where would I go? Here?'

'South of here. There's a cabin in a caravan park, on the books, quite a small one.'

'The cabin?'

'The caravan park. Both, I guess.' A burst of Declan's too-affable laughter. 'It's a nice place, quite picturesque, I'd be happy staying there. If you want to head back to the city, we'd put you up for crisis accommodation. With the kids, you're straight away a priority, but there's a longer waitlist in major cities, and it'll probably be a shorter stay. And it's shared.'

The word 'crisis' shook her. She said, 'I thought we were doing all right.'

Again, the silence. She thought: Oh. Okay. No, we really weren't.

16

So, south again. Her plans for Deniliquin—never well thought out, let's face it—now on hold. But not ditched yet, she told herself. You have to have something to look forward to. Who said that? Probably Heath.

The caravan park was near a lake. It had probably been on the shores of the lake back in the good years, with water lapping at the edges of its manicured lawn. The shoreline was punctuated with dry boat ramps and stranded piers, metres off the ground. There were safety signs on poles in the grass that said No Diving, farcical in their current state. It would be a long walk to reach water these days. But there was a shimmer out in the centre: swans were out there, nesting on mounds of grass and sticks, and on the first day Marnie spotted a small flotilla of pelicans. She pointed them out to the children, who swung their heads everywhere except in the direction of her pointing finger.

The cabin had a bed, a table, a little kitchen, cupboards,

windows, floorspace. It was clean and unremarkable. The door opened onto a grassed area with a picnic table. No bathroom, but that was all right, it was a short walk to the amenities block. The manager's office had geraniums out the front and a rose climbing over a trellis. The caravan park was between the lake and a bitumen road that followed the shoreline most of the way around. Houses with big windows were built side-by-side along this road, gazing out to where the water had been, and might be again. Across the road from the caravan park was a playground, and past this was the main road through town: a supermarket, pub, post office, rural supplies, take-away, hairdresser, chemist and a gallery for local art, which seemed to be closed. There were, as always, empty shops; but also a hospital and a school, public toilets and a mural of waterbirds on a corner. It was sunny, that first day, a high white winter sky. The water in the middle of the lake shone like galvanised steel.

The cabin, fully paid for by the government, was Marnie's for a fortnight. And that was negotiable, Declan told her confidentially, accommodation being so scarce. She didn't know if that meant she might be allowed to stay on after the fortnight, or asked to leave before the fortnight was up. She knew he meant to comfort her with his inside information, but as usual this was not what he managed to achieve. There was money in her bank account again, emergency funds had been organised and her Centrelink money was being adjusted to reflect her 'current situation'. The drive south from Nhill had taken less than two hours. The town she now called home, however temporarily, was Edenhope.

'Nice name,' Rhiannon said when Marnie phoned her a

131

day after they arrived. There was a little edge to Rhi's voice. Marnie could hear it. She had some bridge-building to do.

She said, 'I don't know if the place lives up to it. But it feels nice.'

'Okay, well, thanks for telling me.'

'Have you heard anything? I'm feeling guilty. I need to speak to her.'

'They've gone.'

'Where?'

'I told you. Byron.'

'Byron? You're kidding. You said north, didn't you? I thought maybe the border—I guess I didn't take it in—I thought it was only Brayden.'

'They both went. Took off yesterday.'

'My God. Byron? What kind of job was he getting?'

'My guess is no job, just a bullshit story.'

Marnie shifted the phone to her other ear, as if it would make more sense.

'They hit on me for the bus fare. Said they couldn't spare money for food if they had to pay the bus fare themselves. Multiple buses, apparently. I gave them food, and braided Bray's hair for him.'

'You *what*?'

'It's an intimacy I wasn't looking for, I can say that with my hand on my heart. Lenny is shit at braiding, apparently, way too loose for his standards. He said he needed to keep it neat for the trip.'

They both started laughing, which was a relief. Marnie said, 'Eleanor hates the heat, she hates humidity.'

'Guess she likes Brayden a lot, then.'

More than she likes her children, Marnie thought. Rhi, who may have been thinking the same thing, said, 'So, kids all right?'

'They have impetigo, it's a skin thing.'

'Yeah, I've heard of it. Is it bad?'

'They needed antibiotic cream. And it turns out Koa hasn't had any immunisations, I don't know why I was surprised. Anyway, it's more or less in hand now. Does Eleanor have my number?'

'You told me not to.'

'Yes, yes, sorry, I know. She probably knows it by heart, it's been the same for years. I meant, does she have another phone? Did she give you her number? I probably need to hear her voice. So do the kids.' Marnie thought, Slow down, she'll get her back up, she's not your PA. She added, 'Sorry, I sound like I'm making demands.'

This was followed by a silence that told her she was right, then Rhiannon said, 'Are they missing her?'

Marnie looked at the children pushing plastic cups around the floor with grubby tongue depressors. 'They haven't asked for a while.'

'Is that good?'

'Honestly, I don't know anything about anything.'

'You'd better work it out.' Rhi was not amused, it was in the hardening of her tone. 'And, for the record, people who precede a statement with "honestly" are usually intending to lie.'

*

133

Marnie took the children along the main street. She was restless, increasingly angry. Byron. It was the absurdity of the destination that really boiled her blood. What kind of job would they get up there in that fake old-hippy, wealthy-retiree playground? Answering phones at a yoga retreat? And who in their right mind would employ either of them? People from the south, people like Lenny and Bray, saw Byron Bay as a kind of Nirvana. Sunshine and clean needles and everyone on a high. If Lenny had called her, Marnie would have put her straight. And having no phone was no excuse, there was absolutely no doubt in her mind that Lenny had acquired a new one by now. Of course she knew Marnie's number; she could have gone around to Treen's and got it from them anyway. Lenny was well capable of working things out to her own advantage, she'd been doing it for years.

The hairdresser's was called Chez Colleen. It was open, but seemed to be empty. Two chairs with mirrors in front and a third, higher, chair for children with *Finding Nemo* characters pasted around the mirror, old now and starting to lift at the edges. Through an open door with a view out to a back room, Marnie could see a girl wearing a blue satin frock with puffed sleeves. She was smoking a cigarette and spinning around to make the skirt flare out. Someone with her, just out of sight, was laughing. The girl looked up when Marnie and the children came in and rushed into the salon, holding her cigarette at arm's length.

'Fuckit, I'm gunna go up like a bonfire! Hi! Sorry! I didn't mean to swear. Are you right?'

'Do I need an appointment for a cut?'

The other woman, older, followed behind. 'It's fine. Take that thing off, Krystel, and get that smoke out of here.' To Marnie: 'It's my bridesmaid dress from the eighties, Princess Diana-inspired. We've got this eighties night at the pub. Who's having a haircut?'

'All of us, I guess, if you have time.'

When they left the hairdresser's, Frankie's spider-web snarls were gone and she had a neat bob like Christopher Robin. Koa's curls were shorn off with the number four clippers, his hazelnut-shaped skull now covered in dark fleece. Marnie had gone for a number four, too. She was dismayed, then surprised, then cautiously pleased with the effect. She was utterly grey and her hairline at the front showed the vestiges of a cowlick that made her heart jump, because it was just like Michael's. And, yes, there looked to be the beginnings of style. She fancied she resembled a woman of confidence, which she had never been. Perhaps, with the look nailed, she could fake it.

'Big earrings,' Krystel told her. 'Lots of eyeliner, a dark one or navy, and maybe some new glasses. That's how you carry off a cut like that. When there's a bit of length back in the top you can have blue foils if you like.'

'She doesn't want to go jumping into something like that, you nong,' said the other hairdresser, Colleen, pulling rank. 'It's all right for you young ones, but regrowth is ageing. I'd recommend a colour style mousse, the rose, it'll fade down between cuts. Honestly, it looks magic.'

Marnie noted the use of 'honestly' and said she would think about it.

17

At night in the caravan park plovers called spookily in the dark. Occasionally a car swept past on the road, but it was generally silent. The night after the haircut, Marnie sat outside her cabin in spite of the cold. She thought, can I live here? Can I live like this? She laughed inwardly, could see herself laughing with Eleanor, could hear Eleanor's dry put-down. 'Like you've got options.'

Wealthy people had options. She had never thought of herself as poor, though, until now. She'd always felt there were options. Maybe not expansive ones, but at least she'd always had somewhere to live. After TJ took Michael and went back to his family, while Lenny was still serving her sentence, Marnie had put her modest house in Craigieburn on the market. She couldn't keep up the mortgage, she needed something closer to Eleanor. More importantly, she needed cash to pay Eleanor's fees and fines, some going back years. Her idea—it seemed so logical and clear at the time—was that when Eleanor got out she could move forward without debts, start again in a flat of her own, where Michael could stay. Something to look forward to.

There was no difficulty finding a rental back then. The place she moved to, a pocket-sized flat in Deer Park, was just fine. It had abhorrent shag-pile carpet, but the walls were freshly painted. It was one of twelve flats in a cream-brick block, featureless unless you counted the rubbish overflowing from the bins out the front. There was strip-shopping two streets along and it was a short drive to Dame Phyllis Frost, where Eleanor still had six months to serve.

There was a bus that took longer than the drive, but Marnie preferred it. She liked its eccentric route through minor streets, then past starved paddocks on the final approach to the prison. It gave her time to prepare herself. Going home was less enjoyable. Fellow visitors were travelling back from prison, too. They were often up for a chat, needed to relate their story, their version of it. It was where she met Philip, a sad man whom she slept with twice a week for five months. He was a considerate lover, diligent and unexpectedly skilled. His daughter was a murderer. Of the many stories she heard on that purring bus, she wished Philip's story had not been one of them because it stood between them always, and finally ended the relationship.

Sometimes, after a prison visit, Marnie longed for her mother, a pot of tea on the kitchen table and the crossword from the newspaper. But Joan was long gone.

Did her mother have options? Only limited ones, Marnie now realised, but Joan never seemed to want more. She did not acquire things. Marnie assumed it was because Joan was not interested in the latest dress style or gadget, but maybe, on reflection, it was because she didn't have the money to spare. She had a skirt and two shirts for work, court shoes with small heels. Joan never looked fashionable, but she always looked poised. She had a routine you could rely on, although when Marnie was a teenager she felt the dullness of her mother's life would make her head cave in. But that was the seventies; everyone under the age of twenty-five was planning to get to Kathmandu somehow.

'Where's your dad, then?' Heath asked her once, in the intimacy of the van. Although it wasn't intimate that day, Marko was there, listening. And Hollywood was there. He was new. She had been aware of him from the moment he'd been shown into her office, all through the paperwork and induction, aware of a sweet-salty smell of roasting cashews rising off him. Sitting beside him now, she could feel heat along her side, where their clothes touched. He looked at her from under his lashes, once, then looked away. She did not want to have a conversation with Heath. She wanted to sit in silence and feel Hollywood radiating.

'He died before I was born,' she said.

'Yeah? What of?' Heath always sounded casual.

'He was wounded in the war. He was never right afterwards,' she said.

Heath said, 'That's bad luck, kiddo.'

Marko said nothing. Hollywood said nothing. Marnie felt compelled to add the only other thing she really knew about her father. 'He was in the Rats of Tobruk.'

138

'In a movie? Bullshit!' said Marko.

'Language,' cautioned Heath.

Hollywood said, 'Geez, nuff-nut, she means he *was* a Rat of Tobruk.'

'That so?' said Heath and she nodded breathlessly because Hollywood had understood without having to have it explained.

'He escaped from a prison camp in Italy and walked over the Alps to Switzerland. He was practically a skeleton when he got there.'

'Hooley-dooley,' said Heath.

'Bloody oath,' said Hollywood.

Marko said, 'So bullshit is language, but nuff-nut and bloody are just fine, right? I'm going to talk to my union about double standards, youse bludgers are all on notice.'

Heath clipped him over the ear in a friendly way, reaching around the back of Hollywood to do it. Hollywood eased himself forward to avoid Heath's arm, and even the way he dodged was graceful. That was the end of the conversation.

Hollywood was not his name. Heath had nicknames for them all. Some of them were predictable, like Marko for Mark Rizzoli, and Sheenie for Brian Sheen. Bomba's real name was Terence Graham Fawkes. Their names were written in full on their papers. Bomba was little and wiry, had cut his teeth breaking into shops through tiny toilet windows when he was six—shit-easy, he told them out of Heath's hearing. His first day on the team, they'd done a move that involved two pianos, two sideboards and two flights of stairs. Marnie heard about it later—Heath loved relating job stories and this was one that was trotted out often after the event. At the end of the move, they were so whacked, they pulled up at a park on the way home and lay out on the grass drinking cans of Solo and eating potato cakes. All except Terry, the new kid, who went over to the monkey bars and swung on them for twenty minutes.

'You're a wonder,' Heath told him. 'Bomba the Jungle Boy.' And that was that.

Hollywood's name was Peter James Quint. He stood apart. He never slouched like the others and his long hair was always clean and never fell in his eyes. He had his own languid tempo about everything. If Heath said, 'Come on, lads, get crackin'!' they'd all up the pace, but not Hollywood. He worked hard, seldom rested and was part of the team—but still apart. When the boys kicked a footy between jobs Hollywood would join in, but always waited to be coerced. He could drop-punt a ball dead-centre through the goal posts with the grace of a dancer. 'Ready, Mr DeMille!' Heath sometimes said when they set off in the mornings. But he mostly just called him Hollywood.

It was a mystery to Marnie that Heath sometimes called her Caroline, with an accompanying wink as if she got the joke. 'Go see our Caroline in the office, she'll get your paper-work underway. Make sure you take your manners with you,' he instructed the boys. She never asked. She always explained to them what her real name was, and they accepted it without comment.

They were so held in, those boys. It took weeks to get an opinion out of them. Sausage roll or pie? Creamy soda or

Coke? Window seat or middle (no one wanted the middle). The way they'd shrug and drop their eyes, trying to look cool but only managing to look vulnerable. Hard work, footy, nicknames, Dean Martin and bags of lollies—that was Heath's recipe. '*Relax-ay-voo*,' he sang to the boys. They groaned, blocked their ears and rolled their eyes, and loved him for it.

Anyway, Hollywood turned out to be a bad influence. That was what Heath decided and he wasn't wrong. Marnie wasn't sure if Heath even knew the full story. The younger boys idolised Hollywood; he had a way of provoking admiration. It's possible that Heath got rid of Hollywood because of that: Heath was Top Cat, and there wasn't room in the outfit for two of them.

But it could have been because Hollywood was there on the side of the road a block down from Marnie's place when she drove the ute home from work one evening shortly after he joined the team. She pulled over because she wanted to, and he asked her to come with him for a drink.

'Where?'

'North Melbourne.'

'There's a pub up the road.'

'This is a better one.'

Every cell in her body said yes. 'How are we going to get there?'

He looked at her hands on the steering wheel. She said, 'It's not mine. He lets me drive it home when it's late. I have to pick up Sheenie in the morning.'

'Okay, forget it.' He lifted an eyebrow at her and started

141

walking up the street towards Maribyrnong Road where trams were banging and belling their way to the city and back. It was peak hour.

She got into the ute and drove it past him, then pulled into the kerb, climbed out and waited for him to catch up. He didn't alter his stride.

When he was near enough to hear, she said, 'Why do you want to go out for a drink with me?'

'You're over eighteen, aren't you?'

'I'm nearly twenty.' She was barely nineteen, but back then you wanted to be older, not younger.

'You go to pubs?'

'Sure.' She didn't, except for a counter meal with her mother on special occasions.

'You got something against me?'

'Maybe, how do I know?'

'Come find out.'

'I've got to let my mother know.'

'I'll wait.'

She went home and told her mother she was meeting a couple of friends for a counter meal, and Heath said she could take the ute. Joan thought it was a good idea. Marnie brushed her teeth and grabbed her denim jacket, the coolest article of clothing she owned. She made herself walk back down the road, not run, to where Hollywood was leaning against the ute with his arms crossed. He opened the driver's door for her, closed it after her, then strolled around to the passenger door. Joe Cool, Heath might have said if he'd been there.

Later that night, when Hollywood kissed her, she felt an

electric bolt go through her, mouth to cunt. She'd kissed boys at school, experimentally, and she was satisfied that she had found out what it was like but didn't want more. This was totally different. She didn't want to stop. When he put his hand up her shirt, she let him. When he asked her if she was on the pill and she said no, he sat up frowning.

'Jesus wept,' he said.

She sat up too, breathless and startled.

'What do you usually do?' he said.

'I haven't.' She was too rattled to lie.

'Now you tell me.' He moaned and hit his head, an affectation that she forgave him for at once. 'You're nineteen, aren't you? You're older than me.'

'I'm planning to go on it, obviously,' she said, trying to claw back some credibility.

He started kissing her again, his mouth hot on her throat, travelling down between her breasts. 'You better,' he said. 'Because we're gunna fuck. And don't wear a bra, it gets in the way. No one wears a bra anymore.' He started unzipping her jeans. His breath smelled of beer. She felt ashamed to be so ill-prepared, she would do better, oh God, right at this moment she would do anything.

Hollywood had self-control, of a sort. They didn't have sex that first night, although they came perilously close, but the promise was enough for her. She found a doctor in Moonee Ponds, not the usual family doctor, and went on the pill. She stopped wearing a bra. They hardly spoke at work. When they passed each other at the house or out on a job, she felt his heat. He looked at her face, then her breasts. Every time the same sequence; sometimes he smiled. A fortnight later, travelling in the truck, Hollywood cocked an eyebrow at her, and she nodded.

Ten weeks after that, Heath said Hollywood was being moved on and could she do the paperwork. She did not react to the news, although it felt like a powerful punch to her diaphragm. She kept typing.

'Where's he going?'

'Hell, I reckon,' said Heath. She looked at him sharply, and he grinned at her. 'I'm kidding. Bad influence, that's all. It was a risk taking him on, I always knew it, he's got some maturing to do.'

'He seems pretty mature.'

'Only in the wrong ways.'

She didn't see Hollywood again. At first, she expected to. She drove to the North Melbourne pub several times, but he wasn't there. By then she had developed a raging case of cystitis, compliments of too much cramped and crowded sex while squeezed in the ute with him, although there were also a couple of leisurely Saturday afternoons in her own bedroom while her mother was at cards. Hollywood never met Joan, he didn't want to. He was out the back and over the fence at the first sound of Joan's key in the front door. Marnie found it odd, but no more than that, her powers of discernment being seriously compromised. For those ten weeks she lived in a fog of arousal. Waiting, always waiting, for the next time; thinking about Hollywood between times, avoiding his eyes at work.

A week after he left the job, she went back to the doctor

in Moonee Ponds and received a course of antibiotics for her cystitis, followed by cream for thrush. When the itch persisted, she discovered with real horror that Hollywood's parting gift to her was crabs. She didn't know anything about crabs but she didn't need to, there they were scuttling around in her pubic hair, what else could they be?

This was too shameful to take to the doctor. She treated herself with methylated spirits, then dabbed on turpentine, and finally tipped an entire bottle of Lorna's Rive Gauche over her fanny because it had an impressive alcohol content and she felt that it must, please God, do something. All three treatments burned like blazes and her skin turned crimson and some of it flaked off. Then she shaved her pubic hair, just to be certain; this was also painful. The crabs disappeared, but she remained terrified for months. Finally she thought, 'You fucking bastard, Hollywood. You loser-creep-arse-of-a-shithead. I never want to see you again!'

It was like waking up. Rage and resentment jolted her into the present. She looked around herself and saw change everywhere. Sheenie was moving on. He was applying for the police—that was a turn-up for the books, as Heath said. Bomba was on light duties recovering from glandular fever, had been absent for three weeks and now fell asleep on the packing rugs in the truck every day after lunch. Marko was living at Heath's place because something had gone wrong at the place where he'd been boarding. He had taken over Lorna's sewing room, where there were two sewing machines and a daybed as well as a wardrobe full of fabric and boxes of patterns. Butterick, Simplicity, McCalls. Heath said he'd move

Lorna's stuff out, but Marko wouldn't let him. Everything was about to change for Marko. He had stepped up during Marnie's Hollywood obsession and was now visiting Lorna at the nursing home every night of the week. He was about to cement a lifelong passion and commitment.

Marnie went back to her nursing-home visits feeling chastened. Over the next couple of months, she read Lorna *The Wind in the Willows* and *Vanity Fair*. Marko was always there, listening while he practised cross-stitch and shadow-stitch. Lorna loved seeing his work, she patted it and patted Marko, pointing out needles and thread in her beautiful old workbox, which he always brought along with him. Try this one, try this, she told him. Hold it like this. Marko could understand perfectly the way Lorna spoke now. Marnie recognised that she was jealous of Marko, and tried not to show it.

Heath put some papers in front of Marnie one day. 'You need qualifications, kiddo,' he said. 'This here is nothing you can't do already, it's just the piece of paper with the official stamp you want for your CV. Your mother agrees with me.'

It was a secretarial course with touch-typing and basic bookkeeping. Night classes in the city. Heath paid for it.

18

Two weeks slipped by in the caravan park on the side of the grassy lake. Marnie and the children found a rhythm in their days. They took walks around the lake, visited the playground; the children watched TV in the afternoons while Marnie made dinner, they slept top-to-tail in a single bed opposite Marnie's single bed. Frankie usually found her way to Marnie in the night. Koa woke early and cried to be brought over too, until he learned to navigate his way out of the bed by himself and transfer himself across. He was close to walking. Marnie found lace-up boots for him at the local op shop and he hugged them tightly with his teddy at night and filled them with Octonauts by day. Frankie could sing 'Twinkle Twinkle' and 'The Wheels on the Bus' all the way through without a mistake. Marnie showed her the letters of her name and she made a laborious, crooked, perfectly legible *F* with a felt pen.

Up the street, they were regularly greeted by Krystel or

Colleen at the salon. They now knew the people who ran the take-away and the chemist. The gallery was not closed, as Marnie first thought, but open three days a week. One of the people who volunteered there, a woman called Von, sat at a desk inside the door crocheting knee rugs with donated wool and waved at the children when they passed. Koa cried if he did not see Von in her usual spot.

At the end of a fortnight, Declan arrived. He said she could have another two weeks there if they still wanted it. Marnie said they did. He sat outside at the picnic table and drank tea with her and told her about his upcoming transfer. He was moving to Gippsland, he had a girlfriend there. He'd known her since not long after uni and they'd decided to make a go of it, maybe buy a house.

'You've been having a long-distance relationship for how long?'

'Five years,' he said.

'How did you manage?'

'Okay.'

'It sounds…' She nearly said 'nuts', and was relieved when he supplied a word of his own.

'Problematic? It is, I guess. She was on nursing placements, then Covid came along and she was in a tent outside the hospital just testing, testing, fourteen-hour days. She couldn't get out of the town she was in and I couldn't get across the state. For about eighteen months all we had was FaceTime.' He said, 'And all that didn't kill it, which is mental but in a good way, so we thought maybe we'd have a shot.'

Rather than romantic, it sounded bloodless. Marnie

nodded sympathetically because she knew she should, but she thought, how dreary. No awkward coupling in a car, no trying to hold back, muted cries, rushed finishes, sweaty hands over each other's mouths, ratting around in the dark looking for lost socks. Or perhaps they did all that, Declan and his girl; maybe he was recounting the G-rated version, imagining that Marnie's sensibilities were not up to details. Well, why would he share them, anyway? Though, looking at him, she felt her first impression was more likely to be correct.

Declan told her that he'd been trying to get a child-care placement for her. There was nothing local, but if she could get into Horsham there was a day care that would take both children. Definitely a block of three days available that might bump up to five if there was a vacancy. She was ninety kilometres from Horsham. She had driven randomly, but in the end it had been a circle, like what they used to say about people lost in the desert.

'It'll free you up,' Declan said.

'Do you think I would get work somewhere?'

'Yep, or just have a break. Nearly all kids love it, routine, socialisation, all that. Anyway, you're entitled.' He added, 'Lots of kids in the care of a grandparent, more than you'd know. It's a thing.'

'What happens if my daughter wants them back?'

'She'll get assessed, she's got rights—'

'Of course,' she said, too quickly.

'Byron Bay, you said. Is she working?'

Marnie shrugged.

He glanced at her, his face serious. 'Look, there's just

another thing if you're interested, and you don't have to or anything. But, given the way it is, what you said about your daughter having a bit of a habit—' He took a crumpled pamphlet from his pocket. 'This isn't from work, it's from me, so you can ditch it if there's nil interest. There's a group you can go to, there's meetings in most of the big towns— Horsham's definitely got one. It's for people who get stuffed around by addicts.'

'Thanks.' She looked at the pamphlet. 'Thanks Declan, you're a nice person. I hope it all goes wonderfully for you, the move and everything.'

He said, 'Well, the way I see it, failure is not an option. Which is not me being arrogant, just, I have to make it work.' He looked at her with his earnest blue eyes. 'I'm thirty-one. Time to put the big-boy pants on.'

There were people just naturally like that, she thought in bed later that night, people who just knew how to be, how to get it right. How the hell did it happen?

Both children loved day care. All the initial trepidation was Marnie's. When she left them on the first day, Koa was turbo-crawling through the brightly lit Koala Room towards shelves of activities, while Frankie, after clinging briefly to Marnie's coat, was enticed away to Thunder Cats Room by Miss Tash, divine in a floral dress.

'Are you a princess?' Frankie asked the young woman, and did not even look back.

After all the paperwork was complete, Marnie went to the Plaza and found it cheerless. She drank coffee and watched a parade of locals. Then she went into a department store and bought socks and a sparkly headband, because she had seen how other child-care children were more vibrantly turned out than her two. They needed to fit in, she thought, even if it meant buying unicorns and superheroes on everything. She found cheap jeans and a top for herself to replace Lenny's terrible hoodie. She had glimpsed herself in a mirror at the child-care entrance and realised for the first time that she looked like an ageing junkie. It was a shock. Is this the way she had looked to Declan, and Colleen and Von—and those people at the hospital? She could see now that her new haircut needed help, so she bought modest earrings, probably not striking enough to win Krystel's approval, eyeliner, mascara, foundation. She would look the part from now on. That would help the children too.

In the end, she had nothing to do but wait. She picked out a yellowing paperback from a second-hand bookshop and sat in her car reading until it was home time. The book was called *Ladder of Years* and as she read it, she pictured herself reading it aloud to Lorna.

The next day, in her new clothes, earrings, make-up on, she observed herself cutting a less strung-out figure in the day-care mirror. Frankie hugged her legs for a second before careering into a huddle of girls where the new sparkly headband was entirely appropriate. Koa disappeared on the hip of a worker, waving vaguely back to her, his eyes shining.

Rather than burn 180 km of petrol on the round-trip back to Edenhope, Marnie went to a bargain shop in the Plaza and asked if there was any work. There were vacancies everywhere, Colleen had told her. Ever since lockdown shops were running shorter hours because of a lack of staff. The manager, very young, glanced her over without looking at her face. She could tell straight away she was too old for him to even register her existence. She said, 'I worked in a shop like this, in Melbourne.'

'Where exactly?'

'Niddrie. It was called Treen's.'

He looked it up on his phone, standing in front of her not speaking. Then, eyes on the mobile screen: 'References?'

'Do I have references, is that what you mean?' She was beginning to be embarrassed. He did not bother to confirm, just stared, bored, at her collar. 'Not on me, no.'

'Gotta have references,' he said. 'I'll take your number, if you like.'

She said, 'Thanks for your time,' and walked away. For a few seconds she was sure she had owned the little creep, but then she felt a familiar tremor of humiliation and knew it hadn't been like that at all.

In the car she gave herself a pep talk. No point giving up because of a man-boy experiencing his first taste of power. Of course she should have references. She needed to produce a folder with everything laid out clearly, she needed to look polished, even for a crappy little job like that one. She had acted on impulse and, face it, she was too old to be impulsive. She needed to make a list. She hadn't made a proper one for a while, and the task calmed her.

   a) phone Trinh—references

   b) join the library—access to computer

c) *make an updated CV*
d) *make a list of businesses that might have an interest in
   my skill set*
e) *visit them*

She was quite proud of 'skill set', which had popped out of
the end of her biro unexpectedly. It gave her confidence. She
sat in the car and dialled Treen's. The voice that answered
was unmistakably Patsy.

'Hullo, stranger! I'd told them you'd be back, I said
Marnie'll be back, she's the type, they didn't believe me.'

Marnie heard herself going down the rabbit hole of
niceties, asking after everyone, felt the conversation being
hijacked and found herself hearing a litany of Patsy's
complaints, successes and family additions. She said, squeezing her voice through an infinitesimal gap between clichés,
'Is Trinh there?'

'You're kidding, aren't you? Don't you know?' A note of
triumph in Patsy's tone.

'Is she all right?'

'No. She's not dead but—I'm sorry to be the tither of bad
news—she is not long for the planet. Tom knows it, I know
it, and when she tries to come in of an afternoon it's pathetic,
she just sits there. I kid her along, but I've got work to do and
sorry, but it's pathetic.'

'Is she at home?'

'How long for, we don't know. I told Tom, you can't do
all this without help, that's what nursing homes are for. They
don't have them in their country, so she needs to understand
about the way we do it here. I said, we need to get her in and

comfortable, who's kidding who, I said—she's seventy.'

So young.

'And I can't look after her when she's here. I'm not her nursemaid, not on my wages, I told my husband and he said you'd better just nip that in the butt right now they'll use you up, we all know what they're like.'

Racism and mangled metaphor must be a family thing.

Marnie said, 'I'll call her. Do you have her home number?'

'Darling, trust me, she's too weak to come to the phone.'

'Tom's number, then.'

'She's not happy with you, I'm just telling you because forearmed is better than none.'

'Okay, but I'll still have it please, if you've got it.'

Patsy read out the number, then said, 'Where are you, anyway?'

Marnie said, 'Deniliquin. Thanks, Patsy. Bye.' She ended the call feeling bruised.

She told herself she should not let Patsy change her plans. Of all people, that one should have no influence on her actions. But she found it difficult now to motivate herself to call Tom.

She walked up to the library instead, and signed herself and the children up. She'd had some correspondence from a couple of government departments now—her letters came to the post office in Edenhope—and the librarian said that would be sufficient. There was a library branch in Edenhope, she said, as she handed over library cards.

Marnie wandered around the bank of computers, the printer, the bookshelves and the children's section. She borrowed four books for the children and went back out into the street. So, her list items: not done, done, the last three abandoned for now. The usual thwarting of best intentions.

There was a Staff Wanted sign in the window of a café she was passing. The Honeydew. It was afternoon now, the dull light of day already becoming opaque. A woman with red fingernails and three blue bandaids on the fingers of one hand was bringing chairs in from the street. Marnie said, 'I'm interested in the staff wanted. Who can I talk to?'

'Me,' said the woman. 'Can you help me with the chairs?'

Marnie carried a pile of chairs indoors. 'It's kitchen work, dishes and food prep,' the woman said.

'I've done both. I worked in a child-care centre in Melbourne, and in a fast-food place.'

'Five days?'

'I can only do three. My grandchildren are in my care, and I've only got three days at day care, but they said they'll give me five when they can.'

'Wednesday, Thursday, Friday?'

'Yes.'

'I suppose Saturday is out.'

'Sorry. No child care.'

'Will you try out tomorrow?' The woman stuck out her hand. 'I'm Sam.'

And that was that. Marnie bought pizza for dinner to celebrate, and a punnet of blueberries at an exorbitant price.

Von from the gallery called around to the caravan park one afternoon. She was a small woman with a crooked torso and

155

a limp. She had knitted a green jumper for Koa, and a pink and yellow poncho for Frankie.

'They've got an eighties night at the pub next week,' she said. 'You should think about coming along. It's a fund-raiser for the hospital.'

'I can't leave the children.'

'Bring them, it's family friendly. People ask me about you, they see you around, that's the way it is out here, they won't necessarily go up to you, though. It'd be a chance for you.'

Marnie wasn't sure it was a chance she wanted to take. The thought that she was being spoken about, quite natural she supposed, in a small town, was still unsettling. She said, 'Are you going?'

'No show without Punch,' said Von.

Koa, crawling with one hand only, brought a fistful of tongue depressors over to Von, he pulled himself up to standing at Von's side and emptied his bundle onto her lap. 'Da,' he said.

'You've been blessed,' Marnie said. Von was eighty-eight, she had grandchildren and great-grandchildren dispersed around the continent. She seemed at home in the cabin at the caravan park, sitting at a small table covered with laundry, crusts and toys. She'd farmed on a block just south of the town since she was married at twenty. She was generous with information about herself, told stories of no phone, no electricity, hand-milking at dawn and helping her husband put in fence posts when she was eight months pregnant. Marnie wondered if the talk was in order to hear about Marnie—honesty and sharing serving to disarm the listener. She needed to be careful. It was easy to forget how off-putting the details of her life could be.

Von was kind to Koa, patiently continuing to exchange tongue depressors with him. Frankie brought her book set over and demonstrated the packing and unpacking of the books. 'My mummy does do this,' she told Von. 'When she comes.'

'Did your mummy give you that lovely headband?' asked Von.

Frankie nodded, reaching up to touch the sparkles delicately. She slid a glance at Marnie, who said nothing.

Later, in bed, Frankie said, 'Where's my mummy gone?'

'Byron Bay,' Marnie said. 'Working.' She thought to herself, this is from child care. The others talk of their mothers, so no matter what I do, she feels different. The idea made her stomach hurt.

'Home again?' Frankie said.

'Yes, one day. When we phone her, we'll all say hello.'

'Koa too.'

'All of us.'

'Now?'

'Not now, I don't have her number. But I'm trying to get it.'

'Why?'

'Because I don't know it. I asked Rhiannon.'

'Why?'

Marnie knew that the question was a way of extending the conversation, not requiring a specific answer. She said, 'We all want to speak to Mummy, don't we? You want to tell her about child care...'

'And Von.'

'And Von as well.'

'And...' She held up her teddy.

'And Teddy, too. Time to sleep, baby. Say nigh-night, Koa, nigh-night Teddy, nigh-night Ganny, nigh-night Mummy.'

Frankie repeated each name. She added, 'Nigh-night Miss Tash.'

19

The new caseworker from the Department of Families Fairness and Housing was similar in age to Marnie. Her name was Kaarin. It was probably not spelled that way, but it was pronounced that way and Marnie had to picture the double-A spelling in order to say it correctly. The woman was particular about the pronunciation of her name. She introduced herself with, 'We'll start by getting my name right, will we?'

Kaarin was a squashed-looking woman, small like Von, in a coloured pullover that made her look like a Rubik's cube. Her hair had been cut in an asymmetrical style that was too youthful for her, dyed too dark, with hard grey roots. Marnie heard Colleen's voice in her head: 'Regrowth can be ageing.' Kaarin also dressed for comfort. Marnie could hear Eleanor saying that—'Well. She certainly dresses for comfort'—as a put-down. Not that Eleanor was any fashionista, but she always focused on failings, amplifying them until the failing became the person: Miss ZeroDressSense, Mr PostNasalDrip,

Mrs PleaseLetMeBoreYouAboutMyGrandkids.

Kaarin read out Marnie's recent history to her in a toneless voice, sitting at the table outside the cabin, stodgy in huge runners. She would come inside later, she said, just to look around. She wouldn't take a coffee or a tea. How did Marnie expect she could function if she had a drink at every place she visited? She'd be running to the loo all day. She seemed to want Marnie to feel a rung down from her on an imaginary ladder; also gratitude for Kaarin's time, and possibly a touch of shame for being a bother. Kaarin referred to the Department as 'We' in a way that suggested she occupied an elevated position in the hierarchy.

'I'm afraid we need to clarify a few things,' Kaarin said. 'What date did you commence work at the Honeydew?'

'Oh…last week. I can't remember the date.'

'Why not?'

'If you know I'm working there, then you must have the date of commencement. I phoned through all the information.'

'I know what's written here. I want to hear it from you.'

'Um?'

'Just a question, don't get your hackles up.'

Marnie took out her phone and looked for the date of the call. She showed the caseworker. 'I phoned Centrelink the first day.'

'You didn't need to. You only need to make sure the information is there within two weeks.'

'But there's nothing actually wrong with giving them the information on the first day?'

160

'I didn't say there was, don't put words in my mouth.'

The effect it had on you, the breathlessness you felt when nothing made sense, when you thought you were being suspected of something. She remembered the feeling from working with Patsy. This was different, though. This one (Mrs NoNeckReallyBadRegrowth) wielded actual power.

'Have you heard from your daughter?'

'I don't have her number. She has mine, though.'

'Why wouldn't you have it?' A raising of the eyebrows so that they disappeared under her fringe.

'Her phone was stolen.'

'And you're not aware if she's got herself a new one?'

'I'm sure she has. But she hasn't called me.'

'Family members?'

'There's just me.'

'She has a father.'

If you already know, why are you prying, she thought, but said, 'We've been divorced a long time and Eleanor doesn't have a relationship with him that I know of.'

'Eleanor—'

'Lenny. My daughter. She's on your books as Lenny Odell.' Now she was going red in the face, she could feel it. She wondered if Kaarin was doing this deliberately. She said, 'You have all the details, I know you do, because Declan had them, and they've been passed on. Why are you trying to get me to repeat everything?'

'People make errors.'

'You're trying to catch me in an error?'

'Did I say that?' Kaarin clenched her lips in the shape of

a smile. 'You need to calm down a bit, Marnie, no one's out to get you.'

Anger shivered like a haze at the edges of Marnie's vision. 'Ms Odell,' she heard herself say. 'I prefer that.'

It was a mistake, Marnie knew that before it came out. It was a declaration of war. These are my ground rules, she seemed to be saying, even though they actually weren't. But she could tell that Kaarin would not permit any such declaration from a client; that was not the way this relationship would work. Kaarin collected her paperwork in a pile and packed it into her satchel. Her mouth remained clenched.

'I can see this is not a good time,' she said. 'I'll just have a look inside, then I'll be off.'

She was already walking through the door of the cabin; Marnie, having spoken up, felt she had now expended her one chance to take a stand. She felt sure that this woman, this no-neck Kaarin, should not be free to march into her residence, even if it was paid for by the department.

She called the children to her, swung Koa onto her hip, following along behind, hearing her voice adopt a wheedling cadence. 'It's not tidy, we're just having a quiet day—' Oh, God, make me shut up.

Kaarin looked at the rucked doonas, the plates and cups on the draining board, a used nappy rolled up on the floor, dead centre where it could not be missed. She opened the fridge—could she even do that? 'You've only got this place for another five days,' Kaarin told her, looking over the milk and yoghurt, the orange juice, a shrivelled sweet potato and half a pumpkin before shutting the fridge door again. 'Strictly speaking you've had it longer than we normally permit.'

Marnie stopped speaking. Even her silence was going to be viewed as somehow insolent, she knew. But she felt dammed up. Only fawning thanks might work, possibly, and she couldn't, she would not, do that.

She closed the door on Kaarin without saying goodbye and waited until the car had driven away before opening it up again.

Colleen called to Marnie from the door of the salon later when she walked the children past. She was still feeling bleak and outraged. 'Von said you're coming to the eighties night.'

'I'm not sure...' She'd forgotten the conversation with Von. 'The kids.'

'They'll be in the play area. Krystel's one of the carers, she's got her Working with Children. We've thought of everything, no excuses.'

'I don't have a costume.'

'Don't worry, I've got a plan based on your haircut, it'll be brilliant. Trust me, as the bishop said to the actress.'

Colleen's plan involved dyeing Marnie's hair orange. 'Honestly, it'll wash out, it's only semi. If you use dishwashing liquid on it instead of shampoo it'll be gone even quicker. Trick of the trade.'

Colleen was so fired up that it was impossible to fend her off. She started on the colour as soon as Marnie had murmured a faint assent, flying into action with a basket of broken toys to amuse the children and dragging on latex gloves as she hurled a black apron around Marnie's neck.

While the colour was developing, Colleen brought out a garbage bag of clothes and flung things around feverishly to the delight of the children. 'This looks a mess but I've got a method, half of this is for other people, I've been collecting for ages. But I thought these—' She held up a pair of black vinyl pants. 'They're mine. Okay, you can't believe I ever wore them, I know, but I used to be thin and they will look amazing on you, plus this—' a crumpled black blazer. She held them both up, placing the blazer over the pants for Marnie to see the ensemble.

'I won't fit into that!'

'Try, that's all I'm asking.'

Marnie tried the clothes on. She was surprised that the pants fitted her, they held her soft bits in, giving her the impression of being almost trim. She'd lost weight, she realised.

'Annie Lennox,' said Colleen triumphantly. 'No one else is going as her. We've got that many Boy Georges there's going to be a punch-up before the night's out. You need a shirt, one of my son's old school shirts'll work, and a tie and the right make-up—but it's totally perfect. Am I right?'

Far from perfect, Marnie thought, but she was suddenly happier than she could remember. They looked up Annie Lennox online, found the right era photograph and examined the pale foundation and the cat's eyes in detail. Marnie said she could do it. Sort of, she thought.

'Okay, I'm holding you to this. You do it, you've got four days to practise it, I'll fix it when you arrive.'

'Wow—I didn't know there was a standard!'

Colleen's gusto tempered slightly. She said, 'There's always a standard with me. No one gets to reach it, not even me. That's what's called being a control freak, mate, and why I'm currently single.' Then she smiled. It was a real smile, slightly self-deprecating, no clenching at all.

'How many children do you have?' Marnie asked.

'Three. Two of them don't want to know me, their choice, life's a bitch.' Colleen shrugged and just for the flicker of an instant Marnie saw the hurt chase across her face and vanish like a demon shadow.

It's everyone, she thought. It's all of us.

The man at the take-away was going as Freddie Mercury and his wife and daughters were going as The Bangles. They showed her bits of their costumes when she stopped with the kids to get fish and chips. They already knew Marnie was going along. They reported that Jeff from the council depot was going as Robert Palmer. 'He fancies himself,' one of the girls said. The other one said, 'He's got a red velvet tux from the seventies, that's all. And he's got that much of a gut it'll never do up.' The girls ignited like a Catherine wheel.

There were posters all over town, in Apsley and Harrow, Goroke, as far as Horsham. The supermarket had eighties hits on its muzak loop. Colleen was organising a DJ, and the publican had a veto over the playlist. 'Which is a worry,' confided Krystel. 'His musical knowledge is totally country— which is fine, but it's not the theme, is it? Even I know more about eighties music than Lester, and I wasn't born until eighty-nine.'

Von would be collecting money at the door. 'No costume?' Marnie asked her.

'Colleen's got some idea about something. I told her: I'll do what I'm told.' She looked at Marnie and added, 'You can't fight city hall where Colleen's concerned. I'm knitting legwarmers now,' she said. 'If anyone tries to get in without a costume, they've got to put legwarmers on, that's her rule.'

The couple who ran the caravan park were going, too. Marnie went to see them to organise another week's accommodation when her time ran out. She paid in advance and they expressed satisfaction that she was staying on.

'We've had some bad experiences,' the woman told her. 'Not mentioning names or anything, some people can't help it.'

'People who just won't follow rules,' the man explained.

'Sometimes they don't know how, they never learned,' the woman corrected him.

Marnie felt gratified that she was not lumped in with the rule-breakers who came through DFFH, and tried not to look guilty on their behalf.

20

On the night of the fundraiser, she felt confident and included enough to wave to the couple as they headed off in their leotards with headbands, wristbands and legwarmers, and Walkmans attached at the waist. 'See you at the shindig!' they called. They were going on foot so they could have a few drinks. Marnie could tell they were excited about walking along the main street in their fluoro outfits.

The kids were jumping with exhilaration. Marnie tried to apply her make-up, checking the pictures on her phone, while Frankie and Koa bounced around her, aware that something was about to take place. There was no full-length mirror to check herself, so she smoothed herself down, struggled with a Windsor knot, and loaded the children into the car, aware that she was trying to defuse her own excitement. How long since she had felt like this?

Of course she would not be there late. The children would be tired and cranky by eight-thirty, if they even lasted until then. Settle down, she told herself. She tried to think of Kaarin, but even that couldn't deflate her.

The hotel was lit up, balloons everywhere, the DJ was playing a relentlessly buoyant song to get everyone in the mood—'Break My Stride'. The words came into Marnie's head as if they'd never been gone. Colleen appeared at the door, a startling apparition in a polyester tutu, a tuxedo jacket, bowler hat and hair extensions. She grabbed the children and conveyed them inside, shouting back to Marnie, 'Wait there. I have to check your make-up.' She reappeared moments later with a tackle box and pushed Marnie into a chair on the porch under a bright light as if she were about to experience a hostile cross-examination.

'Not bad,' said Colleen. 'Not bad. More definition needed, some shading. We really need green contact lenses.'

'Huh?'

'I haven't got any, it's just I wish I did.' She made deft movements with a brush and eye pencil.

'Brilliant,' she said finally. 'Clear for take-off. You're one of the first. Make an entrance.' She left Marnie's side and ran outside to greet the next arrivals.

Von appeared to be wearing used Christmas wrap, but it turned out to be a mauve shell suit several sizes too large. She was positioned behind a cash register at a table inside the door. 'Colleen needs to take a chill pill,' she remarked to Marnie. 'I'm not one to push drugs, but…'

Marnie paid her ten-dollar entry and received a raffle ticket. 'What's it for?' she said.

'Door prize. I can always tell country people from city

people. Country people never ask, they just take their ticket and hope they don't win. It's never anything special. You look very nice, are you meant to be a boy?'

'Annie Lennox.'

Von looked blank but nodded approvingly and said, 'Glad you came.'

'Who is Colleen dressed as?'

'Sandy someone. Loper. Looks damn silly, but you didn't hear that from me.'

Cyndi Lauper. Of course. A relief to know, it would be a frightful faux pas to get it wrong. The room was dim, the bar lit up, an adjoining room was cordoned off with six or seven wired children in it, watched over by Krystel in the Princess Diana-inspired bridesmaid's dress.

Marnie was aware of shadowy figures standing in groups. She waved to the couple from the caravan park. A man was leaning across the bar in one corner, not participating by the looks of it: jeans, ripped flannel shirt, moccasins, Bombers beanie. He was talking to the publican, who was decked out in a cowboy shirt complete with pearl snap buttons and bolo tie.

'Who the hell did you come as, Lester?' someone called to him.

The publican looked up and said, 'What's it look like? Slim!'

A woman said, 'An eighties icon?'

'Then, now and always!'

The publican caught sight of Marnie and stepped backwards in a show of delight, shouting across the room,

'Sweet dreams are made of this! My beating, bloody heart! It's my poster girl!'

Everyone's eyes were on Marnie for a few seconds. There was a smattering of applause.

She stayed longer than she'd intended. When the crowds had gathered—this included three Boy Georges, Adam Ant, a Bowie, Tina Turner and Debbie Harry plus an assortment of other less-recognisable figures with oversized shoulder pads, cinch-waisted jeans and naked ankles—the music ramped up. Marnie danced with Colleen and sang 'Come On Eileen' with Von. Krystel appeared for 'Wake Me UP', looped her skirt into her sash, and kicked up her heels in orange tooled riding boots. Who is watching the children, Marnie thought and went looking, but there they were safe in the other room throwing cushions, while Von, drinking tea in a corner and shrinking steadily into her shell suit, watched over them.

A couple of hours in, there were speeches and an auction of a weekend at someone's beach house in Port Macdonnell. Frankie, glassy-eyed with tiredness, came looking for Marnie and crawled up on her knee for a while before being coerced back to the children's room with the promise of ice cream.

The drinker at the bar, a regular who had resentfully paid his ten-dollar entry to appease Colleen, won the door prize which turned out to be a paper plate of home-made biscuits and a bottle of Riccadonna spumante. He looked at both with a kind of bewilderment and glanced around the room as if just noticing the throng, allowing his bloodshot eyes to rest on Marnie for a second before moving on. Then he said to the assembly, 'All right, nothing to see, play on.' And turned back to the bar, plonking his prizes on the seat beside him.

Von confided in Marnie's ear, 'The problem with Razza is he goes from drunk to nasty like flicking a switch. Who's taking him home, I wonder? I'll just go ask Kaylene.'

She went to the bar and spoke to the publican's wife, who was dressed as Nefertiti. The music became less frantic and Lester, the publican, appeared at Marnie's shoulder suddenly.

'Come on, this is our dance,' he said. 'I've loved you for forty years, make an old bastard happy.'

The music was 'Dance Me to the End of Love', and Lester knew how to dance, the knowledge was there in the pressure of his hand on her elbow before they'd even begun. 'Sorry, mate, I'm old school,' Lester said, reaching around her waist. 'Just go with the flow,' which suggested there might be a choice, although she wasn't aware of one. She couldn't remember the last time she'd danced, had always been self-conscious at Gerald's work-dos and random weddings. But she felt capable now with the confident pressure of Lester the publican's hand at her back, his whole body manoeuvring hers around. She looked over his shoulder and saw that she was being watched: his wife at the beer taps, Razza the barfly from under his unkempt eyebrows, beer glass to his lips. She tried to look as if it was a joke, but it felt so nice, so right, that she was nervous her pleasure showed too plainly. She was glad when other people began to dance, too. For four minutes she felt completely new, and then the music ended and she was laughing and clapping because it was all such a huge joke. Lester went back to his wife at the bar, looking plump and

171

balding and ridiculous in his cowboy costume.

Marnie collected the children after that. Koa was asleep under a chair and Frankie was staggering. When she came back into the main room with them, speeches of thanks were going on, featuring Colleen's name prominently. She was stopped from leaving by Colleen, who chased her to the door and thrust a sixpack into her arms.

'You got the costume prize!' she said.

It was vodka mixed with something improbable. Turkish delight? 'You earned it. You have it,' said Marnie, pushing it back into Colleen's hands. 'Where's Von?'

'Drove Razza home. No, you keep it,' pushing the drinks back at her. 'It looks pukeworthy, but I want to try one at least. I'll drop in.' She called out, 'Annie Lennox is leaving the building!' but the music was back on—'Heart of Glass'—and no one heard, thank goodness. Marnie slipped out into cold air carrying both children, her bag and nappy bag. The Milky Way was a frosty wash over their heads.

It never left you, she thought later, lying sleepless in bed. Desire, like an exotic warmth, that pulse of blood in her thighs, that want, sending heat branching through her, her whole pelvis both light and heavy with it. Not desire for Lester the publican, or Ged, God help him, or any of those others going all the way back to Hollywood. But it was there. Purposeful yet undirected, a fire that would not go out. Sixty-three years old and lying awake, filled with it.

21

In the style of a bad joke—predictable and tedious—Kaarin called by the next morning.

'It's Saturday,' Marnie bleated, opening the door on a dismal day. The lake was invisible behind a wall of mist. From the doorstep, Kaarin regarded her from under her sinister fringe, beaded with rain. Marnie knew she was taking mental note of the orange hair dye, badly slept on, the vestiges of make-up, Marnie's dressing gown over trackpants.

'I'm in transit, it's convenient for me,' Kaarin said.

Marnie held the door open. 'You'd better come in, you're getting wet.'

The children were on her bed in a doona and pillow cubby house. The sixpack of Turkish delight Cruisers was lying on its side on the sink. Vegemite toast crusts and a banana skin were making their presence known from a plate on the floor which Marnie picked up quickly.

Kaarin said, 'We've had contact with your daughter.'

'We? You've spoken to her?'

'I'm not her case worker. The department has spoken to her. She's been trying to contact you.'

Marnie picked up her phone and switched it on, unplugging it so that she could bring it over to the table. 'I've had no messages. She can't have forgotten my number, it's been this for years. Is she all right?' She stared at her phone screen, rather than look at Kaarin. There was something even more smug and withheld about Kaarin today. Marnie said, 'It's old, it'll take a moment to fire up,' and repeated: 'Is Eleanor all right?'

'I just said I didn't speak to her personally.'

'Please don't talk to me like this. I only want to know about my daughter, you must have details, I know you do. They keep a profile with all the calls, I've dealt with DHS for years,' searching her memory, 'a dossier, or something.'

'DFFH. It's been called that for a while.' Kaarin appeared to be admonishing her.

Marnie might have responded, but Frankie and Koa were fighting with each other now. Marnie unearthed them from the doona and sat them on her knee. They blinked at Kaarin.

'All I know is, your daughter's concerned about her children,' Kaarin said.

'Well, I should hope so!' Marnie's mobile belled a wake-up alert, followed by a series of pings. An unknown number, but a recognisable text, repeated ten times.

Mum whr R U?

Followed by a variation on the eleventh text:

Call me, plz.

'Oh hell,' said Marnie. 'We were out last night, I didn't see these, I just plugged the phone in and went to sleep.' She glanced up at Kaarin. 'A fundraiser at the hotel.'

Kaarin said nothing. Oh, how much power was conveyed by silence. It made Marnie furious with Kaarin and also with herself for being intimidated. 'Please tell me,' she said again. 'Is everything all right?'

'Phone her and find out.'

'Not with you here! Can I have privacy? What is this about?' Anger made her incautious. 'This is my daughter, their mother. Where is Brayden, can you tell me that, at least?'

'I don't have that kind of information. Tell me this, though, are you feeling well?'

The question surprised her. 'I'm not sure I understand you.'

'Simple enough, isn't it?'

'I'm fine. Thanks.'

'Can you tell me today's date?'

'Yes.'

Kaarin waited.

'I need you to tell me what's going on,' Marnie said more quietly.

'Humour me.'

'I'm not required to humour you.'

'You can be compelled to undergo a medical assessment.'

'Sorry? On what grounds?'

'Diminished responsibility.'

175

Oh my giddy aunt! What new nonsense was this? What had Eleanor said? Denying it, getting into a tizzy, that would make her look guilty and, yes, unhinged. Marnie said, 'I don't know what you're talking about, but I will phone my daughter. I don't even know why you've called by, but thanks for alerting me to the fact that my daughter has messaged me, which I would have found out anyway as soon as I turned on my phone. I really don't know what else to say to you.'

Kaarin was on her feet, bestowing her smile. 'You'll have to be out of here on Monday, we spoke about that.'

'I've made arrangements. Thanks for the reminder.'

'We'll need your new contact details.'

'Contact details all exactly the same. I'll give you the address within two weeks. Thanks for calling.'

This time she felt cautiously confident that her tone was right but knew there would be repercussions. Kaarin was the kind of person who exacted revenge slowly.

And so, the inevitable phone call. Eleanor: 'Oh my God, Mum, where are you?'

'Where are *you*?'

'Up north. I am so upset, Mum. Everything's shit.'

'Are you working?'

'A bit.' That meant no, Marnie thought.

Eleanor said, 'Brayden left me.'

The sound of misery in her voice, the crack of emotion, it didn't matter that Marnie hated him, she felt her chest tighten. 'Oh, baby, what happened?'

'Where do I start? It's just shit and now I've got nowhere to live.'

'Where did he go?'

'Tweed Heads is what he said, but he's not even answering my calls. I've sent a billion messages.'

Poor tactic, no point telling her. Eleanor's misery rolled out, waves of it, a griping stream of complaint. The job at Byron that never eventuated, the accommodation that was a rip-off, the camping on the beach, the storms, the tides, the humidity. Yes, there was emergency help, it was flooding all up the east coast.

'It's biblical, Mum,'

'I've seen the news. I thought the worst of it was past.'

'No, you have no idea. I mean biblical. Brayden went all paranoid one night and said we had to get ready like the world was ending and the next day he just fucking went. I was getting us breakfast. He was in the tent when I left and then he wasn't and all his stuff—some of my stuff too, the prick—all just gone and I'm sitting there with my sleeping bag and my backpack, he even took the toilet paper and about a hundred dollars' worth of other stuff.' Which meant weed, probably. 'He left me with seven fucking dollars, Mum.'

Marnie was sitting outside at the picnic table. Frankie came from the cabin looking for her, turning back to assist Koa to crawl backwards down the front steps. Seeing that simple gesture of solidarity, Marnie felt pain in her chest.

She said to Lenny, 'Where are you now?'

'In a gym on a fucking army cot with about a gazillion other people and their dogs. I have to do Covid tests every

177

fucking day practically. They're saying I might not be eligible for assistance because I didn't lose a house. It's totally unfair.'

'Can you get back here?'

'With what? Aren't you hearing me? Seven fucking dollars, Mum. They've cut my money off.'

'They can't have.'

'Yeah, well it's your fault. You've got the kids, and the money's got redirected to you.' Now it was coming out.

'I didn't ask for them to do that, they just did, they worked it out. And they couldn't have taken all your money. Only what you get for the kids.'

'I want them back, you took them. They're my kids, Mum.'

A skitter of panic. 'You wanted a break, Brayden agreed. I didn't even know you went up to Byron!'

'I'm not *in* Byron, I'm north of it. Some shithole that Bray said he knew someone from, and that person wasn't even here anymore.'

'You told Rhiannon you were going to Byron, that's all I knew.'

'Fucking Rhiannon, don't get me started on her. She's a bitch.'

'She's not, and she has nothing to do with anything so leave her out of it.'

'It's pathetic the way you let people run your life.'

'Tell me what you want to do, just let's talk calmly, let me see if I can help.'

Frankie said, 'My mummy?'

'Yes, honey-kitten, it is. Frankie's here. Do you want to speak to her?'

'Not now! I can't cope with her right now, Mum. Jesus, you really don't get it, I'm stressed out of my mind!'

'Just say hello.' She put the phone to Frankie's ear and heard Eleanor's tone lighten instantly making sounds of caring and concern.

'I go to Miss Tash,' Frankie told her. Then she tried to tell the story of Marnie's hair colour but didn't have the vocabulary to explain herself. 'Ganny has got all sort, sort hair all gone now and Coween did make it go onage.'

'Sorry baby, put Ganny back on.' Impatience in Eleanor's voice.

'I'm here,' said Marnie. 'You need to come home. It doesn't sound like there's much hope of work or anything up there.'

'Can't you bring them here?'

'No. I don't have the money for a drive like that, I wouldn't be able to pay for accommodation. I have a job down here.'

'That job was shit.'

'It was a job, Eleanor. Shit or not. And I don't have that one anymore. I'm not in Niddrie, I'm in Edenhope.'

'Where's that?' Bewilderment in Lenny's voice, as if she was just catching up.

'Western Victoria. Come back. You can take a bus to Horsham.'

'Holy shit, Mum.' Silence on the phone, then she said, 'Did you have a party for Ko?'

The birthday date that Marnie could not remember. 'I thought I'd save it for when we were all together. Koa doesn't know, or care.'

'Is he walking?'

'Really close.'

'Mummy, I'm really scared.'

'I know, baby, I know. Tell them at Centrelink. Just explain that you have to come here. They'll help you.'

'You say stuff like that, but it's not true. You live in a dream world, Mum.'

22

She tried not to let Eleanor get to her. She'd been trying, sometimes succeeding, for how long? Following that phone call, old thoughts came back—shabby memories on rafts of guilt. Eleanor at primary school, refusing to wear her school socks, refusing to go along to sports carnivals. Eleanor at secondary school, obdurate. Phone calls home, 'Your daughter is not at school. We'd like to remind you of our policy...' As if Eleanor's behaviour was something that Marnie approved of. Sometimes Marnie left work and drove around the streets, then Eleanor would be there at the end of the day, sauntering in, kicking her bag through her bedroom door. Marnie tried asking, then begging, then threatening. Where do you go? Why do you go? If you hate school, let's please talk about it.

By year eight Marnie had cut a groove to the principal's door in two schools. Gerald was away a lot, a glorified salesman. In her night-time panics over Eleanor, she resented Ged's absences, her revenge fantasies filled with acts of violence. But when he was there, she kept the peace.

Had she loved him once? Or just been overwhelmed by the smart suits, the lamentable coloured shirts with white collars?

Gerald represented a world she thought she ought to belong to, that world she glimpsed when she did the secretarial course. The others in the course, all female, had social lives and boyfriends. She went along with them to department-store sales and aerobics classes. They weren't readers but it didn't matter, she wasn't reading much herself just then. One of the girls knitted Fair Isle jumpers, breathtaking in their complexity, another went in for ballroom dancing competitions. They all styled their hair like Charlie's Angels. Marnie admired them but felt no deep connection.

The world was full of polarisations and Marnie didn't know where she belonged; she can't have been the only one. That was the first truthful realisation she ever had about herself, twenty years old, 1979, her disastrous fling with Hollywood behind her. Where the hell did she belong? Since there was no answer, she finished the course. Her mother was keen, Heath was keen, and let's face it, she learned heaps of useful stuff.

She undertook three work placements and had to take time off from Heath's, time away from Lorna. At her first placement, her supervisor liked to give her shoulder massages, pausing at her desk to chat and press his short, hairy fingers around her neck. At the second place, no one spoke to her at all and she spent the first three days looking for the stationery cupboard. At the third placement, in a company that sold microprocessor components and software development systems, she met Gerald Odell.

There was no doubt in her mind, even then, that Ged liked himself just fine. He was good-looking, and enthusiastic about his work—he called it a sunrise industry. He liked the company of the computer engineers he worked with, she could tell by the boyish way he behaved when he was with them, but they weren't particularly friendly to her. They either ogled her or talked to one another over her head. Sometimes they attempted to explain the inner electronics of obscure instruments by drawing on napkins, but this was less to help her understand than to show her how clever they were.

Ged was learning PL-M and Algol, languages they would all know one day when they worked from home on TRS 80s, or Commodore 64s. It was the new world, it was coming, apparently, and she had no reason to dispute it. Ged told her his company supplied components that went into Space Invaders consoles, and she was duly impressed. He said there would be a million new toys on the market soon that could speak to you, ask questions about arithmetic and spelling and supply answers. These toys, he promised, would revolutionise education.

He wasn't wrong. If anything he was limited in his vision of an industry that was drawing up around them like a tidal wave, ready for the deluge. His enthusiasm about it all wasn't the problem with them as a couple, it was that he had no interest, not even the slightest, in her.

After she finished the secretarial course, Marnie settled back into working for Heath, visiting Lorna, going out with

Ged on the weekend. But she also enrolled in an arts degree, part time—literature and Latin. She started out keen as mustard, but felt gauche. A girl with Farrah Fawcett hair reading Conrad, Woolf and T. S. Eliot—surely everyone could see through the pretence. She showed her books to Lorna and read some of them aloud.

Marko was always at the nursing home in the evenings. He was earning money now, sewing tutus for a local ballet school. He listened to Marnie's books, stopping her to clarify things sometimes, throwing his hands up halfway through *To the Lighthouse*, to say, 'When is she just going to go there, for fuck's sake?'

Marnie explained ablative declensions to Joan. She taught Heath a few Latin quips. But Gerald; Gerald never once asked her a question, never even referred to the night lectures from which she travelled home by tram, although he often collected her from the stop. She repaid his utter indifference by dropping out of her course and marrying him when she was twenty-four and he was thirty.

Heath was unimpressed with Gerald. He didn't say so, but it was evident. If she'd asked Heath, would he have told her why? Years later, when the marriage was done, she suspected any explanation from Heath would have included a robust criticism of her for choosing Ged in the first place. Heath could be direct.

His on-switch was cheerful-chatty, but he left gaps for other people to speak. He didn't mind silence in the van, and he didn't mind if the conversation turned serious. He often spoke about self-esteem, as he had that first day she met him.

He explained to her that the boys all suffered from a lack of self-esteem, even the really crass ones. It was easy to feel sorry for the quiet ones, but the mouthy ones made you want to tighten your lips and turn away. Or worse, you wanted to cut them down to size. Heath understood the impulse, but he never gave in to it. He told Marnie that when those boys allowed themselves to express a truthful opinion and you took the time to listen and acknowledge them, it was like opening a door. You could see in, and those smart-arsed, brutish boys could see out. Most things came down to self-esteem, Heath said: good choices, bad choices, love, hate—the lot.

Was that the single, pathetic reason she allowed herself to be subsumed into Gerald's life the way she did? Now, as in the past, after a few hours of catastrophising in the dead of night, she pitched up at that question. But it followed a path blocked by a wall she could never breach.

Without Gerald, there would have been no Eleanor. Whatever else happened in her world, whatever shitty path she was on, there was Eleanor.

23

Marnie resisted the urge to call Eleanor. Over the next few days she texted twice and received monosyllabic replies. She sent love hearts and smiley faces from the children once, and then let it rest. 'You don't have to suck up.' Rhiannon's advice from long ago. She slept badly. Same old, same old.

Colleen called by late one night at the end of the week. They sat in the cabin and cracked open the Turkish delight vodkas. 'So, news,' Colleen said, opening a bag of chips and tipping them onto the tabletop. 'Me first.'

Colleen's news was that Von had broken her hip the night of the fundraiser. Von had driven Razza home—he lived in a cottage in a bluegum plantation a few kilometres past Von's. Von had dropped him off, driven back to her own place, stepped out of the car in her carport and tripped over the strap of her handbag, which had fallen out of the car in front of her. Lucky she was in the carport and not outside, Colleen said, because she spent the rest of the night on the concrete and it got down to nearly freezing. The only good thing was that she was wearing the shell suit over her normal clothes and she'd been holding her overcoat when she started climbing out, along with Razza's beanie which he'd left behind, so she had them. Her phone was, unfortunately, on the dashboard.

'She could have died,' said Marnie.

'It would take a bit to kill Von,' said Colleen opening another drink. 'Anyway, Razza came back next morning to get his beanie, and he found her and called an ambulance.'

The ambulance had taken Von to Horsham and from there she'd been airlifted to Melbourne.

'I guess it's good that Razza arrived.'

'The least he could do. And he always does the very least, believe me.'

'You've spoken to her.'

'Totally ropable. They gave her morphine and it made her throw up, so they gave her something else and she went woozy—her words—and missed the whole flight to Melbourne, which she would have enjoyed, she said. Plus the family's circling like vultures—also her words—trying to get her to go into a home. Don't get me wrong, they're all right, I went to school with most of them. But it's not what she wants. Have you ever had morphine?' Colleen asked.

'No.'

'Von said she saw mice dropping down off the ceiling and floating around her in the hospital room. Does everyone get that, do you think?'

'No idea.'

'Don't tell anyone. She said you need to be careful what

you tell people when you're her age. They'll say it's dementia, next thing they're moving in on a carer's allowance and all your independence is gone.'

Marnie's problems seemed to pale a little by comparison. She reported that she had one more week at the caravan park, so she was officially house-hunting in Horsham—she could pay rent or petrol but not both. She wanted to keep the children at child care, her job was working out all right. The downside was, there was a massive shortage of rentals. She also told Colleen that her daughter had been in contact. Eleanor was stuck up north; but she wanted the children back. Marnie hadn't said anything about her daughter before this. She wasn't sure why she said anything now.

'How do you feel about that?' asked Colleen, opening another bottle and sliding it across the tabletop. 'Is it just the alcohol kicking in, or does this stuff grow on you?'

'I don't know, it's weird,' Marnie said.

'Your daughter, or the plonk?'

Marnie looked at her and looked away. 'Don't get me wrong,' she said, 'she loves them and they love her. But she doesn't make good choices.'

'So what are you going to do?' said Colleen.

'Wait for the next fiasco.'

'Story of my life,' said Colleen.

Of course, that was it. Marnie woke up next morning with a mild hangover and a vision of Von's sky-diving mice in her head. That was why Kaarin had asked about her 'wellness'— Eleanor had concocted some story. She thought it might get her some money, of course, why else would she do it? She would have no compunction about casting aspersions on her mother's sanity if there was a fortnightly carer's cheque involved; no loyalty, no altruism, no qualms whatever. And horrible Kaarin would buy it. It was in her nature to believe the worst. She would swallow the most complicated story from the most unreliable source, just as long as it fitted her assumptions. Of course, of course, of course!

Marnie sat up, furious. Then she remembered that she had been dreaming and that she was likely off on a tangent. She might be correct about some things, but the whole conspiracy was too fantastical to be true. She really knew nothing about Kaarin except that she didn't like her. And hadn't Kaarin clearly stated she had not spoken to Eleanor? Marnie reminded herself that she was never entirely right about anything, that her imagination was Crazyville. She told herself to take five deep breaths and to follow that up with a to-do list. Something achievable. Just for today.

On the third breath, her phone pinged with a text from Vincent.

Have bond. Where can I send it? Would like to get it to you safely. Please advise. V Russo

Bless Vincent. And bless his sister Sylvie, who would have instructed him.

It was rare to be awake before the children, this was a golden morning. Marnie made herself tea and pondered her reply. The bond was $1500. Perhaps they would take some money out for cleaning, that would be fair, but she had assumed they'd keep the lot on account of her shooting through the way she did. This was a windfall. It meant she had money for another bond, or some of it anyway. Would it be pushing goodwill to ask Vincent for a reference? Rhi would advise her. She made her list over tea.

    a) Tidy up

    b) Call Rhiannon

    c) Text Vincent

    d) House-hunting

All do-able. She would tick the list off by the end of the day and feel organised and fulfilled.

Colleen blew in while she was dressing the children. 'On my way to the salon,' she said. 'Got a proposition.'

She'd been on the phone to Von, and Von had suggested that Marnie go to her place and look after things while she was away. Von would be in hospital for at least two weeks, then rehab, then a short stay with her daughter. It could be two months before she was home.

'Two months is best possible scenario. They're being positive to keep her spirits up. Von's ancient, let's not kid ourselves, it'll be longer for sure. What do you think?' said Colleen.

'I don't know.'

'It's not Horsham, but you said you could pay petrol, or rent.'

'How much rent does she want, though?'

'Nothing, that's my point, are you even listening? She wants a house-sitter. It's not so cushy as you think. I know, I'm doing some of it now, and so is Razza who's useless, and about five other people. It'd be easier handing it all over to one person.'

Colleen went on to list the jobs. Von had chickens, two bottle-fed lambs, a geriatric Jack Russell and a scary cat. She also had a vegetable garden and orchard, and about an acre of lawn that needed to be kept mown. There was a woodpile by the shed, but Marnie would have to haul the wood in with a wheelbarrow. Also, if Marnie could do one of Von's shifts at the gallery that'd be good, but no pressure.

'It sounds perfect,' said Marnie.

Colleen held up a hand. 'Yeah, no, I'm telling you, once you've slogged through the frost at six a.m. and had a frigging lamb suck the teat off the top of the bottle and drench itself, so you have to go back to the house and start again, you'll be calling me every name in the book. Plus, the dog vomits for no reason. Usually on your shoes.'

But it was perfect. Seeing Von's house through a veil of fog later that day, paddocks behind it and misty blue gums to one side, it was about as picture-perfect as a house could be. It was plain, functional, constructed of home-made bricks from the earth it stood on painted a peach colour. Its windows were odd-sized, reminding Marnie of her place at Vincent's. There were bare roses around the front veranda, bedraggled iris beds, camellia trees weighted down with fat buds.

But that wasn't where she'd be staying, Colleen said, and pointed to a little weatherboard cottage to one side of the vast front lawn. An old shearer's cottage, shabby, but renovated in a piecemeal way. The kitchen had a wood stove, plus a microwave and electric kettle if she didn't want to bother with the stove. Colleen explained that the oven took only small-sized logs and Marnie would have to cut down the big ones using the hatchet outside the kitchen door. 'It'll give you splinters,' she warned, 'as well as the shits. My advice, just use the microwave.' There was even an old highchair. Luxury.

Colleen's idea, and Von had okayed it, was that the family could have the big house. If anyone decided to come up and stay, then Marnie wouldn't be disturbed, and the family would retain their sense of ownership. Families need that, Colleen assured her—in the country no one really trusted newcomers for years. 'No offence!'

The cottage was used sporadically by Von's family during general get-togethers when growing numbers spilled over from the house. It was sparsely furnished, unadorned except for a *No smoking in this house please* sign on the refrigerator. It had two bedrooms and a bathroom painted blue with a stained blue bath in it and a blue pedestal basin. There was a tiny living area that made an L shape with the kitchen. The black and white lino tiles on the bathroom and kitchen floors were so old and cracked they looked like they might shatter at any moment. The carpet through the rest of the house was antediluvian—cabbage roses on brown, worn to threads in the traffic areas—but warm-looking.

'And when she comes home,' Colleen confided, 'if you're still okay with it all, you won't have to move out. She'll be glad to have someone close and actually they'll probably tell her she needs someone there. See?' She tapped the side of her head. 'Thinkin'!'

24

Mornings were icy now, winter upon them with its bruised skies and short bursts of pale sunlight, a plunge in temperature approaching night. Von's lambs began bleating as soon as the rooster woke them around 4 a.m. Colleen had said don't bother about them until six, but Marnie could only stand the noise for so long. The lambs had stronger wills than hers. Greater need, too.

She made up bottles in the kitchen from a sack of powdered milk. The bottles were glass lemonade bottles dating back to the sixties, the teats were in a margarine tub, a selection of colours and shapes and flow capacities. Evidently, lamb-raising was something that Von had been doing for years. Marnie shook up the bottles and tested the temperature, just as she had done for Michael and for Frankie, then she jammed them into her overcoat pockets, slid her feet into cold gumboots and stomped up to the tractor shed in the dark.

The lambs could hear the screen door click shut no matter

how quiet she tried to be. Their cries ratcheted from insistent to frantic as she stepped off the veranda, the noise guiding her through the winter fog. She felt for the light switch in the tractor shed. The hanging bulb lit up an old Fergie first. The walls around it were fuzzy with dust, trailing ancient spiderwebs. Blinking lambs tumbled over each other to reach her, nosing in the folds of her coat after the smell of milk. They were grotty, frail yet strong, they smelled of cheese, lanolin, sweet shit.

Marnie found a working pattern for the feeds after a few days of clumsiness and mis-timings. She sat on an old kitchen chair and let the big lamb latch on to the first bottle, taking care to hold the teat. Colleen was right, he sucked the teat off twice in the first two days and soaked them both. Marnie was wise to it now. She wedged the bottle between her knees once she felt the suck pressure lessen, letting him get on with it. She guided the second bottle into the smaller lamb's bawling mouth. Then came silence.

She grew to love that silence, the easing of desperation, the fulfillment of desire, however temporary, the absurd fluttering of shit-caked tails. When they were finished, she rubbed their blunt little heads and spoke to them. Did Von do that? Did she also find those sticking-out ears and those dumb eyes heartbreaking?

On her walk back to the house, her eyes adjusting to the darkness, she could sometimes make out the shape of the house roof, the outline of trees. She could hear chickens rustling on their perch in the chook shed, sometimes there was movement in the bushes along the fence. Occasionally, a wallaby skittered sideways across her path and thudded into the gloom. She shed her overcoat on the kitchen floor, washed her hands and went back to bed for one more hour before the children woke her and her day officially began.

Von's dog and cat adjusted to the cottage without diffi-culty. The dog yapped hysterically the first day they were there, but it accepted dinner from Marnie's hands and transplanted itself from the doormat of the big house to the doormat of the cottage thereafter. The cat, elderly like the dog, appeared at mealtimes for several days before allowing anyone to touch it, and sat on the veranda rail of the cottage gazing in at them. Colleen couldn't remember their names, so Marnie called them Noisy and Shadow. Shadow slept in the feed shed where he apparently kept the mice down. He sometimes materialised when she was feeding the lambs and sat at Marnie's side like a benevolent overseer.

She spoke by phone to Von to assure her that everything was in hand, and to thank her. Von told her that Razza might call past and cadge eggs, it usually happened when his pension ran out. So Marnie was not surprised to see a figure in a torn coat, Bombers beanie and mud-caked boots coming through the house gates. He stopped at a distance when he saw Marnie and the children. She was trying to hatchet splin-ters off large lumps of firewood to fit the wood stove. She felt him watching her.

'How's Von?' he called when she looked up.

'Okay, I think.'

'You getting on?' His eyes, under the shadow of his brow, assessed her.

'Yes. There's about four eggs. I'll put a carton in the mailbox, Von told me you'd want them.'

'Yeah, whatever.' He half-turned away, then turned back. 'Annie Lennox,' he said, remembering. 'At the pub.'

'Yep,' she said. 'Marnie.'

He turned away and she watched him head out the gate again. He appeared to be walking into town. She knew Von took him casseroles. Should she do that too? She didn't want him too close; even from a distance he smelled of sheep.

When she arrived back from Horsham with the children the next day there was a pile of kindling on the ground outside the cottage. He must have come past and cut the logs down to size for her. He understood about the wood stove. She felt awkward about it. Grateful, too; mostly awkward.

The children tried to help with the lambs during the day and grew accustomed to being knocked over in that desperate stampede for milk. Frankie threw feed to the chickens and ran in terror from the rooster. They watched crimson and green parrots fluff up and splash about in the puddles along the driveway. Koa took three steps towards the cat one day, hauled on the creature's back leg, and was scratched across his face. Marnie applied multiple bandaids to his arms and legs and face to appease him, and stuck a few on Frankie too, so she wouldn't feel left out. She hoped it would not be a day that Kaarin decided to call in, and it wasn't. The children played in the blue bath at night until the skin on their fingers pleated and turned white.

'So you're staying there?' asked Rhiannon.

'For now.'

'Until...'

'Lenny comes. She will.'

'Like death and taxes,' said Rhiannon.

'Yep, well, she's my daughter, Rhi.'

'Sorry, shitty thing to say.'

'It's okay, it's true, it's the way it's been for so long I don't know any other way.'

'You sound okay.'

'I am, I think. Never speak too soon. How are you?'

'Learning bongos.'

'Wow—bongos?'

'I couldn't do it when the dog was alive, he used to freak. So now I am. It's kind of...' She's going to say 'cathartic' thought Marnie, and Rhiannon said, 'cathartic. There's a group I go to, so it's not all at home, shitting off the neighbours.' She added: 'It makes me happy. That and meetings and work.'

'That's fantastic.'

'The thing is, you might as well just say it when you feel it. I'm happy. It's not speaking too soon, it's living in the moment. It's what we're meant to do.'

Waiting for the kettle to boil, later that evening, Marnie considered saying I'm happy, because there was no one around to tell her she was wrong. She knew what happiness was. It was finishing a day of hard work at Heath's and having him say, 'Good job today, kiddo. I didn't think we'd make it this time, and we did.' It was reading the last paragraph of *Dombey and Son*, and looking across and seeing Lorna's eyes shining. It was lifting Michael onto a slippery-dip and seeing his face as he slid all the way down. 'A-den? Ganny? A-den?' It was morning sun slanting across the breakfast table, her mother exchanging smiles with her as they watched Eleanor turn her toast over in tiny, sticky hands so it went into her mouth jam side down.

Of course, for every action there is an equal and opposite reaction.

25

Two and half weeks later, Eleanor arrived. Marnie knew she was coming. The text messages began the moment the train pulled out of Southern Cross. They became more frequent after she transferred to a bus at Ararat for the last leg of the journey.

    — *OMG will this trip never END???*
    — *150 squillion sheep. What is this place???*
    — *Are you going 2 pick me up?*
    — *Seriosly over this. Man bside me Bad BO*
    — *PLz b thre. I don't know where2 go, Mum.*
    — *Mountains amazing.*
    — *fucking raining and I ned smoke*
    — *I am neva doing this trip again. EVAH*

And on and on. Marnie answered a few of the texts but after a while they became background clutter. She remained surprisingly calm, as if she'd stepped out of her body. She assured Eleanor she would be picking her up; the children would be with her, they would drive the last ninety-kilometre leg back to Edenhope.

   – *90???? Holy crap Mum! This is HELL!!!!*

Marnie expected that reaction and had sent the detail as a kind of bear-poke. She wanted to see Eleanor, but didn't mind if she suffered a bit first.

It was Monday: no work. There had been a period of sunshine mid-morning, but when they drove into Horsham it was cheerless again, dull brown light that lowers all expectations. They arrived early and visited the Plaza, where they bought leopard-print gumboots for Eleanor at the discount shop before meeting the bus mid-afternoon. Marnie tried not to anticipate the arrival. She expected Eleanor to be in a bad mood, and knew she would find plenty to disapprove of. 'Just don't let her ruin everything,' she thought, then didn't know why she was thinking that. Was everything so damn jolly that it could be ruined? Her stomach knotted as if locking her into her body again, that pleasant out-of-body feeling gone for good.

The children were fractious. Frankie had an understanding about who was coming. She was quieter than Koa, but still shrieked the Plaza nearly to a standstill when Koa started yanking on the new gumboots that she was cradling to her chest. 'No, Ko, *no!*' she roared at him, Brayden's savage voice rearing up from the past. Both children dissolved into squeals and Marnie thought, this is what it will be like now.

She thought, if the bus crashes it'll all be over. But it wouldn't be. It would just be shittier. Get a grip, she thought.

It was beginning to rain when Lenny spilled out of the

bus, thin and grey-faced, puffy around the eyes. She was wearing black jeans and thongs instead of shoes, a bulging cloth bag over her shoulder. She was feeling in her pockets, not looking for the children or Marnie.

'Fuck, Mum,' she said when Marnie called to her. 'I left my lighter on the bus.' She glanced at the children. 'I just need my lighter,' she explained, her voice bright suddenly, but turning her back on them at the same time.

'Boots!' said Frankie running to her and tripping over the boots. She didn't hurt herself, but she was embarrassed, you could see it in her eyes. Marnie put Koa down so she could retrieve Frankie and the boots, thanking random people who helped to get the wailing child upright. Koa stood on the pavement saying, 'No! No! No!' The crowd dispersed and for a moment it seemed that Lenny was gone too. Then she was coming down from the bus again, already lighting a cigarette.

'Oh, baby, honey,' she said, blowing smoke out the side of her mouth from her first famished draw. She crouched down and put her arms around Koa and kissed Frankie. 'Are these for Mummy? Oh, baby, I love them. Look.'

She stepped out of her thongs straight into the boots and ran in a little circle and suddenly Frankie was laughing. 'They're the best, honey, they're the best! Do I look like Elsa?' She picked up Koa, who resisted her. 'He's grown. Are you walking? My big boy! Is he walking, Frankie? Hi, Mum.' A cursory air-kiss. 'Interesting haircut,' she said. 'Lesbian chic.' Koa started to fuss, and she transferred him back to Marnie.

Lenny needed McDonald's. They went through the drive-thru and finished up with a car full of rubbish. The children sucked down thick shakes and Lenny sat in the front eating soft hamburgers, reading the writing on her coffee cup while stark sodden Wimmera paddocks flashed past and rain clouds folded and unfolded overhead. At one stage Lenny unlatched the glove box, as if idly filling in time, and looked inside.

The pawn-shop cash. Well, Lenny was welcome to look, good luck to her, the money was gone. Marnie told herself to settle, to not become enraged, to say nothing. It was hard to say nothing when there was so much to be said. But even given the perfect opportunity, it would still have been impossible to know where to start.

They had a birthday cake for Koa that afternoon. It had one large candle in the middle surrounded by hundreds and thousands, and a little car jammed into the icing. Eleanor had arrived with nothing for the children, which rankled, but she sat on the floor with them and rolled the car and played with Octonauts while Marnie fed the lambs. When the children went to bed, Lenny read their books to them. Frankie, who knew her Seasons books off by heart, corrected Lenny when she skipped bits.

'Where do I sleep?' Eleanor asked, coming out to the kitchen again.

'In there, you can have the top bunk or the single bed. The children seem to do better in the same bed.'

'Who's in the other house?' asked Eleanor, looking through the kitchen cupboards.

Marnie explained about the arrangement.

'Pity they gave you the shit place.'

'It's bigger than the one I had. It's fine, it's easy to keep warm. We're fine with it.'

'Is there even wi-fi?'

'Magnet on the fridge with the login.'

'Thank fuck,' Lenny muttered, fetching it. 'Still no washing machine.'

'Yes, in the outhouse over at the back of the main house. Washing machine, dryer and a freezer full of meat, which I'm allowed to use if I want. The occasional snake in summer, they told me.'

'*In* the freezer?'

'Under it.'

'Shit.'

'The kids will show you the chickens tomorrow, and the lambs.' She added, 'It's nice for them here, they know people. They love child care.'

Eleanor said, 'Who did the haircuts?'

'Local hairdresser.'

'Jesus, Mum, Frankie looks like she's stepped out of 1960.'

Marnie felt a thrumming inside her, rage or guilt she wasn't sure. She said, 'It was all knots, I couldn't get them out. It was the best Colleen could do at the time.' She told herself to shut up. Nothing she said would smooth things over if Lenny wanted to be disagreeable.

There was a short silence while Lenny ate a spoonful of peanut butter. Marnie said, 'Have you been in contact with Brayden?'

'No.' Further silence. Lenny threw herself into the armchair. She said, 'The kids look good,' flicking through channels with the remote control, not staying on any of them long enough to find out what was on.

'They'll want you to see child care. Frankie especially.'

'I need to go to Centrelink.'

'You can do both, it's all back in Horsham.'

'What are you doing living so far away, then?'

'It's how it worked out. Look, it's free. Housing is terrible at the moment.'

'Are you telling me because you think I don't know?' Eleanor glared at her mother, her forehead creased, eyes hot.

'Sorry, baby, I'm just glad you're here. I'm sorry it didn't work out with Bray. I'm sorry about everything.'

Back to channel surfing. 'Got anything to drink?'

Marnie felt guilty that she hadn't thought of it earlier. She should have anticipated. Alcohol would probably calm everything down, if there wasn't too much. She didn't have to be all temperance for Lenny. 'I saw a half bottle of brandy in the back of the kitchen cupboard. I guess it won't matter to drink it. I think it's a leftover from Christmas or something.'

Eleanor was on her feet. 'Any Coke?'

'I didn't think.'

'Shit.' She poured herself a glass of neat brandy.

Marnie said brightly, 'I won some vodka Cruisers at the pub. Turkish delight flavour.'

'Ooh-la-la. You drink them?'

'With a friend.'

Eleanor took her brandy to the veranda and sat in the cold, smoking, looking out at the black night. Marnie heard her speaking to the dog and the cat. Later, when Lenny had gone to bed, Marnie let the animals inside because it was going to be frosty. She was pretty sure Von wouldn't approve, but what the hell. She made up bottles for the lambs and took herself to bed, finally, where she lay sleepless in the dark. When the cat came in, smelling pleasantly of hay, and curled up next to her she rolled over and stroked it and it purred into her hand. She thought, everything stays the same in the end.

26

Eleanor slept, rolled in a doona like a bear, until late the next two mornings. She didn't stir when Marnie was dressing the children, feeding them, letting them hullabaloo around the house. On Wednesday, when they called out goodbye to her, Eleanor shifted and moaned. When Marnie brought the children home from child care, Eleanor was asleep in front of the TV, although there were tell-tale signs that she'd been up and about—dishes in the sink, food out of the cupboard, her phone charging on the floor below a power point.

After the evening meal, she showed signs of life. She sat with the children when they had their bath, eyes fixed on her phone. She read them goodnight stories rapidly, tonelessly. She watched TV and she went to bed long after Marnie did, streaming God-knows-what on her phone in the dark. It was all so familiar, that feeling of watching her daughter across an abyss. No response when Marnie tried to make contact: it seemed worse now than when they'd been at Niddrie.

Whatever else you could say about Brayden, Eleanor was more connected with him around. She showed little real interest in the children. Marnie half-wished Kaarin would call in so she could see it like this, so she could understand.

On the fourth night, Lenny asked for the car. She needed cigarettes, she would drive into Edenhope, maybe get some grog. Marnie gave her the keys. She said, 'There's not much fuel. Enough for Edenhope, that's about it.'

'What's the pub like?'

'Okay. I've only been once.'

'Cool. Thanks, Mum. I need to get out.' She kissed Marnie, passing her quickly, such a rush to get away. 'Got any money? I'll bring us home a cask or something.'

Marnie handed over twenty dollars and watched the car drive away. She'd forgotten to warn Lenny about kangaroos. She almost phoned her, then didn't.

'Good,' said Rhiannon when Marnie called her. 'You can't infantilise her.'

'I know.'

'How old is she, anyway?'

'Thirty-seven.'

'Brayden looked about twenty.'

'Closer to thirty. I'm beginning to think he might have been good for her.'

'He wasn't. In my opinion. Sorry, I'm not trying to be an expert. How are you going, anyway?'

'If you'd asked me a week ago I would have said okay, right now I feel like everything's going to hell.'

'Same here.'

'How come? How's bongos?'

'Good. Some days everything feels bad. Doesn't have to be logical. How are the kids?'

'I'll send you a photo with the lambs. They're so fierce.'

'The lambs are?'

'Children and lambs, both. Not savage-fierce, fierce about life. Like nothing's going to stop them surviving. I don't know where they get it from.'

'Maybe from you.'

'I wish. I need to learn it from them.'

The pub shut at eleven. Marnie lay awake listening for the car. It arrived back at midnight. That was a whole hour for a ten-minute drive. She heard the car door slam followed by the clunk of Lenny kicking off her boots on the doorstep.

'Mum, you awake?'

'Yes. How did you go?'

'Good, everyone was really friendly.' She sounded upbeat. 'I got a cask for us, do you want a drink?'

'I'm in bed.'

'Come on.'

Marnie got up and came out to the living room, Lenny handed her a glass of white wine and snuggled into the armchair, she was wrapped in her doona and smelled of weed. She reported that she'd played pool and won free drinks. She'd spoken to the man at the bar.

'Lester? The owner?'

'Yep. He remembered you from this eighties-night thing. Said you looked stunning.'

'I didn't.'

'Yeah, I told him he must've been drunk. Anyway a few people asked about you, they said you should come to the pub more.'

'Not my thing.'

'I told them you were a wowser. And I drove that guy Razza home. Said he lived next door and it turned out to be about ten kilometres up the road, I mean, are they seriously challenged about distances around here?'

'You drove Razza home?' Marnie put her glass down, flustered suddenly.

'Yeah, so?'

'He's a bit unpredictable, I heard.'

'Pissed to buggery, so what?'

'Nothing, doesn't matter. I'm glad you got back safely.'

'He lives in this falling-down place on a plantation. He gets it cheap, he said there's lots of them in the blue gums, better than his one.' She said, after a moment, 'How do you find out about those places?'

Marnie looked at her. 'Are you thinking about staying?'

'Got nowhere else.'

'You can stay here, baby. I'm not pushing you out.'

Eleanor said, 'The thing is, Mum, I'm not a baby and I don't want to live with you. What self-respecting grown-up wants to live with their mother? Oh, yeah, of course you did. You stayed with Gran in that house until she died.'

'She was sick, we couldn't leave.'

'How did Dad feel about it?'

Where was this coming from, this sudden sympathy for

her father? Marnie said, 'I guess you've worked out a whole scenario and you probably don't want to hear the truth, but your dad was fine with it. We were saving for a house, he was desperate to live in a better suburb, so he was happy to wait until Gran died and we inherited her house. It suited him just fine, Eleanor.'

'Ooh, touchy,' Eleanor poured herself another drink. She was thinking things through, Marnie could see the cogs going around. Of course, Eleanor couldn't know why choices were made back then, of course she would reach her own conclusions. The decisions Marnie made with Ged didn't include Eleanor at an adult level, she was in primary school, she was expected to tag along. Marnie fought a desire to keep talking, to justify—what? She told herself it would be pointless, it would be too much explanation, most of it unimportant. She said, 'You didn't mind living with Gran, did you? I thought you liked it.'

'I loved Gran.'

'I'm glad. Sometimes I think I get everything wrong. I lie awake and everything I remember feels like it was just wrong.'

'Me too,' Eleanor said.

The silence between them was different, a sudden warmth in it. Marnie picked up her drink again. 'Do you remember Heath?' she said.

'God yes, that messy house.'

'My office wasn't messy.'

'Oh all right, Saint Marnie, your office was a shrine.' Eleanor added: 'The painting of the stag with those huge antlers, remember that, and the one with the church?

210

Terrifying. What happened to that house?'

'Marko got it. Heath left everything to Marko.'

'I saw Marko in a magazine. All about his work at the Stuttgart. I didn't even know he went to Germany. He's amazing.'

'When was that?'

'Few years ago.'

'He made you those dresses, you probably don't remember, you were little. Hand-smocked, stunning.'

'I remember.'

'I kept them for years.'

'How did he get so famous?'

'He was good at what he did, and he worked at it. He really worked hard.'

Eleanor groaned. 'Now you sound like a frigging social worker. Maybe he just sucked up to the right people. Maybe he was just lucky.'

'Oh, honey, Marko wasn't lucky. He really wasn't. He had a horrible life before Heath got him. I only knew bits, but it was bad. He was going straight down the toilet. Then he found Lorna's sewing stuff and it was like lights going on.'

'TJ said that,' Eleanor said.

'TJ never met Marko—'

'About lights going on.'

Marnie was silent. It was so rare for Eleanor to mention TJ that she was afraid to say anything.

Eleanor said, 'The time he came to visit me before he took Michael, he said that's what happened to him. The lights went on.' She looked into her glass. 'Prick.'

It must have seemed like that, so simple, so sudden. Marnie remembered it differently. She was there, TJ and Michael were living with her in Craigieburn. Eleanor was still in Dame Phyllis Frost and didn't see all the negotiations—phone calls, lawyers, court appearances, social workers; that priest who came down from the country to set him straight. A whopping safety net was spread out for TJ. If anyone was lucky, it was TJ.

The priest—what was his name? He just arrived on the doorstep one day. Middle-aged, trained voice, silver hair—looked like a used-car salesman, the full cliché. He introduced himself, he was there from TJ's parents to see that TJ was getting on all right. Could he talk to TJ—just the two of them? Marnie invited him in. She made tea and took it to them on a tray. He sat in the backyard with TJ, watching Michael making roads in his sandpit.

Father Dom, that was it. He came every day for a week to start with, then less often, but he spent an hour or so each time. When TJ informed her one evening they were going out to a meeting, the priest and him together, she was a bit confused.

'Meeting?'

'Narcotics Anonymous.' He said it quickly, embarrassed.

'Well, good Teej, good idea. I can mind Mikey.'

'No, we want Michael to come along.' The priest speaking.

'He's only four.'

'That's TJ's look-out.'

'Sure,' said TJ, with less conviction than the priest.

Later that day Father Dom came and stood nearby while

she was pegging out washing. He wasn't dressed like a priest in the movies, like *Going My Way*, but he had a gold cross on the lapel of his sports coat. It glinted in the sunshine.

'He needs to get it through his head, there's no going back,' he said to Marnie. 'He needs to hear stories from people who've been there and feel the weight of that little boy on his knee while he's listening. He needs to confront it—he's a dad now, his childhood is over.'

She said, 'I only offered to help.'

'I know. But he doesn't need help. He needs a backbone.'

She was annoyed later that Father Dom had just stood there, not even handed her a peg. Laundry was women's work, after all. The priest needed to grow up, she thought. That measured voice, so full of self-importance, acting out his role without ever having to do real stuff in the real world. He probably had some woman washing his jocks and boiling eggs for him every morning.

27

Eleanor visited child care a couple of times, wandered around town while Marnie worked, and was there ready to be driven home at the end of the day. Marnie introduced her daughter to Sam at Honeydew, hoping there might be the offer of a job, but it was clear Eleanor's disdainful expression was off-putting.

'She looks like a cow,' Eleanor said on the way home.

'She's fine. Sam works as hard as anyone.'

'I don't want to grate onions and wash pots. Haven't they got a dishwasher?'

'Yes. Me.'

'People use you,' said Eleanor.

'You think?' Marnie's voice had a sarcastic edge—why did she let that happen? Eleanor said something that sounded like 'bitch' under her breath and didn't speak for the rest of the drive.

The upshot of that was that Marnie, not Lenny, was

offered more work at her next shift, on the strength of the children having someone to mind them now. More than an offer, it felt like a requirement. Marnie agreed, and immediately started worrying.

'We'll have a great time, too easy,' said Eleanor, turning to the children in the back of the car. 'You'll be with Mummy while Ganny works, okay?'

The children didn't seem to mind.

Coming home from work the following Monday, bringing leftover lasagne and carrot cake for dinner, she found the children watching television while Eleanor relaxed in the bath with the door open—her nod to child monitoring—drinking cask wine from a coffee mug. Not what Marnie would have classified as 'a great time' but the kids seemed unfazed. The next day was more promising—she found Eleanor making soup when she arrived home—but the lambs were bellowing from the house paddock; she had forgotten to bring them in to the tractor shed and give them their bottles.

'It'll take me a couple of days to get it together,' she said, off-hand, and poured Marnie a drink. The next three days were child-care days. Eleanor stayed home alone. There was evidence of genuine activity: the clothes horse was draped with washing in front of the stove, toys were stowed in a carboard carton, towels had been picked up off the bathroom floor. Eleanor went to the pub after dinner on Thursday and Friday, and came home in good spirits both times, not too far gone. It was all right, thought Marnie in bed, they could keep this up.

The next week, Eleanor went to the pub on Saturday night

and didn't come home. Marnie gave herself until lunchtime on Sunday before making a call to Colleen. She kept her tone light, no need to scare the horses.

'She was definitely at the pub,' Colleen said. 'I didn't take much notice, I was doing book club in the ladies' lounge.' Colleen promised to wander up the street and see if the car was parked outside the pub still. 'She might have been too pissed to drive,' she said. 'Wouldn't be the first.'

The Subaru came down the driveway with mud spattered across its windscreen while Marnie was waiting for Colleen's report, so she texted her quickly—*Forget it All good* with a smiley face—and took the children up to the chickens so Lenny wouldn't know how sick she felt. When they came back to the house Lenny was already in bed. She slept the rest of the day, getting up just before midnight to raid the fridge and turn the TV on.

Starting the car Monday morning, Marnie saw the petrol light come on as Lenny and the kids stood on the veranda and waved her away. Marnie nursed the car along to Horsham, arriving by the skin of her teeth.

'Are you okay?' asked Sam, because of course it showed.

'Yep, excellent,' was all she said. She tied on her apron, got going, hardly took a break, went like the clappers until the Honeydew closed and she could get back in her car. The day's work hadn't calmed her. She banged her head twice on the steering wheel before starting the engine. 'Don't overreact,' she told herself, and pulled into the nearest servo.

When she arrived home, it was not quite dark and there was a light on in the main house. She thought, oh shit—Von's family, and then she saw through the windows Lenny's stooped shape moving from room to room. She ran inside the cottage and found the children in front of the TV. They both wanted to be picked up. She carried them over to Von's house.

'Eleanor, I'm home.' She stepped inside the front door, trying to sound casual.

'Oh, hi,' said Eleanor, appearing from a room down the hall.

'We're not supposed to be here.'

'The door wasn't locked.'

'It probably never is.' Von's house was cold but still redolent of roast dinners, fruitcakes, old woollen blankets. There were photos of weddings on the wall inside the door, and clusters of photos of children of varying ages all up the narrow hall.

Lenny said, 'I was looking for a tin of tomatoes. She's not going to miss one tin, is she?' She hadn't come from the kitchen, she'd come from a bedroom.

Marnie said, 'There's half a jar of pasta sauce in our fridge.'

'Okay, whatever. They should have let you have this place. It's way bigger.'

'I don't need bigger.'

'What is it with you? You always settle for crap.'

Marnie said, 'Let's go and get dinner on.'

Eleanor stood her ground suddenly. Her voice remained mild. 'You go. I want to look around. I haven't finished.'

'It's not our house!'

'No one's here, no one will know. Stop being a drama queen.'

There was a moment of silence between them, punctuated by distant bleating. Frankie gave an exaggerated sigh. 'Dats da lambs,' she said. 'Fucking pests!'

'Im-PES!' repeated Koa with emphasis.

Lenny grinned at Marnie. 'Oopsie,' she said.

The next day when Marnie got home, the house smelled of sheep.

'Have you had the lambs in here?' she asked.

'Oh, shit, the lambs,' said Lenny. 'I forgot about them again. Sorry.'

She went past Marnie into the kitchen and started banging bottles about. Frankie said, 'Ganny, up,' and lifted her arms to Marnie from the floor. Frankie's forehead was creased, her eyes looked hot. Koa had a swollen lump under one eye. 'Did Ko knock himself?' Marnie called.

'On the table leg. He's goes about two steps and falls over, you've seen him do it. Nothing's changed since this morning, Mum.'

Marnie said to Frankie. 'Did Koey fall over?'

'He falled over me,' said Frankie, with her arms around Marnie's neck.

'Did you get hurt too?'

'Koey sooked.'

'He's only little.'

'Mum, they're fine,' Lenny shouted at her from the kitchen. 'You let them cry over everything. They need to suck it up. How are they going to go at school if they start frigging wussing about every little thing that goes wrong?'

'They need to show their feelings.'

'Okay, of course, I'm always wrong, you know best.' Her shortness was a hair's-breadth away from anger.

Marnie waited a few seconds, and then said, too brightly, 'Do you want me to do the lambs?'

'So you can accuse me of forgetting to do my chores? And ground me? No thanks all the same, Ma Walton.'

'Eleanor—'

'Lenny! It's Lenny! You know I hate Eleanor, you just say it to get at me.'

'I'm sorry. Look, let me do the lambs.' Marnie disentangled herself from the children.

'Fucking do them, then.' Eleanor slammed the bottles onto the kitchen bench and went into the children's bedroom, slamming the door.

Marnie went up to the lambs, taking the children with her, trailed by the dog and the cat. The bottles were too hot. She sat them in a puddle to cool them down while the lambs bawled so hard they made her ears vibrate. 'Shut up bad lambs!' Frankie shouted at them.

Marnie said, 'They're not bad, honey-kitten, they're just hungry.'

Frankie threw a handful of straw at their heads and then looked at Marnie, challenging her.

When the lambs were finally fed, and while the children were occupied building a tower out of loose straw over the top of the dog, Marnie called Rhiannon.

'I'm a bit scared of her right now,' she told her.

'Has she taken anything?'

'She's been home all day, I had the car, so I don't know how she could have.'

'Still—it sounds like, you know, guilt. Or boredom, lots of reasons to work up a drama. But also substance. I guess you have to assume she got something from somewhere.'

'I didn't check the wine cask.'

'Don't bother checking anything, it won't make you feel better. Just be aware that she may be on something and stay out of her way. Work on having a good evening.'

'I don't think you know how hard that is.'

'I do, though.'

Oh God. 'Sorry, I'm sorry Rhi.'

'Forget it.'

'I don't know why I said that.'

'I do, forget it. All I can say is, don't get into an argument while she's like this. You'll lose.'

Arguments, however, have an energy of their own. If one participant wants one, there is rarely a clear path of retreat.

As soon as Marnie was back in the house, she could see that Eleanor was antsy. She found fault with dinner preparation, then dinner itself, then the children. Koa reached over to her cup and tipped it over on the table, spilling wine everywhere, and she slapped his hand away. Both children started wailing, wanting Marnie, wanting to be away from Eleanor. That infuriated her, too.

'That's what you've been working towards—well done, Mum. You've turned them against me.'

'I haven't. They got a fright. You need to see things the

way they are. Koa didn't mean to spill anything, he was just curious. He's fourteen months old.'

'Yeah, yeah, give me the full psych breakdown on my own children, such an expert.'

That jeering tone. Marnie backed down. 'Hey, can we just finish dinner?'

'I'm finished.' Lenny stood up and went for her cigarettes, lighting up in the kitchen, then coming back into the living room to the armchair, blowing smoke about. Marnie recognised the action as incitement. She said nothing.

But Frankie made the mistake of saying, 'No smoking in dis house!' in a sermonising way, pointing to the sign on the fridge, which Marnie had read out to her one day.

'You better not take that tone with me,' Lenny said, glaring her down.

Frankie retreated rapidly, white-faced, and slid under the kitchen table.

'That's it, is it?' Marnie heard herself say. Her voice was surprisingly quiet. 'That's the length and breadth of your power—scaring little kids? You're better than this, Lenny.'

'You don't know anything about me.'

'I know you learned how to bully little children from Brayden. He was the big hero, too, wasn't he?'

Why did she say that? What possible good could it do to even refer to Brayden? She could hear the voice in her head telling her to shut up, but there was something else urging her on, wanting to really hurt Eleanor. Anyway, it was said. Now, the best she could do was shut up and let it subside.

Unfortunately, Koa's crying had turned into anger. He

said, 'No! No! No!' from his highchair, and Eleanor rounded on him.

'Just. You. Fucking. *Shut up,*' she said, her voice low and fierce. Koa froze on an intake of breath.

Marnie swept him up and started patting his back. 'Stop it, please, stop it, Lenny. This is my fault, I'm sorry. Don't take it out on them, you'll hate yourself later, you know you will.'

There was a thin, keening sound from under the table, a sound strangled tight to shut it down, but squeezing out anyway. Marnie put Koa down and pushed him under to Frankie, who grabbed him. Koa was hiccupping now, breathing at least, she was relieved to hear it.

Lenny said, 'You know nothing about me, nothing about anything, you have no right to have the kids, they're mine.' Then: 'You let them take Michael away—'

'I didn't!'

'What did you do to stop it?'

'It was a court order!'

'You could have done something.'

'What? What could I have done? I never wanted Mikey to go, it nearly killed me!'

'It did kill me! It did! Don't fucking even try to say "nearly" like it counts!'

'Lenny, we have to stop this, we can't solve it.'

'No, *you* can't. You think you can get the kids away from me, well you can't. I'm not letting them go. They're mine.'

'I'm not trying—you said you needed a break.'

'I don't remember saying that.'

'I said it to both of you, Brayden was good with it, he

was "oh, yeah, great," don't you remember?' Now she was inventing, and it was just spewing out of her. She let it. 'And then I couldn't phone you. Do you think I didn't try? I didn't know what was going on. I didn't know you lost your phone. I just did the thing I said I'd do, which you said you wanted—a break from them—and I thought, well, you'll ring when you can.'

She stopped, the story was too detailed, too desperate. Then she remembered her trump card. 'You never even tried to tell me you were going to Byron, you just went! Where did the kids fit into that plan?'

'You're talking shit. Everything you're saying.'

'And what about the engagement ring you took to Cash Converters? You were going to tell me about that, were you? After it was gone for good?'

'It was mine.'

'It was my mother's. And it was in my house, not yours. What happened to it? Straight up your arm, right?'

'I was going to get it back, I had a plan!'

'No. Don't start that, it's all fake. Tomorrow I'll get better, tomorrow I'll stop using, tomorrow I'll get a job and retrieve all the stuff I've put through pawn shops over the last twenty years—it's not possible Eleanor, it doesn't happen that way. If you wanted Michael back you needed to get straight, and that means change. You could have gone back to the rehab.'

'It was shit!'

'Oh, sorry, was it meant to be a breeze? What, then? How? What's the next plan? Oh, actually, I think I know what it was—say your mother has dementia, something like

223

that? And get a pension for supposedly looking after me? Except you wouldn't have, would you, even if I did need it? Just another scheme for getting easy money—'

'It was Brayden's idea!' There was genuine surprise in Lenny's voice.

So it was true. Marnie was taken aback for a second, the sheer boldness of it, the shock of her daughter's disloyalty. She took a breath. In that moment of silence, she saw Eleanor's face. Confused? Haunted? She couldn't tell. Why, why was it she could never read her own child's emotions?

'We didn't go ahead. How did you find out?'

'Forget it, we don't have to trawl over stuff, we shouldn't, it's poison.'

'I didn't mean it, Mum.'

Marnie could believe it. But that wouldn't have stopped her, she thought, if the road had been smooth. Someone in the application process stopped it. Not Lenny and not Bray. Someone said, 'prove it' or 'provide documentation from a doctor', and they backed down.

She said, 'Rhi told me once, it never does any good looking back, it's just so hard not to do it—'

Now Lenny was firing up again. 'Rhi, Rhi, Rhi—she totally dominates you! You're pathetic, running to her all the time, letting her get in your ear about me.'

'She doesn't.' Marnie was calmer now, her voice slowing, she could hear it. They were on a seesaw, the two of them. She said, 'Rhiannon gets in my ear about me. That's her job.'

'Job!'

'Her role. She's my sponsor. She doesn't talk about you

much at all. She keeps reminding me that you're on your own journey. She's there for me.'

And silence. Finally, silence. Eleanor lit another cigarette. Marnie sat on the floor and looked for the children, the sight of them huddled under the table pressed a weight on her chest that would always be there, never expelled, never alleviated. She beckoned to them and they crawled out to her.

'What kind of sponsor?' asked Eleanor when she'd finished her cigarette, while she lit the next one.

'I started going to meetings after Ko was born. You and Brayden just went off—do you know how that felt? He was three weeks old! I needed help. I went along and they said find someone from the meetings to be a sponsor, it'll get you going faster.' She stretched her legs out on the floor, leaned back on the wall, the children against her like weighted backpacks.

After a few minutes of silence, she added, 'When I started going, it was incredible to me, the number of people all messed up, just like I am. How did they find out? How did I never find out till so late, I mean? Anyway, that's where Rhi was. That's the story.'

Silence again. Marnie thought about Declan, that sweet, seemingly untroubled boy. He had given her the pamphlet and she hadn't told him she already knew, she'd already been going along. God knows why she didn't say. Maybe because she was guilty for stopping the meetings, for trying to get herself together on her own, or because she was in the throes of doing something that the people in her meeting might have counselled her against, taking the children away from Lenny.

225

The revelation had created a shift in the room, somehow. The silence was changed. No longer fraught, just silence.

Marnie said, suddenly, 'Baby—back when you were little. When you used to come and visit me at work—Heath didn't…he didn't interfere with you, did he?'

Eleanor said, 'Where did that come from?'

'I don't know.'

A second of silence, and then: 'He was a sad old fuck.'

'Meaning?'

'All those lollies he fed me—he should have been put in gaol for trashing my teeth.'

She hesitated then, and Marnie said nothing. They both knew the truth about her teeth. It wasn't the lollies that trashed them.

28

Getting ready for work the next day, Marnie allowed herself to be hopeful that their argument had cleared the air. Eleanor came out dressed and ready for the day, clear-eyed, and said, 'I'll come with you. I need to go to Centrelink, there's a couple of jobs on Seek.' She showed Marnie her phone—carer, kitchen hand at a local pub, salesperson wool brokers. 'What's wool brokers?' she asked.

Marnie said, reading it, 'Selling wool? But this looks like office work probably,' keeping her tone casual, no hint of surprise.

'So long as they don't ask me to shear anything.'

'Never say never. Could be a new career path.'

Lenny gave a short laugh. She ate dry cereal from the box and watched Marnie cutting banana onto Koa's plate. She said with her mouth full, 'So, I'll go in the library and do all that stuff. And I need a skirt or something for interviews, and some shoes. Where do I look?'

'Main Street, or Plaza.' Marnie took notes from her wallet. 'Here. Put this towards the clothes.'

'Hey thanks, Mum.'

Lenny pocketed the twenty and two tens and flashed a smile at her. 'I'm sorry about last night,' she said.

'Me too, baby.' It was a relief to say it. Marnie thought: I should have said it first.

Eleanor said, 'I can pick up the kids, and we'll come around to Honeydew after you finish. Four o'clock, right?'

It sounded so normal. Marnie said, 'If you like, we could get a counter meal.'

'Now you're talking,' said Lenny. 'Hear that, Frankie? Dinner at the pub! Woo-hoo!'

'Woo-hoo!' said Frankie.

But at four o'clock, Lenny wasn't at Honeydew. Marnie waited ten minutes before texting.

– *Ready out front. Where R U?*

There was no reply, so Marnie phoned her, but the call went to messagebank.

She walked around to child care, where she learned that the children hadn't come in at all that day. Eleanor had phoned at eight-thirty, reporting that they all had Covid symptoms, including Marnie, who had lost her voice. As Miss Tash related this, and realised the implications of what she was saying, her face seemed to lose expression. Her voice faltered. 'I mean…It sounded so okay, the reason for her phoning, and not you. Oh Marnie. I'm—I don't know what to say. I'm getting my manager.'

228

Marnie nodded, 'I'll check the car.' Miss Tash was already running from the room.

Marnie went outside and found her car in the place she'd parked it. She was comforted by this for about three seconds. She opened the boot and saw that the stroller was gone. Well, that was logical enough, but the empty space where the stroller was usually stored sent a pricking over her scalp. Lenny had waved her away, standing by the car in her leopard-print gumboots, a child on each side of her. 'See you later, Ganny. Wave, Koa!' The business of blowing kisses, three vertical jumps from Koa because he could, and Marnie had walked away from them all, trusting her daughter to take them in to child care. Oh, God. Trusting her.

Now, she walked slowly back to child care and entered an atmosphere of mute tension. She heard herself, surprisingly composed, reassuring them. Her daughter had probably kept the children with her for the day. Perhaps Lenny believed she had no choice, that there was some rule that she had to drop them off, so she lied. Miss Tash asked her manager in a murmur, should they call the police? The manager continued scrolling through documents on her computer. 'It's all right, it's all right,' she said, not listening.

And it was, because no law had been broken. The relief on the manager's face when she found no directive from Child Protection on the files transcended all immediate concerns. Her face became tranquil, there was no point overreacting, she reminded them. It could be just a case of jumping to conclusions.

And yet they all knew. The small gathering of staff, the

manager, the cook, Marnie, their tacit looks, they all knew what had happened.

After nearly an hour and many unanswered calls to Lenny's phone, Marnie went around to the Centrelink office in the vain hope that someone might tell her if Eleanor had been in, which had been the plan. It was all she could think of. It was close to closing time. 'This is probably for CPS,' said a woman in a Centrelink shirt, removing her coat and turning her monitor back on.

'Yes, I guess.'

'Oh, good!' said the woman to her monitor, scrolling through pages of information. 'Kaarin's got your case, I just saw her in the tearoom a few minutes ago. I'll fetch her.'

Marnie said, 'No.' But the woman had left the office. Marnie looked at her phone blankly.

Sometime later Kaarin came into the office girded, overcoat on, shoulder bag across her chest, car keys in her hands. 'Ms Odell.' Patches of pink on her face. 'How can I help you?'

'You know, they've told you.'

'Yes, the children are with your daughter. Can you tell me what the problem is?'

'They're in danger.'

'Is there a parenting order in your favour?'

'You know there isn't.'

'There is no problem then, is there?' Was that triumph in her eyes?

'Of course there's a problem!' Marnie walked to the office door and looked out for assistance, the place was empty. She turned back to Kaarin. 'I believe my children are in danger.'

'Your *children?*' an emphasis that both challenged and derided. How could a person live with such a need to humiliate?

'My grandchildren. You know what I'm telling you, why are you making this difficult?' Her phone pinged. She looked at the message.

    — *Stop calling. Were fine. Kids with me. Call u later.*

She showed it to Kaarin, who said, 'I think that's answered your question. Make an appointment to come in if you have any concerns.'

She opened the door and held it for Marnie to pass.

She waited in town until it was fully dark. Shops closed around her. People turned keys in shopfront entry ways, shrugging on jackets as they moved along the street. She drove to the supermarket, where the lights would stay on. Sat there in the cooling car with her mobile on her knee. She resisted the urge to call or message Eleanor again. She had already made how many calls? She didn't know. Too many, anyhow. Too many to seem in control.

She thought she should phone Rhiannon but didn't. She thought she might phone Colleen but couldn't. Blankness engulfed her. When finally she looked at her watch she saw that another hour had ticked by. She allowed herself one more text.

    Can you just tell me where you are?

An answer came back.

All good. Later.

She drove to the bus station. The timetable showed her the movement of buses all day. Adelaide or Melbourne, also Ballarat, Nhill, Murtoa, Dimboola, Stawell, St Arnaud, Bendigo. All points of the compass, really. Eleanor could have taken a bus to any of them, what would she care? She had burnt so many bridges that it wouldn't matter where she washed up with two children and a stroller. Although, Marnie thought, it would be somewhere big, that was what she was used to, and wasn't it true that people tend to gravitate towards the familiar? Bendigo or Ballarat, then; Melbourne or Adelaide.

Or perhaps Eleanor had got a lift home? Could she have met up with someone she knew from the pub? Lester, the publican—in her mind always dressed in chaps and bolo; Razza, even—no he didn't have a car. And, of course, it would be the kind of thing she would let Marnie know about via text. *Got lift home.* Or, *Sick of waiting, took kids home.* Hope, like a bubble, surfaced and burst. Marnie drove out of town in the gloom. There were things she needed to do. Feed the lambs, the dog, the cat. She must get on.

She drove slowly. The paddocks in every direction were maroon-coloured. Cars and trucks overtook her; she couldn't seem to accelerate.

Her head was empty, but thoughts came like fish, swimming up from depths, twisting and turning, flashing out, then in again. She saw the children this morning blowing kisses; the tender lump under Koa's eye. Then, a distant memory, she saw Michael's face staring at her through the car window, smiling and then frowning as the car drove off, his perfect white brow wrinkling right up to his cowlick, his face changing, subtly changing shape, as he began to understand that he was being taken away from her.

A road train overtook her, its draft pushing at the side panels of her car. A baritone blast of rage from the truck's horn swerving her onto the blue-metal shoulder. She corrected untidily as another vehicle shot past her with another horn blast.

Okay, she needed to pull over, maybe at the next town, but she found she was through Natimuk and passing paddocks again before she could make her mind up to do it. Then, without warning, she could not breathe.

The rumbling of the car over the blacktop seemed to suck all the oxygen from around her. She swung off and braked abruptly, jerking forward into her seatbelt, fumbled for the engine switch and fell through the driver's door into cold air. Was it a heart attack? Was this what it felt like? Now she was on the ground with gravel pressing through her trousers, sticking in her hands. Now she was crouching, no air getting in, her chest locked.

She did not know how long she stayed there. She covered her head with her arms. Passing vehicles sent air pummelling over her. She wanted to breathe but couldn't remember the action, couldn't make herself do it, yet she was conscious— how could she be? She was breathing, she must be. She heard air in her chest but it was drawing in as if through stone. She felt it, sure enough, listened to the miracle of it, not daring to move. Air in, air out, breathing. She counted one for in and two for out. If she kept still, she could do it. She reached fifty-six. She should stand up. But she couldn't yet. She would have to wait.

Then lights, slamming car doors, a crackle of electronic sound, finally a voice close at her ear. 'Police. Can you hear me?'

'Yes,' she said, and felt suddenly ridiculous, ashamed. She didn't lift her head. The pulse of blue light hurt her eyes.

A male voice: 'Okay, we're here because you were reported in difficulties. We just want to check you out. Can you tell me if you're in pain?'

'I couldn't breathe,' she said.

'Can you say that again? I didn't catch it.'

'Breathe,' she said.

'Are you asthmatic?'

'No.' It all seemed pointless, now, the questions and the answers, because she could tell she was recovering.

Was she on medication? Had this happened before? What was her name? Could she stand? Could she locate her driver's licence? The person asking the questions relayed instructions from time to time to someone else, standing behind them.

'Car's all right,' the other voice said. Then: 'Ambulance on its way.'

'What's your name, love?' The first voice, close range. The question again, this time enhanced with a glib endearment.

'My name is Marnie,' she said, lifting her head slowly, squinting away from the flashing lights. She found herself close up to a bulky police vest. Hi-vis stripes, badges, a burbling mouthpiece. The other figure was further back, in shadow. Questions came at her again. She said she didn't think she could stand up, but maybe in a minute. She apologised, once, twice. After the third time she heard Rhi's voice inside her head, telling her to quit with the goddamn apologies.

'Marnie.' The voice close in, conversational, unfussed. 'Always liked that name. I knew a Marnie, yonks ago. My first job. Furniture removals.'

She opened her eyes but could not make out more than shadow and cheekbone. She nodded at the figure.

'Are you...' The voice rose several notes. 'Is it *Marnie Guest?*'

She looked harder, her eyes wouldn't focus. There was a tone of disbelief in the voice now, a tightening of a hand on her arm. 'It's me, Brian. You remember. Sheenie!'

Was this a trick? A ghost?

'Geez, Marnie Guest! This is a weird way to catch up with an old mate!' His arms were around her, professional circumspection abandoned. Two strong arms were bracing her, helping her stand, she could smell him. Sheenie. From a distance came the wail of an approaching ambulance.

29

Overkill, she told Colleen, who came to get her from the hospital at Horsham some hours later. She didn't know it was just a panic attack, that was the problem. She should have realised.

'Just?'

'You know.'

'Yeah, not sure I do.'

They were driving back along the highway, looking for Marnie's car. Sheenie had moved it well off the road for her, assured her that he would call in. He knew Von's house. Sheenie. Sheenie lived in the area, just a bit northeast of her. She barely recognised him. He was bigger, his head was shaved. He was sixty-two.

'Sheenie's been around here a few years,' Colleen told her. 'He's our local copper. He was at the eighties night, didn't you see him?'

Marnie's brain was numb. It was disconcerting. She

thought back, obediently, to please Colleen. 'Dressed as?'

'The police. Didn't stay, just called in. I mean, he was in actual uniform, on the job, not Sting-Police. But that would have been funny, I wish I'd thought of it.'

Marnie had no recollection.

Colleen said, 'This is giving me a head spin! How long since you worked together?'

'Long time.' She had a sudden, touching memory. 'Last time I saw him was at a funeral. He had more hair.' The memory was of her finding a tissue in her handbag and passing it to Sheenie. It was Heath's funeral. Sheenie was crying.

'I can't picture him with hair. He's nice. Shy.' Colleen's voice was different. She wanted to talk about Brian Sheen more than about the children, and Lenny. Or was she trying to keep off the topic? She said, 'Man—I actually can't get over that you know him.' Then: 'So has he always been single? No ex-wife anywhere? No kids?'

Marnie said, 'I wouldn't know.'

Colleen rolled on, 'I thought maybe gay, but I don't think so. Okay, now we're cookin'.'

Her headlights had found the flank of Marnie's car, nose-in to a milk-churn letterbox on a farm driveway. She slowed. 'Phase two. Can you do this?'

'Of course.'

'You drive in front, I'll follow. You shouldn't be driving at all, probably.'

'I'm not drunk.'

'Did they give you anything?'

'Panadol and a cup of tea.'

'Jesus, what do you have to do to get actual drugs these days?'

On the drive home, glad to be in silence again, Colleen's headlights bolstering her from behind, Marnie heard two messages ping through to her phone. She didn't stop driving. She didn't know what would happen if she stopped.

She read her messages when she was home. They were both from Eleanor, both useless. The next morning she called the Honeydew to arrange time off work, and Sam sounded put out. Marnie promised to be back on Friday and work all day Saturday to make up. She could hear herself speaking as if from a distance. 'I'm sorry,' she said, 'a few things happened.'

'The kids?'

'Their mother has them.'

A silence, but the silence of an ally. She remembered Sam's narrow-eyed look in Eleanor's direction, summing her up. Sam said, 'Take it easy, then. See you Friday.'

Marnie tried to take it easy, whatever that meant. She fed lambs, cleaned the house and hung washing on the line, dragging it in when rain swept through in the late afternoon. She collected up Octonauts and teddies, shoes and pyjamas. Tried not to feel furious that so much had been left behind— what were the children wearing a day later? Had they slept in their clothes, in their gumboots? She made soup, which was tasteless, put it to one side and drank tea instead of eating.

Razza came by on his evening trek into town.

'You good?' he said from the doorstep, casually swatting

the dog away from his boot.

She said she was. She wondered what he knew, if word was already out about last night on the road. Would Colleen have said something? She said, 'The chickens are laying better. Do you want eggs?'

'Nah, stop offering, they shit me. Von makes me take them.' He added: 'Don't tell her.'

Marnie nodded, and for a second her eyes grew hot and hazy. Okay, this was not a functional way to respond to a throwaway conversation.

'Where's Lenny?' he said.

'Don't know. Why?'

'She owes me fifty.'

She stared at him in disbelief. 'You sold her drugs?'

He met her gaze for a second, those eyes that bothered her, that might have been sexy once. He said, 'What of it?'

'Why would you do that? You absolute bastard, I'm not going to pay you!'

She slammed the door on him and watched through the window as he walked slowly back to the road.

For an hour afterwards she seethed, walking about the house and the yard, followed everywhere by the dog. When she was calmer, Marnie read through her two phone messages from Eleanor again, hoping there might be more. There weren't.

All good here. Need space. Don't worry.

Followed by: *Thanks for what you did Mum. Luv U.*

Still meaningless, not comforting, not anything. Marnie couldn't formulate a reply. But would that make Eleanor think she was giving her the cold shoulder? Was that good? Should she send something? If not words, a smiley face? Enraged again; she picked up the phone and piffed it across the room. Oh God, a drink would be good. The cupboard was bare, of course. She went back to pacing.

Sheenie arrived in the early evening, as promised. She watched him through her window, walking from the police Ranger to her door, minus his safety vest. She could see the familiar heavy thighs, his large palms and short fingers. He was thicker in the waist now. Trying to saunter, she thought, trying to be casual. Same shy boy, even at sixty-two. Now he was pausing to greet the dog. She went to the door and met him on the step, reaching her arms around his neck, pulling him close, hugging him, breathing in his aftershave. Sheenie. She didn't want to let him go.

'There you go,' he said gently disengaging, red in the face. She remembered, then, that hugging someone for an extended time was awkward when you were old. Even Sheenie.

But he wasn't uncaring. He said, 'Okay, kiddo?' Just what Heath might have said.

While she boiled the kettle, Sheenie told her what he knew. He'd put out a broadcast after he got back to the station. Transit police were all over it, but unfortunately it was already too late. If Lenny and the children had arrived at Southern Cross, it could have been as early as 5 p.m., depending on when they'd got on the bus.

'If they got on the bus,' she said.

He said there was an alert out on them around Horsham, but nothing had come of it so far. In his opinion, Lenny had definitely left town, but he said Marnie shouldn't give up. Lenny would surface, she would need housing, she would need money and food. He had already put a report through to Child Protection. She mentioned the difficulty she had with the current caseworker, only in passing, she didn't want to put up obstacles. It would make her seem inured to the system, that old-hand tone that was always unsympathetic. Sheenie assured her that if she kept her nerve, kept pushing her case, something would come up. 'Something always does.' And she wondered if he only said it to comfort her, because she was certain it was not true. She made her eyes look hopeful, allowed him to believe his comforting had worked.

They drank tea in front of the heater. 'Geez, this is all right,' he said, stretching out his feet in linty socks. 'Von's the complete package, you know?'

'Yes.'

'Colleen picked you up last night?'

'Yep.' Adding, for Colleen's benefit, 'She thinks you're a really nice guy. She told me.'

Mottled colour on his cheeks. Marnie thought *Glory be to God for dappled things*. Sheenie said, 'You tell her about me?'

'About what? You being Heath's biggest success story?'

'Settle down!' He hid his pleasure behind his mug of tea. How could he still be so self-effacing? He spoke about his career in the force. 'No big deal,' he said. 'Just holding steady, you know?'

He told her that after he made it through the first rough years, he was encouraged to take a path into Youth Liaison because of his background. He thought it would be good too,

241

but it wasn't. 'Nearly finished me,' he said. 'The stress, those kids, it brought everything back, you know? Did my head in.'

He spent some time as a patient in a mental health unit, he said, but didn't elaborate, then he took a country posting. This was his third, his last. He liked it here. Had he ever married? He stared at the heater, he said he came close once. It wasn't the woman's fault, it was him always anticipating disaster, always expecting her to show him the door.

'Didn't anyone ever tell you that you're a prize?' Marnie said. Being with Sheenie made her the calmest she'd been for weeks, reminded her of what it had been like to be in charge, way back then.

'Consolation prize?'

'Come on! Heath told you how proud he was of you!'

Sheenie looked at his hands, 'I never believe the good stuff, you know?' He said that a lot: *you know?* A conversational tic she didn't remember from the old days.

He wanted to change the topic, she could tell. So she told him her story, a shortened version. She said, 'If you want to hear about failure...' and pointed at herself.

He laughed. 'Not buying it. Beautiful Marnie Guest. I didn't even know your name for weeks. Heath called you Caroline. Or Miss Marnie, sometimes, didn't he? I thought that was your name, Caroline Marnie you know, like Marnie was a surname? Marko put me straight.'

'You ever see him?'

'Oh sure, well not for a while, but I see most of the crew I worked with.'

This was unexpected. 'You do?'

He was embarrassed. 'I'm like a sheepdog, got eyes on all of them. Every couple of years I'd end up having lunch with Marko, hearing the goss, you know? I'd have to drive down to Melbourne, he never came to me. Reckons he's allergic to country air, typical Marko bulldust. Haven't seen him since he went to Germany to that ballet job.'

Her eagerness surprised her. 'What about the others?'

He named boys she could hardly remember, Ack, Floyd, Iceberg. Of course, Iceberg! A boy so gangly and uncoordinated Heath pronounced him a danger to shipping. Sheenie knew where they'd ended up, whether they'd made a go of it, which ones were dead. He told her Bomba was gone, glassed in a laneway, some sort of territory war. 'Bomba never got out of the groove. Two stints in gaol, always picking up with any crim who needed errands done. Poor little guy.'

'Last time I saw him was Heath's funeral. He was pretty wasted-looking.'

'Still, it was good he fronted.' Sheenie, Sheenie, always finding the good. 'He was that quick, you know? Sharp. I think now they'd say ADHD, and he would've got help. We were all messed up.' He looked over to her. 'I couldn't read or write when Heath took me on. Did you know that?'

She avoided replying. Of course she knew. She'd filled in the forms for him when she saw him flushing and switching the biro from hand to hand. She had pointed with her finger where he needed to sign, watched him carving tiny letters into the paper, his ears scarlet.

Sheenie said, 'Heath fixed me up with classes, some old nun friend of Lorna's in a flat near the tram stop. I go, I don't want no nun teaching me, I had nuns in prep and grade one, belting me for being a leftie. Heath goes, they messed you up, they can fix you up.'

'And it worked?'

'Went to her for two years, geez she was a nice bird, then Heath got me in at night school.'

She said, 'He put me through night school, too.'

'He got Iceberg wearing glasses—the guy didn't even know he was half-blind, can you believe it? He got dress-making lessons for Marko. Marko ended up doing a diploma or something, didn't he?'

Marnie said casually, 'Hey—ever catch up with Hollywood?'

Sheenie glanced at her, reading her disingenuousness. 'Sure,' he said. 'You liked him for a while, didn't you?' He knew enough of the story, obviously. 'Good-looking guy. Bit of a prick.'

'Heath got rid of him.'

'He had this way of putting people down, you know? Really bullied Bomba. Called me a fat shithead; called Marko a poof all the time. Other stuff, way worse. Always making out it was a joke.'

Yes, that was Hollywood. She remembered how out of kilter he made her feel, not always in a sexual way. You could never call him on anything, never take issue because he'd say you were being a sook, no sense of humour, couldn't take a bit of fooling around. The problem wasn't ever Hollywood.

'Where is he?'

'Pilbara, fly-in fly-out. May not have lasted after they

brought in stricter drug-testing. Hates a beer.'

She said, 'This is going to sound silly—when I first came here, you know that guy Razza who lives up the road from here?'

'Everyone knows Razza.' Sheenie gave a short laugh.

'He reminded me of Hollywood. Not seriously I guess, but still.'

You could say things like that to Sheenie. He said, 'Yeah, makes sense, but he's a local boy—footy star—got picked up by Essendon, didn't last—too many concussions, you know?'

'Alky, is he?'

'Got some kind of brain problem anyway, lives on meds. Von looks after him a bit.' He was gazing at the heater, but he lifted his head and glanced at her, then looked away.

'I'm glad you found me,' she said. He nodded.

The calm feeling didn't last. After Sheenie was gone, with night lowering over the house and yard, she found herself pacing again. She ate a piece of bread for dinner. Later she squeezed a tube of the children's yoghurt into her mouth. The television blatted voices at her, cheerful voices, sing-song voices, voices overstating situations and emotions, building drama out of inconsequence. She realised her chest was tight-ening again, it was probably the TV doing it. She turned the sound off, buried her face in her knees and sat crouched in the recliner, the chair that Lenny had claimed for herself. Curled up in that chair, she felt Lenny inhabiting her. She looked around the room and felt that she saw it with Lenny's eyes, how shabby and plain it was, how...not enough. She felt it, the want that was always there, that would never be satisfied, would never allow her daughter to be happy.

She watched an infomercial without sound, all about miraculous ointment that melted away wrinkles. When she found herself looking at another one, about a miraculous ladder, she turned everything off and took herself to bed.

In the dark everything came back. Sheenie had talked about it, the feelings that came back. It wasn't fair—couldn't the past just disappear into the past? Couldn't you look forward into clear air without shadows always lurking, threatening, muscling up as soon as there was a moment of silence or a space?

She felt a wave of outrage, and even that was familiar. Outrage, regret, fear and, yes, emptiness, all the ghosts magnifying around her bed like creatures from the black lagoon. She should turn on her light, maybe. Phone Rhiannon, make a list, do some damn thing. She wanted Sheenie to come back, but maybe it was Sheenie who had brought the battalions inhabiting the room right now.

Hollywood, Gerald, the Rats of Tobruk father she had never known. She told herself to settle down for God's sake, why do they still matter? Lorna, Joan, Heath. They died one after the other, yes, but separated by years. Now their passing seemed compressed in time and space, a domino-fall of abandonment.

Lorna—poor, poor Lorna—died first. There was Heath, sitting with her that last week, all day and every night. Marnie and Marko couldn't get past the door of the room, there was no space for them, the air filled up to choking point with Lorna and Heath.

'Are we ever going to love people like that, and get loved back?' Marko asked her in the ute on the way home.

'No,' she said.

And afterwards, Heath sitting in his backyard in spring sunshine, surrounded by overgrown bushes, in a racket of bees, staring at the fence. It was Joan who got him going. She came around and sat with him. Marnie watched them together from her office window over the course of a week. Once she saw Heath's head on her mother's shoulder.

Marko went back on the truck. He said he was out of practice, and he was. He took compassionate leave from the Australian Ballet, where he had a job in the wardrobe department. Marko, Marko, in overalls and steelcaps, coordinating the boys until Heath could take the reins again. It was the beginning of the end of the business, but they didn't know it yet.

Then Joan. It was years later when Joan became ill, Eleanor was ten. Heath was retired, shambling up the hill to their house most mornings to sit with Joan while Marnie was at work. He was often there when Eleanor came home from school. Sometimes, when Marnie came through the door—she was bursar at a primary school now—she found the three of them clumped together on Joan's Queen Anne bed, playing Uno.

Ged wasn't good with sick people. He announced it with a kind of bashful pride, his face a parody of regret. This is the way I am, his tone implied, soliciting sympathy. He went interstate a lot, no great loss. Right at the end Marnie was with her mother every day, helping out when the nurses came around and Gerald, she knew, would have been pained and put out, a drain on her. She knew, even then, the house was simply easier without Ged in it.

Joan endured, Joan lingered. In the last days, the bad days, she lapsed into vacuity and then, without warning, woke inconsolable. One day, she said, 'Marnie—I had it wrong.'

'What, Mum?'

'I thought he would snap out of it. I got so fed up with all the pills.' Her tiny hands were weightless, they waved and plucked at the sheet.

'What pills, what are you saying, Mum?'

Joan's face, lined with effort. 'No, listen. It was PSP-something, I saw it on the telly. Post trauma something.'

'Post-Traumatic Stress Disorder?'

Astonishingly, tears came spilling out of Joan's eyes, down her papery cheeks, disappearing in the fleshless folds of her neck. 'I was ashamed of him. Crying all the time, a grown man.'

'Mum don't, please!'

'Post trauma thing—on the telly about the ones who went to Vietnam, but it was what your father had only they didn't call it that. They gave him pills, they said depression.' Joan's lower lip puckering, her voice cracking. 'I should have been kinder.'

When Marnie unearthed the documentation for Joan's death certificate, which included her father's death certificate, she read that her father had died by suicide. Her mother had never mentioned it.

Heath said, 'Don't hold it against her. It was like that, after the war.'

Five or so years later, when she and Gerald and Eleanor were in the new place in Ivanhoe, Marko rang to tell her Heath was dead. Emphysema, blood pressure, rampant diabetes—one or all of them had finished him, as he had been warned many times they would. Even Gerald fronted for that funeral. Eleanor's face was full of studs, her hair jet black and holes in her tights. Her first tattoo, some sort of Celtic knot, was scabby and inflamed along her soft inside forearm. Marnie could not look at it.

Brian Sheen was there, upstanding in his police uniform. Marko, resplendent in the sharpest suit money could buy, satin waistcoat, silk handkerchief, shoe-uppers like mirrors, slender and tanned. Iceberg, Floyd and, that's right, Bomba was also there, where had he come from? Unwashed, jaunty, most of his teeth gone, wearing new trackpants for the occasion.

Marko nudged Lenny and pointed out the Best and Less label dangling from Bomba's waistband at the back and they both dissolved, handfuls of tissues over their faces to hide the hilarity. But it was okay because the man from the church, giving the eulogy, was saying that Heath's name really was Heathcliff—Heathcliff William Wavell Woolley—and that got everyone going. This was followed by stories about Heath's penchant for soppy songs, his disasters in the ruck for the local footy team, his appetite for dolly mixture. Lots of references to Dean Martin, of course, the way Heath used song quotes as philosophy. Everyone was laughing. Then it got serious at the end, when the priest spoke about Heath's tour of duty in Korea, his bravery medal, his marriage, his prison work and youth work, his Order of Australia, which Marnie had never,

ever, heard him mention—a staggering list of achievements. 'It is within all of us to fly the standard that Jesus raised for us. Some succeed in small ways, and some of us are giants,' the priest said. Then it was over. The priest's voice broke during the final blessing, and Dino sang Heath out: 'Return to Me'. The coffin was balanced on the boys' shoulders, Marko, Sheenie, a couple she didn't know. Even Bomba fronted for the task, shorter than everyone, making the coffin lopsided. On top of that, he was incapable of keeping in step. It was a brief but nerve-racking journey from altar to hearse.

After the funeral, Gerald confessed to Marnie that he was seeing someone else, the catering manager of a golf club in Surfers. Marnie wondered why he included the new woman's employment information, and then realised it was because he was impressed by it. He packed his bags and moved to Queensland.

Some men are giants. And some aren't.

30

Another week passed: no word from Eleanor. Marnie drove
to work in morning gloom and drove home in evening murk.
Sheets of rain hung over flat paddocks, every indentation in
the landscape was filled with water.

At night, the dog and cat slept in front of the heater.
The lambs ran beside Marnie, leaping and twisting, into the
paddock each day then back to the shed in the evenings. Late
in the week, she arrived home to find a new pile of firewood
at her door and Razza leaning the splitter up against the
wall. He started walking to the gate while she parked. She
felt guilty and called, 'Thanks. It's good of you.'

He hesitated, half-turning to her. 'Those lambs weaned?'

'I'm not sure how I'm supposed to do it.'

'Leave them in the paddock and stop feeding them.
They're fucken sumos.' He was unshaven, his beanie sitting
nearly over his eyes. He turned back to the gate, and she called
out to him.

'I'm sorry I lost it with you.' He stopped walking and half-turned back. She said, 'What did my daughter buy off you?'

'Weed.'

'You grow it?'

He said, not answering the question, 'She paid half in pills. The fifty was what was left.' He started walking again: no intention of engaging with her further on the subject.

Sheenie called by in civvies with a list of things for her to do, and she told him what Razza had said. Sheenie was unsurprised. 'If it's pills, it'll be one of the contins. That's Razza's downfall.'

'I don't know where Lenny would have got them.'

'When you're in the scene, you just know. Sorry,' he added, 'but you do.'

He gave her instructions; he'd put some thought into it. She needed to create a paper trail with DFFH, she could bypass Kaarin, she could make a formal complaint or just say she felt they didn't understand each other, keep it vague. She needed legal advice—Legal Aid would help her—she needed them to take formal Family Law Act proceedings, she needed protection orders, at the very least. She needed to start the ball rolling, that was the thing.

'I still don't know where they are,' she said. Just saying it gave her a pain that travelled through her to the balls of her feet.

'Your daughter's in the system. She's getting paid, right?'

She was. Marnie's pension had been adjusted already.

Lenny had expertly organised the financials. When Marnie had made enquiries about Lenny's address, she had been blocked.

'Is she on the methadone register?'

'I'm not sure. It's just that she was gone for a year.'

'Well, that's two ways we can track her, that's all I'm saying, you know? My advice is get a lawyer. I'm not up with all the legal stuff, but Legal Aid will sort you out with someone,' Sheenie said. 'Come to the pub. Just for a quick one.'

But she couldn't. She waved him off and went back inside the house. Later she picked up Sheenie's list and read through it with a feeling of defeat. The next day she rang in sick for work and stayed in bed. She made up her mind to quit the Honeydew job entirely. It didn't matter, the bond money was in her account from Vincent. She would live on that until it was gone. It didn't matter.

Rhi phoned her, but she didn't answer. Colleen phoned too, and threatened to turn up unannounced if she didn't reply. She texted back that she was fine, she was working long hours and tired, that was all. Yet another lie, but so what? You had to protect yourself.

Anyway, she didn't want to see Colleen. Colleen was in love. Marnie had inadvertently brought her together with Sheenie, and now he had a glow about him, too. Yes, it was lovely, straight out of the pages of a cheap romance novel. Marnie had no stomach for them, or their glow.

A week passed in a blur of no-action and sunless skies. Then Razza showed up again one morning, driving through the gate in a twin-cab ute. He said, 'Gotta do a job. You can help.'

'I don't want to.'

'Colleen said you have to.'

'Do what?'

'Sit in the ute.'

She didn't know why, but she put on her gumboots and sat in the wet, wool-smelling cabin of the ute, mud on the floor and all up the insides of the door, a film of cigarette smoke on the windscreen, everything foul. She was now sitting closer to Razza than she ever wanted to be. They drove out the gate and up the road a way, then in through a farm gate, past woolsheds and hay sheds, equipment sheds, across paddocks, vast stretches of grass punctuated with wild carrot and mallow, skirting around dams and finally onto a laneway between paddocks, potholed but sound.

It was quieter here than anywhere else, she thought. Sheep were all around them, clusters of new lambs creched in piles of fallen timber, troops of bigger lambs chasing follow-the-leader around dam walls, backwards and forwards. Mothers feeding, moving slowly. There were dead lambs too, startling-ly white, flat in the grass like discarded handtowels. Razza picked them up and put them in the ute tray.

'Don't look,' he said.

'Why do they die?'

'Law of averages.' He added as mitigation: 'It's been an all-right season. Ninety-seven per cent.'

'Is this your farm?'

'Taking care of it for a couple of weeks.'

They came to a paddock with new lambs in it. Razza

pointed out triplets clustered around their mother. 'She's a keeper,' he said. 'Knows her job.'

They found a dying sheep beside a dead lamb. 'Don't look,' Razza said again, pulling up. Marnie looked away. After a few minutes she felt the thud of the sheep's body in the ute. They drove on. Clouds churned; rain misted across the windscreen, then petered out. Why am I here? Marnie thought. Did Colleen actually think I would enjoy this? She thought of Razza saying law of averages. That was all anything was; they were all part of it, randomly, hopelessly. The law of averages.

Razza gave a wide berth to a sheep in the throes of lambing, on its side in a copse of wattles. The creature's efforts made Marnie want to cry, its dread-filled eyes rolling at the sight of the ute—that now, on top of everything else.

Further along, Razza stopped the ute. 'You can get out,' he said. She thought for a moment he was going to leave her there. He was walking away, so she followed him.

But there was a sheep down. Part of a lamb's head protruding from the back of it, grey and dead-looking. The sheep struggled to stand when it saw them approaching. Razza leapt forward with unexpected agility and restrained it.

He beckoned to Marnie. 'I'll hold her, you push the head back in. It needs to come out feet first, got it?'

Marnie put her hands on the unborn lamb's head, was startled by its warmth. 'It's alive,' she said, involuntarily, a gasp in her voice.

'Push it in, then get the feet, you'll feel them.'

She did as instructed. There was life in the feet too, just a little way up that humid birth canal, she could feel the heat of them. She held the feet in her hand and pulled. The feet came forward, for a second alarming her, then the whole lamb followed, sliding, wet and alive, like it wanted to, like it was meant to—no awkward stopping or wrenching or twisting, almost no effort at all. Razza picked up the lamb and shook it a bit, before laying it out in the grass by its mother. Both creatures were still.

'Are they dead?' she said.

'Prob'ly not.'

They went back to the ute and drove for another ten minutes, up to the highest point of land, a modest rise, notable only for a cluster of boulders. Razza pulled up and got out of the ute again without a word. Without a word she followed him. Thin sunlight had located an aperture in the clouds. The gunmetal paddocks were transformed into improbable iridescence. Nearby, shelducks foraged in groundwater. Razza lit a cigarette and Marnie sat on a lichen-covered boulder, waiting.

After Razza finished his cigarette—one long, last suck, holding the smoke in lovingly—he said, 'Good spot.'

She nodded.

He said, 'My mother died last week.'

She turned to look at him. He was staring over the paddocks. She thought, no, please I don't want to hear this. He said, 'Ninety-four. They didn't want me at the funeral.'

'Who didn't?'

'My sisters. Bossy cows.'

Marnie wondered if he would have called brothers that. She was tired of the conversation, she'd grown used to his silence, she did not want his confidences. 'I'm sorry,' she said, reluctantly.

He stubbed his butt on the ground, then put it in his shirt pocket, a surprising act of neatness. 'Not their fault. They didn't want any dramas.'

'Then maybe they're not bossy cows.'

'They're not,' he said. 'They're over me, that's all. I was going to send them a card. Don't know what to say in it.'

'Yes, you do,' she said, standing up. 'You know exactly what to say. Just damn well do it.'

He followed her back to the ute.

On the way back through the paddocks, he pointed out a fox trotting purposefully along in the shadow of a line of trees. Head down, tail down but not cowed. Razza said, 'Bastard knows I haven't got my shottie. Could be after your lamb.' But when they drove by the spot, they found the ewe upright and the lamb Marnie had pulled staggering at its mother's side.

Further along, among the wattle, newborn twins butted at their mother's belly in a soft hail of blossom.

Razza dropped her back at Von's and drove away. Marnie stood under a warm shower, resting her head on the bathroom wall.

When she was dressed again, she took her clothes over to the laundry at the back of Von's house. While the machine was on, she went around to the front door of the main house, pushed it open and walked inside.

The air was cold, the rooms dim. She imagined the way Eleanor had explored it and moved along the main corridor in her daughter's tracks, pushing open doors and looking in. Beds with chenille covers, bookshelves filled with farm journals and magazines, a pianola in a wood-panelled room, standing on the same cabbage-rose carpet as the one in the cottage. In the living room was a wall cabinet from the 1970s stuffed with holy pictures, birthday cards, dusty trophies. There was a bottle of Tia Maria on one shelf, unopened, beside a half-empty bottle of marsala—both blasts from the past. The marsala bottle had a glass next to it containing residue. Marnie smelled it and saw that the remains were recent enough to be still liquid. Lenny had not even tried to cover her tracks.

In the narrow bathroom with pink and black tiles, she found cupboard doors ajar, contents ransacked.

Marnie stood there and felt Eleanor's eyes looking through her. The cupboards contained the usual motley assortment of household drugs, some dating back years. Ford Pills (good lord, how old must they be); mercurochrome, cough syrups, Vaseline, castor oil, oil of cloves. There was a bundle of repeat prescriptions that had been bound together with a rubber band, but the rubber band was lying on the floor and the prescriptions were thumbed through and discarded. A small plastic tub, lid off, contents tipped out. There were sheets of paracetamol, aspirin and ibuprofen; tablets for indigestion, for blood pressure, for underactive thyroid. There were tablets in bottles with names she did not recognise. The recipients of the medication printed on the boxes were Veronica Concannon or Noel Concannon. Von's husband had been dead seven years, Colleen had told her that. Cancer. There were boxes of drugs with his name on them, all open now, all empty. She read the labels, which she could have predicted to the letter. Oxycontin, Endone; oh yes, good old Diazepam. Eleanor had sifted methodically through everything.

What should she do, Marnie wondered, put the empty boxes back? Would Von even know what had happened? How much had Eleanor got hold of? After all this time, perhaps the drugs would have lost their potency. But how likely was that?

Marnie sat on the bathroom floor. So still for so long that she saw a mouse emerge from under the iron bathtub, slip across the floor and disappear down the hallway. That was the other smell, she thought—mice. Perhaps she should put Shadow the cat into the house for a day, to see what he could do. The thought made her tired. She started packing the drugs up, removing the empty boxes. She found a half-sheet of Endone in the bottom of a box—Lenny must have missed it—and put it in her pocket. Then she went back to the cottage and burned the cardboard in the stove.

Later, curled in the old recliner, wrapped in a doona, she swilled the four remaining Endone down with water and waited for something to happen—floating white mice, anything at all.

It was not what she was hoping. Within twenty minutes, having barely made it to the bathroom, she was vomiting spectacularly and peeing herself. By the time she was able to sit back, away from the toilet bowl, she was shuddering like jelly. Her mouth tasted like the inside of one of Heath's horrible ashtrays. She crawled into the shower and sat under a warm stream of water to wash the smell off, thinking she had never known water to be so consoling. She would stay here, stay right here, because there was nowhere else to be.

Eventually, a voice in Marnie's head began to suggest at least some part of the drugs had made it into her bloodstream and the love affair she was having with warm water was not authentic. Also, the water was cooling. She dragged herself to her feet and fumbled the water off, felt her way out of the shower and could not find a towel. But her doona was somewhere, she had discarded it on the floor outside the bathroom. She went to it but could not pick it up. It was simpler to go down to the doona. She found her way onto the carpet, pulled the doona around her and allowed herself to drop into the pacifying embrace of the dark. *I fled him down the nights and down the days.* She wondered why she had ever bothered. *All things betray thee, who betrayest me.* This feeling was God, and Lenny had always known the truth.

31

The melancholy days of August continued their run of rain. The weather report called it unprecedented. People spoke about it in the supermarket and in the street, using the word again and again, because it had been on the telly. Tractors sat bogged in paddocks and sinkholes opened on roads. Mud rose up the legs of cattle, thickening into clumps around their tails. Over at the caravan park, the lake rose to kiss the old piers. Eventually, Marnie took a phone call from Rhiannon.

'It's just that I have nothing to say,' she explained to her.

'Have you heard anything?'

'No. I said to her, Just send a photo, and she didn't.'

'Are you working?' Rhiannon asked her.

'No.'

'Help me, can you—are you doing anything?'

'Watching TV. I meet a friend for coffee sometimes.'

'Is that enough?'

Marnie didn't answer the question. It didn't even make

sense to her. 'I have a list of things. Sheenie gave it to me. He's a copper.'

Rhi's voice was relieved. 'What's on top of the list?'

'Get legal advice.'

'Have you done that?'

'I haven't done anything.' She said, 'I'm sorry, I have to hang up. I'm sorry.' She ended the call. Then she sent a text apologising. After that she switched her phone off.

That evening, Colleen came around and walked into the house, startling Marnie, who was in front of the TV.

'No one can reach you,' she said, putting a four-pack of prosecco cans on the table.

'Wow, are we celebrating?'

'Well, I'm relieved you're alive I guess.' Colleen hunted up glasses. 'This place is depressing, what have you got against pubs? Lost your phone?'

'Turned it off.'

'Von's been trying to reach you, she's coming home on Friday with Meg, that's her oldest.'

'Is she all right?'

'Not according to Meg, but Von won't take advice. She's coming home. Good on her. I never thought she'd last away from here this long.'

'How long has it been?'

'The eighties night was—what—nine weeks ago? How long have you been here? Six, seven weeks?'

Seven weeks. Maybe eight. Holy crap.

Marnie drank prosecco with Colleen, but she couldn't converse the way she used to. She couldn't ask questions, or answer them. She didn't want to hear news from town, news about Sheenie, about any of them. Colleen rattled on and Marnie thought about her next move. She certainly couldn't stay now that Von was coming back. Oh, Colleen thought it would be all right, but Marnie knew otherwise. To Von's family she was an interloper, living there rent-free to make matters worse, someone to distrust. She couldn't feel indignant about this because, let's face it, they were justified. When they noticed the clean-out of drugs in the bathroom there would be assumptions, maybe outright accusations. They would want her gone.

Truth be told, Marnie didn't know if Lenny had taken more stuff—money, jewellery, anything. Probably. All that aside, in the unlikely event that the family noticed nothing, Von would need Marnie to help her. That was key to Colleen's plan for her, bless Colleen and curse her, too, because there was no capacity within Marnie for anything like that. She was full up to the brim with blankness. The knowledge made her pragmatic.

Colleen said, 'So there'll be a message on your phone from Von, just phone back and let her know how everything is. How are the lambs?'

'Weaned. Razza made me.'

'Dog okay?'

'Dog, cat, everyone. I haven't mowed.'

'No one has, the whole district's a swamp. Anyway, Von just wants to hear about it, you know how it is. She's homesick.'

'I don't know what else to tell her. She has mice. But does

she really want to know that right now?'

Colleen went uncharacteristically silent. Then: 'Razza said you were bad. You need to get help, mate.'

Suddenly Razza was someone whose opinions should be valued?

'I'm just sick of it all,' Marnie heard herself say. 'I'm fine, you don't have to worry about me, I'm just sick of it.'

Over the next three days, Marnie cleaned. She cleaned and washed everything in the cottage. She lit the wood fire at Von's every day and felt the place come to life again. She wiped dust from surfaces. She changed Von's bedsheets and tidied her bedroom in readiness for her. She made a fruit cake, put fresh milk and butter into the refrigerator, fresh towels in the bathroom. She wrote Von a note thanking her, explaining as well as she could what had happened in the bathroom. She apologised for her daughter's behaviour and hoped that Von would understand. She left a hundred dollars on the dining table under a cut-glass vase stuffed with branches of rosemary—which was all she could find in the garden that looked passable since all Von's camellias had been pulverised by the rain.

On the third day, she fed the animals and sent a text to Colleen. Then she packed her things into her car and drove away. Out on the highway she thought—Deniliquin or Melbourne? But she knew the answer already. Eleanor would never have gone to Deniliquin. She turned south.

She spent one night in a cabin by another little lake and then drove the final leg into Melbourne. Fifty kilometres out, between hills, the city buildings poked up through brown haze, jagged, like broken teeth.

Over the Westgate Bridge, creeping forward in noisome traffic, buildings rising glassy around her, she questioned her impulse to come at all, but it was too late.

She knew the streets well enough. She parked in the corner of a supermarket carpark in Flemington and took a tram into town. The city streets were shadowed, winter sunlight appeared at odd moments, sliding away along gutters, under broken awnings and into cold doorways.

She walked around the markets, council flats, took a tram to Clarendon Street where Lenny had spent time, years ago, with Zac. Once she thought she saw Lenny in the window of a florist, of all places. But it was her own reflection, framed by bird of paradise stems, hundreds of them. Her face startled among foliage.

She walked the streets and laneways of the city centre, up Collins Street and down Bourke Street. She sat in the Mall and watched buskers do their schtick, was weirdly grateful for the general discordance of competing sounds. She watched cranes moving overhead against towers of ash-coloured clouds. She felt the afternoon collapse around her.

At the end of the day Marnie went back to Flemington and shifted her car, then she returned to the city and took a bed at a backpackers near Southern Cross station. The person at reception showed no curiosity, took her cash, gave her directions to her room. It was empty when she got there and she tried to believe she was glad to be there. During the night the three other beds in her room filled up: a crumpled girl who coughed and smelled of cigarettes. Two spectacular young Swedish women, who spoke quietly together and glared at the smoking girl over the top of their face masks, appealing to Marnie with their eyes to join in their disapproval. She nodded to them, a show of support, although she would have preferred not to engage.

Anyway, the shower was hot, the mattress was okay. Marnie left the backpackers in the morning. She took a tram to St Kilda and walked around the streets, then crossed the highway and walked the length of the shopping strip in Balaclava. In a little carpark behind a main street, she saw a woman lying on the ground and went over to her.

'Are you all right?' she said, collecting up the woman's bag, stuffing spilled belongings back into it. She was a bony woman, somewhere between thirty and fifty, dressed in a tight skirt and ankle boots with thin heels. She wore a leather jacket, unzipped, decorated with fancy stud work, cracked with age.

The woman turned her head with effort in response to Marnie's question. Her cheek showed indentations from being pressed on the gravel. Her voice was muffled. 'Sure, yeah, sure.'

'Your stuff has fallen out, look I'm putting it back. I'm putting your bag here by your head.'

'Thanks, darling.'

'Do you want me to help you stand up?'

'I'll be okay. Thanks, darling, thanks.' The woman only wanted to sleep. She dropped her head back to the gravel and closed her eyes. Marnie sat on the ground beside her. After ten minutes, the woman turned her head again. She said, 'Do I know you?'

'Marnie. I just thought you might be safer if I stay here for a while.'

'That's kind, thanks, darling. Thanks, Marley.' She closed her eyes again.

A few people passed them, heading to cars. Couples with shopping trolleys looked at them. One man smiled at her. 'Okay?'

Marnie nodded.

'You a friend of Charlie?' he opened his car boot and loaded his groceries into it.

Marnie shook her head.

'She's here a lot. They keep an eye on her.' Who, she wondered, were 'they'? He said, 'You her mum?'

'No.'

'She'll be all right, she always is,' he said. He closed his boot and pushed the trolley into the curb near Charlie's head. 'Shame, though.' He climbed into his car and drove away.

Marnie shifted the trolley away. A while later, Charlie woke and tried to sit up, pulling her bag onto her lap and looking through it vaguely. 'You okay?' she said, noticing Marnie. 'Marley, isn't it?'

'Yep. Marnie. You?'

'I will be when I find my smokes.' She stopped her search, and closed her eyes for a while, as if exhausted by the task. When she opened her eyes again, she looked at Marnie and said, 'Still here?'

'I wanted to know if you know my daughter, Lenny. She has a couple of kids with her.'

'On the spike?'

'Yes.'

'Sorry, darling.' Charlie went back to turning over the contents of her bag, sighing. 'Sounds like a shitful—' She lost the next word, searched for it, then abandoned the task. 'Can you see them?' She held out her bag to Marnie, who located the cigarette packet and handed it to her. The business of finding her lighter began, the same struggle. 'Jesus, you do it, will you? I trust you, darling. Where does your daughter live?'

'I don't know.'

'Maybe she doesn't want you around, sorry, sometimes you got to say it.'

'It's okay. You're right. It's the children.' Marnie unearthed the lighter from an unpleasant flotsam of used tissues and face masks, loose tampons, hair ties, a dirty comb and a cherry-red bra. She brought the lighter to the surface, along with a brass NA medallion with a 3 on it. Three months. She said, 'You got three months clean.'

Charlie laughed, exhaling a stream of smoke, coughing over the last of it. 'Worst seven years of my life.' She added, 'Only joking, darl. I'll do it again, I'm working up to it. This time it'll be for longer. I got a plan.'

'Gotta have a plan.' Marnie said it with irony, but the woman nodded emphatically.

'Sure do, sister.' Her laughter and her cough were indistinguishable from each other. When Marnie got up to leave, she said, 'Thanks, darling, thank you. God bless.'

In the tram, heading back to Flemington, Marnie got out her notebook with Sheenie's list folded inside it. She looked up Legal Aid on her phone and waded through pages of advice and suggestions. When she was back at her car, she summoned her nerve and made a phone call which, after some time, resulted in her securing an appointment with a family lawyer. Why was it so daunting? Hadn't she spent years navigating red tape? Surely she could just do it now, without feeling like she was working under wet cement. Get yourself together, she told herself. Get a backbone.

That smarmy priest was right. She resented him like crazy, but he was right. She resented TJ for getting a backbone, resented TJ's family for being there for him, for giving him a home where Michael could grow up and not be part of her life anymore. A home with a piano.

She wept behind her steering wheel for a few livid minutes, then she drove to Moonee Ponds and bought a pie and a coffee and ate them in a park with ducks. She found a police station and told them who she was, and asked if there was any news. They looked her up, checked their internal circulars…yes, the case was under investigation. They'd be glad of any more information, had Marnie had contact with her daughter? But there was nothing Marnie could add, except to tell them she was in Melbourne now, too. That's why she'd come in, to let them know. She gave them Rhiannon's address and felt guilty about it. She would have to phone Rhiannon and tell her. She would.

From there to a Centrelink office, a vastly bigger place than the office in Nhill with its Daffodil Room. This one was busy but quiet, heaving with disgruntlement. 'You can do this online,' she was advised at the front desk. 'It's preferred.'

Marnie explained that she did not have a computer, that she had no charge on her phone, that she needed to upgrade her employment status, she needed Child Protection input, that she was at the end of her tether. She said, 'I'm sorry if I'm doing this the wrong way, but I'm here now. I know you're overworked, but I need help.'

They took her into a cubicle and the whole rigmarole of statement and cross-checking recommenced. She gave her Melbourne address as Rhiannon's. They wanted to know if she had left her job willingly. She explained that she'd had to, she had to come to Melbourne to find her grandchildren. She had no choice. Did she realise that it might make getting assistance difficult for a few weeks? She knew. She had heard it all before. Perhaps because of that, she did not allow herself to be deflated.

When weak daylight was reverting to night shadow and drizzle was once again coating the world, she found herself in her car putting ticks beside the items on Sheenie's list. How those marks buoyed her—it was mental. That nice boy Declan had used that word and it was perfect. It was mental that she could get pleasure from biro marks on paper. She traced over her ticks until they were thick and dark. When the night became complete around her, she held her notebook against her heart. She could feel the ticks, even when she couldn't see them.

She spent the night in a carpark outside a swimming pool in Kensington. In the morning, when the pool opened, she went in and swam up and down for a while, then showered and tried to make herself neat. It was still hours before her Legal Aid appointment, so she indulged in a nostalgic drive around.

First, northwest of the city to Bree-Maree Avenue, where Michael had spent his first years. The street seemed shrunken. The houses, all built on jaunty angles along the curving roadway, seemed to have outlived their promise. Lawns were a wreck, and the garden statues she remembered—they had appeared in beds of tanbark all along the street—were either gone or needed to be. At the time she moved in, Marnie had thought how optimistic they were: children hugging, coy girls holding back petticoats, dogs, cats; in one case a giraffe. Her own house was disappointingly grungy. She had planted jasmine on a side fence; it was gargantuan now, brown in clumps. The curtains in the front windows—the ones she had installed, cheap as she could find—were pulled shut, limp behind dull glass, backing shredded.

She drove to Deer Park and looked at her second-floor flat. Here was a surprise: it was neater, the block now painted white, the bin area fenced in with fancy panels. How the unexpected things change, she thought. A sign at the front said Residents Parking Only in clear fresh lettering, and the car spaces were marked with a number. No weeds poking untidy heads from cracks and concrete edges.

She felt an unexpected wave of nostalgia for the tiny kitchen, the adjoining lounge room, the portable TV balanced on her one bookcase. It was where she slept with Philip the murderer's father, who, she realised now, was the only sexual partner she'd had who she remembered with real affection.

It was where Frankie learned to crawl, to walk, to run into Marnie's outstretched arms. It was where, for a short time, Eleanor was clean.

In the early afternoon she drove back to Maribyrnong, circling her school, the shopping centre where the chemist had once stood, then finally her old street. She parked outside her childhood home. It was hemmed in on all sides by flats and larger houses, no vacant blocks left now. The street had big trees in it, a profusion of green, not the scrappy, stunted prunus of the sixties. House rooftops shimmered with solar panels. Her own house had been extended upwards in timber so that orange-coloured brick was no longer its dominant feature, the backyard was overflowing with greenery. There was a new fence at the front with a climber on it. Joan wouldn't have allowed it. She liked to keep plants away from structures. She liked straight lines and neatness. But this, Marnie thought, was better. She would have liked to live, back then, in the house as it was now.

She drove around to Heath's, and it seemed a shorter drive than she remembered. That wasn't possible of course. The illusion was momentarily disorientating. But Heath's house was unmistakable despite its changed context. It had been a large corner block with an empty block beside it that held a tall garage where the van and truck were housed. Gone now, replaced by a smart modern house with a row of ornamental pears along the fence line, furred with buds. Heath used to park the ute outside in the driveway, she remembered. She thought about her nights with Hollywood in that ute. Hollywood who would always be part of her story, no blotting

272

him out even if she wanted to. Hollywood, possibly in the Pilbara now, possibly drinking himself to death.

Anyway, this was definitely Heath and Lorna's house, older than Joan's, with a casement window jutting out from the bedroom, brick steps up to a square, solid porch. The big old fence was the same one, but grander without the hedge rambling over it. There were hydrangeas on the east side. The tulip tree was still in the centre of the front yard, looking beautiful even without leaves, better than it had looked in her memory, being used mostly as a leaning post for truck parts, old tyres and general refuse. There were standard roses around the house, not Lorna's unkempt bushes. These were pruned to knobs by someone who knew how to do it. Hellebores beneath the roses, claret heads nodding at the ground, and miniature hedges winding around flower-beds. There was a weeping cherry starting to blossom and a birdbath inside a low circle of box, where once had been only poxy weeds masquerading as lawn.

Marnie walked up to the fence to get a better look at the garden and see if she could place the rooms that overlooked it. The main bedroom was clear enough, and the sitting room. Her office was there. Underneath the office window, she saw a man weeding around a gardenia. He was bent over, a pudgy backside covered in faded work trousers, a line of flesh showing between waistband and windcheater. It might have been Heath, except of course Heath had never gardened, and only mowed when the grass was so long you could lose your car keys if you dropped them. In her time, it was usually Bomba who mowed. Bomba loved the Victa.

Marnie watched the old man straighten his back and pick up his bucket of weeds. His salt and pepper hair was thin on top, curly around his ears. His thick-rimmed spectacles, chrome-coloured and chic, took her by surprise. He was looking directly at her now and she knew him at once.

'My, my,' said Marko, removing his gardening gloves and dropping them in the bucket. 'Look what the cat dragged in.'

32

No, he had never sold up. Why would he? Marko, large as life and twice as sardonic, took her on a whirlwind tour through Heath and Lorna's house to the kitchen.

It was not the house she remembered, although there were familiar elements—even some of the old furniture was there. The muddle was decisively obliterated, the nicotine-stained walls were now white. 'Biscotti,' Marko corrected her. The drapes were gone, it was all roman blinds now, folded up at the tops of windows so that light came in everywhere. The carpet was gone—what an improvement! The floorboards were golden.

'When did you do all this? You were overseas.'

'Oh, you know, boomeranged back like a Millennial. Broken relationship—back to Melbourne. Between jobs— back to Melbourne. Lockdown in Germany—well, that was the clincher. I thought, what's the point, we're all going down in a pandemic, why fight it? I'm sixty. I was at the time,' he corrected himself. 'Now I'm sixty-two. Which makes you sixty-four.'

'Very nearly, thanks for the reminder. I never thought you'd hang around.'

'You might be overestimating me. I think I'm flattered.'

He left her in the kitchen while he changed his clothes. In the silence, she took in the restoration all over again. The deco cornices, the furniture that skated between the 1940s and the 1950s, it all managed to look harmonious. The kitchen table was, of course, Formica. The chairs were iron-framed, kidney-shaped, covered in hard vinyl. There was an old Mixmaster like an anvil on the benchtop. The floor in the kitchen was linoleum squares, black, brick, bone.

'Tea or coffee?' Marko reappeared in a smart shirt, hair combed, looking ten years younger than he had looked five minutes earlier. His neck was red. Was he nervous?

'Where are her books?' she said.

He showed her the living room, furnished with Lorna's chairs, re-upholstered. The treadle sewing machine was under a window, polished up: a curio. Three prints of ballerinas, the kind that had been in every house in the 1950s, hung side by side along one wall. The old bookcases were painted white, there were fewer books, interspersed with cloisonné boxes, Royal Doulton animals, also an elaborate silver beer stein.

'I had to chuck some, they were too near the briquette heater.'

Marnie lifted out *Lorna Doone*. She heard Marko take a breath. 'Sorry,' she said, replacing it.

'No, it's fine. All good. Dombey's still there.' He pointed. 'I wanted to throw out *The Hound of Heaven*, but it wouldn't let me.'

'You read them?'

'I don't read. I look at pictures.'

She gave him a look. He said, 'What?'

'You can read!'

'I'm better at listening. You were the reader. I was the comic relief.'

There was a moment between them. She wanted to hug him, but didn't.

She noticed movement on the other side of the room and glanced over at a long, low TV unit, blonde wood, late 1950s. The TV screen seemed to be showing a nature show. She looked closer and realised it was, in fact, a shell. What she was seeing was a pair of stodgy cats, curled together as one, two square faces blinking at her through curved glass.

Marko said, 'My fur babies. Do *not* laugh.'

Otto and Heinz were street cats. He had adopted them from a shelter in Germany, brought them back to Australia, put them through vaccinations, a flight, quarantine. Now here they were.

'I thought you'd be into exotics,' she said.

'More fool you.'

They sat together at the kitchen table and drank coffee. He congratulated her on ditching Gerald.

'He ditched me,' she said.

'Were you sorry?'

'I can't remember. Yes, for a while.'

'You're allowed a minute's grief for Gerald, but even that's fifty-five seconds too long. He was a tool.'

'Thanks.'

'You had abysmal taste in men. That's one of the many things we had in common.'

'You never fancied Gerald.'

'Shit, no. I finished up with a dancer, hazard of the job. Seven years though, record for me.'

'And now?'

'I'm telling myself I'm over relationships. Who the fuck did your hair, by the way?'

She told him about the recent past, was defensive about her hair, which, she reported, had made her look like Annie Lennox at an eighties night in a country pub and she'd won a prize.

'There is so much in that story I want to unpack,' he said drily. 'But let's not dwell. You need work.'

'Thanks, I actually came here to have my self-esteem walloped.'

'You never had self-esteem, gorgeous,' he said. 'That's why Heath gathered you in.'

After that, it was all banter. He was the old Marko in so many ways: smart, guarded, occasionally candid. He said he wasn't surprised about Eleanor. 'Well, she dressed like an apprentice junkie when she was at school.'

Marnie felt herself recoil. 'Steady, you're talking to her mother.'

Marko stopped speaking at once. It really was Marko, she thought. He had a conscience, never could carry off ridicule.

278

She said, letting him off the hook, 'Anyway, that was her Goth phase.'

He said, 'Silly me. That makes all the difference.'

The cats, both boofheaded tabbies, strolled into the kitchen and he introduced them. He spoke to them in German, and they listened as if they understood. He made jokes about them but when they climbed onto his lap, she saw his fingers exploring their cheeks and ears and their soft chests with tenderness, saw them lean their big heads on him and rub their faces in the palms of his hands.

'You can stay here,' he said to her, not making eye contact. 'I've got four bedrooms. Couch-surfing is never something you should brag about down at the dole office. Although admittedly it goes with your hair.'

'Will you give me a break?'

He said he was only jealous because his hair tended to go down the plughole after every shower these days. He said he was looking more and more like Friar Tuck.

She said, 'Still got the sewing room?'

An instant softening. 'Got all her stuff. Patterns, bolts of cloth, photos of all the wedding dresses she sewed up, so much petticoat netting I could cover the Westgate Bridge with it— who uses petticoat netting anymore?—the whole shebang. I call it the Lorna Woolley Soft Furnishing Memorial Room. If you stayed, you wouldn't have to sleep there.'

'You did.'

'Thought I was in heaven, honest to God. Such a douche.'

On the wall behind Marko, Marnie saw a cluster of coloured tiles with sayings on them. She remembered each one—the

St Francis prayer, the Irish Blessing decorated with shamrocks, a funny one with a monk holding up a glass of beer that read, *Oh Lord, make me virtuous, but not yet.* Another, with a picture of the sun peeking out over clouds, that had been on the toilet wall, above the roll holder. It said, *The prayer of a humble man pierces the clouds.* Funny that these, too, had been so lovingly kept.

She put her cup on the table. 'Thanks,' she said. 'It's so weird being here—good weird—I'm a bit overwhelmed.'

'Me too.'

Later, they exchanged phone numbers. Marko walked her to the car. She said, 'It's really nice of you to offer me a bed, but—I think it'd be hard for me, and for you.'

He was visibly relieved. 'I didn't want to say anything,' he said. 'But when you put your coffee cup on the table beside the coaster, I literally felt my arteries hardening.'

She kissed him. 'I still love you, Marko,' she said.

'Yeah, yeah. Piss off.' Then he added in a grumbling way, 'I'll get my OCD under control for your next visit.'

When she climbed into her car, he said, '*Komm bald wieder,*' which she took to mean goodbye. His Heston Blumenthal spectacles were fogged up.

The solicitor's office was in Carlton, a gloomy room at the back of a terrace shop which sold expensive and mostly useless giftware. Marnie held her nerve while she went through the initial paperwork, and watched the solicitor's arthritic hand scribbling notes. His name was Richard Tregonning—well past retiring age, she thought, curly white hair, smile creases around his eyes. She thought, why is he still doing this? He had to endure all the stories, sort a path through a morass of dysfunction. He would never go home with a song in his heart after sitting in a drab office with people like her. She thought, maybe he's a weirdo, has a gambling debt, a couple of ex-wives, several entitled adult children with cocaine habits. But he looked at her every so often, straight into her eyes, and once he smiled at her.

She tried not to ramble, hearing Rhi's advice in her head. She held on to Sheenie's sheet of paper but didn't look at it. Yes, she was told, going on the history as she had related it, a court may decide that a parenting order should be made in Marnie's favour.

'How long have they been in your care?' he said, looking at his notes.

'Well, this time, since April. But before that she was living with me. We helped each other. I mean, I helped her. She became pregnant again, and then she had a new boyfriend, and they took the children interstate.'

'Not the father.'

'Not. Yes. I mean no. Sorry.' Marnie said, more slowly, 'She doesn't know who.' It was hard to keep speaking. It sounded like betrayal. She said, 'She hasn't stopped me from seeing them. I don't want to mislead you. They went away and I couldn't follow because the borders were closed.'

'Is she trying to stop you now? Do you think?'

'She's not answering my calls. Her phone might be lost…' She couldn't finish her sentences. What was happening to her? She said, 'Sorry.' And then, 'I don't mean to keep saying sorry.

It's just that everything sounds confusing and it makes me embarrassed because I can't just answer you. Simply, I mean.'

He waited a moment longer. Marnie waited too. Then she said, 'You probably can't do anything until they're found.'

Mr Tregonning said that there were several things they could do and went on to list them: they could put in an application for a location order, and a recovery order if it became necessary. He said it was customary to attend dispute resolution before commencing legal proceedings, but without the mother this was not an option and there could be an 'ex parte' interim hearing, he would seek to list it as urgent. Did she feel the children were in danger? She told him that the police had flagged the case as high risk. She said she worried that it might be an overreaction.

'Do you think it's an overreaction?' he said, one eyebrow slightly raised.

She said she wasn't sure. There was a short silence in the room. He looked at her, not expectantly, she felt no pressure to speak. So she told him that Lenny had taken no extra clothes, socks, pyjamas, nothing for the children to change into, no nappies for the baby. She pictured Frankie while she was speaking, Frankie frightened in a new place—and what sort of frightful place it might be—not knowing where the toilet was, maybe wetting herself. What would Lenny put on her if her undies were wet? Who would be there to help? She said, 'No, it's not an overreaction.'

She explained that Michael had been placed into his father's care. Of course, it had impacted Eleanor. She would fight to keep hold of the other two. She agreed that Lenny's ability to care for her children was compromised. The feeling of treachery crept up again while she spoke. In the end, she said, 'My daughter loves them. I don't want you to think she doesn't. I don't doubt it, I never doubted it. She loved Michael, too. He was a loved child, he still is.'

The solicitor said, 'But your daughter's habit comes first.'

She couldn't answer. It was obvious anyhow. She looked at her hands.

Richard Tregonning said nothing. She knew he'd heard it all before. He knew, as she did, that love was not enough.

33

Nights were the worst. Loneliness settled over her like a weight that evening while she sat in her car in a shopping-centre carpark. This particular night was possibly the worst yet. Talking to the solicitor about the children had brought them into the forefront of her mind and she couldn't get them out. There was nothing for her to focus on, to plan for, she had ticked off the items on Sheenie's list and now the little pleasure hit of the achievement was gone. Now it was just graphic premonitions of disaster.

She sent a text to Lenny with a love heart.

How are you doing? How are the kids? Thinking of you.

She looked over the traffic of texts from Colleen and sent a cheery one to her.

Nothing yet but all okay. How are you?

There was a new text with no ID which began:

Hello, my name is Margaret and I'm writing on behalf

She thought it was spam and nearly deleted it when the name Von caught her eye, so she opened it.

Hello, my name is Margaret and I'm writing on behalf of my mother Von Concannon. She wants to say thanks for looking after everything also please don't worry she understands & feels it was her fault for leaving old meds in the cupboard and the Lord's Prayer says lead us not into temptation. She would be happy to hear from you. Tip and Puss look well and thanks. I will also tell you there is a jar of coins missing she does not want me to say it but I feel you should know. There is no need to pay anything back it was right out on the bench. But thank you for the money you left under the vase. I've told Mum she should keep it. We are sorry for your trouble.
Margaret Herbert (Von's daughter)

She wanted to call Von, but not now. What could she say? How could she do justice to such understanding? And why did it make her feel bitter? Also, she did not really want to get into a discussion with the daughter, who might pick up the call for her mother.

Later that night, when the carpark had emptied, a security guard tapped on her window and told her to move on, they were putting up night barriers to stop hoons. He did not make eye contact with her all the time he was speaking.

She drove out onto the road and parked in a nearby street. She ran through her options as she listened to rain drumming on the roof.

She should go around to Marko's. Maybe. Was she

being an idiot for not taking up his—let's face it, not very generous—invitation? Probably. But it had been years since they were close, you couldn't resurrect a relationship in five minutes. Maybe it would never be resurrected; it was a flimsy thing, two people thrown together by work, by circumstance, by Heath Woolley.

She spent the night near the swimming pool again. In the morning, a brief swim and a longer shower. As she dressed she saw herself in the mirror through Marko's eyes. Wet hair didn't help. She'd make another list with *Haircut* at the top, but she needed to hold back on spending until her Centrelink payments were readjusted. She combed her hair, put on face moisturiser and what remained of her make-up and went to the police station to inquire after her report. Had they heard anything? A young constable narrowed his eyes into the middle distance and told her that if they'd heard anything they would have contacted her. He was inexperienced, she knew. She was not going to be intimidated by him. She could see, in fact, that he was intimidated by her. By her age, her shabby appearance, and by her asking things he couldn't supply a ready answer for. She said, 'It's my daughter and my grandchildren. You must understand how worried I am. I'm not here to mess up your day.'

He backed down slightly, a mental regrouping, you could see in his eyes. He said, 'You need to get home and have a cup of tea and just calm down.'

'Thanks,' she said, and nearly walked away.

Then she turned back. 'But that's a facile thing to say. Sorry, but it is. If it was your children missing, do you think you would be glad to hear someone say that to you?'

'Sorry?' he was startled by her resistance, it made him bristle. His apology was just another regrouping, the forerunner of confrontation. Of course he didn't have children, she should have known better than to take that line with him. But she kept going.

'Tea isn't going to help,' she said. 'I'm just telling you, so you know for next time when someone comes in. I can't give you the right answer, I don't know it. I'm just telling you that what you said is the wrong answer, and it's belittling.'

She had spoken gently, she thought, but she saw the barriers go up behind his stare, could imagine him disparaging her in the tearoom later, when he could indulge his hostility. She walked back to her car and sat there for a couple of hours listening to the exchange replay in her head, with variations.

In the evening, seeking company, she went to a meeting.

It was at a hall in Footscray. People on chairs, a circle two rows deep, and a hot-water urn steaming on a trestle table against a side wall. She made a coffee. A man standing at the table offered her a biscuit.

'First time?' he said.

She shook her head.

'Good to see you.'

She took a back-row seat, near the door, thinking she might walk out if it got too much. But it didn't. Rather than making her unhappy, the meeting made her sleepy. She drank her coffee and listened to familiar keywords, stories of sickness and loss, partners and children. Someone spoke of wanting a miracle. This was a newcomer speaking for only the second time—it was pointed out—angry at the world, outraged by the madness of his situation, scoffing at tropes and at the acceptance he was hearing from other speakers. Acceptance was passive, it did not fix lives that were unravelling. People who accepted things were waiting for a miracle, he said, and would never get it. You had to make your own miracles. He wanted them to all wake up to it, to get busy and force a solution. Otherwise what was the point of meetings like this?

There was a short silence, then another speaker, and another. They asked Marnie if she'd like to comment. She waved her hand in the negative. But while the meeting continued around her, she thought about what she might have said. She could have told them the story of Lenny leaving Michael, twenty-two months old, in a locked car behind the Collingwood Woolworths one summer morning before going off with a Stanley knife and robbing a 7-Eleven. And how, coming back to the car forty minutes later after a short detour to her dealer, pockets full of cash and drugs, she found an ambulance and a dozen onlookers, a police officer smashing in a passenger window of her car while another pulled the child out. That while they stood there remonstrating with her, the police received a call about the robbery along with a photograph and were able to arrest her on the spot. Lenny put up a struggle, a not-very-effective one since she was already off her face, and the onlookers cheered while she was handcuffed. 'It isn't even a hot day,' she kept yelling at them. 'He was just fucking asleep!'

When they read the medical report out in court, there was

an audible wave of anger. It described the temperature inside the car as reaching thirty-three degrees and Michael in evident distress. He had been hospitalised for three days following the ordeal. Yes, the car had been parked in shade but Lenny had not accounted for the movement of the sun. During the police report there were snorts of laughter, because Lenny's protests were repeated by the police prosecutor verbatim, in a deadpan voice. *It isn't even a hot day. He was just fucking asleep!* It was the insanity they were laughing at, Marnie knew, the brazen stupidity of it all. And they could afford to laugh on this occasion, because Michael hadn't died.

At the end of the meeting she slipped away. When she was back in her car, she switched on her phone and saw two missed calls. Caller Unknown. No point fretting. She switched on her engine and at the same time her phone lit up and commenced its repetitive patter. Colleen. She answered it.

'Well, hallelujah! I'm totally done with talking to your message bank.'

'Sorry.'

'Any news?'

'No. That's why I haven't called. Sorry.'

'Okay, shut up and let me speak. I've got a proposal. From Brian, both of us.' Brian, now? Not good-mate Sheenie? The relationship was consolidating. Colleen added: 'We're moving in together.'

'Wow.'

'Don't say quick work, or I'll frigging detonate. We've heard it. What do they think we are, teenagers?'

'Well, congratulations—can I say that?'

'He's in his sixties, and I'm fifty-seven. Seize the day, right?'

'Right. Sure.' She was thinking of ways to end the conversation and felt guilty about it.

'So, he's got a spare house. It's only little but we think you should come and live in it. It's in Pimpinio, which is getting to be okay, bits of it are. It's not Edenhope but it's close to Horsham and the house is little but renovated, nearly fully. I'd live in it like a shot, but I need to be close to the salon, so he's coming here.'

Unbelievable. 'You're offering me a house?'

'I'm getting in early because Von is still talking about you coming back there. So look, Brian wants you to have it free, for the first six months I thought, then we can work something out. Don't say no without thinking about it.'

'I don't know what to say.'

'Yes!'

'But I don't know what's happening, it could be ages.'

She could hear Sheenie's voice in the background.

Colleen said, 'I know, I know, Brian's telling me to dial the pitch down, so just think about it. We want you back, mate, whatever happens. Okay? You'll think about it?'

Marnie said she would. She tried to say the right things, to be grateful, feeling that she could never match Colleen's intensity.

When the call was over, she sat still for some time. It wasn't a miracle, but it brought hope crashing in, jackhammering around on her bedrock of dread that she'd got used to. It wasn't a miracle, miracles shouldn't be unwelcome, in fact it was unsettling enough for her to want it to go away. Whatever happens, Colleen had said. That was presupposing Marnie could survive a calamity.

She returned to the backpackers for two nights, but only stayed for one. It wasn't that there weren't older people there, there were travellers of varying ages. They were friendly even, some of them. But the whole place made her feel sad and she couldn't sleep, which rather defeated the purpose. She checked in at the police station each morning, then drove around randomly in the afternoons.

She found a second-hand book exchange and bought two books that she had difficulty concentrating on: *I Capture the Castle*, a hardback, yellow with age and *Plainsong*, a newish paperback, fuzzy at the edges. The first was too sweet to bear, a fairy tale, a story for a happier time. She had read it aloud to Lorna once, but the pleasure she'd taken in it then was not available to her now. The second spoke to the emptiness inside her, spoke to the cold outside the car that seeped in around the door edges and moved through the windows like a ghoul when the engine was off, even now as the calendar clicked across to spring.

But with this book she found her reading space finally, read it through twice, and then read chapters separately. It comforted her, and it validated her. She wanted her mother suddenly, hopelessly, to read the book to. She would say, 'Just listen, Mum. You'll like it. I know you will.' And her mother would listen patiently, because she had been asked to. This mother, Joan but not quite Joan, would not look for excuses, but just listen. And after a while they'd talk about the characters, and then Marnie would bring her mother up to date on Eleanor and the children, and they would think about the situation together, without reaching a solution—because there wasn't one that could be reached, they both would know it—and Marnie would be comforted.

34

She went back to Richard Tregonning's Dickensian office on the appointed day. He made a plunger of coffee for them both.

'My office assistant retired recently. I should have explained that to you when you came. I'm slower over the paperwork than her.'

Marnie wondered if he were about to tell her that it was all a mistake and he couldn't help her.

'She was with me for a longer time than I was married,' he said, pushing the milk jug across his desk to Marnie. He explained that his wife had died thirteen years ago, when they were in their late fifties. He'd never remarried. He had two moderately successful sons who lived in different states. He had grandchildren whose visits he quite enjoyed. He was winding down his practice, well, he guessed that was obvious to her. Just a few cases to keep his hand in. 'I hope that's not off-putting,' he said. 'I'm sincere in my interest. I hope you understand that.'

She said she did, although she didn't particularly understand why he had chosen this moment to disclose so much personal detail. It unsettled her.

But the moment was past. The solicitor was telling her now that he had prepared documents for an urgent ex parte interim hearing he hoped would take place next week. Marnie tried to focus. She wanted to stop him speaking while she found her notebook and pen. The information was too fast and too foreign. The application, he said, would be listed down the track.

'Application for...' She was embarrassed interrupting him.

'Parenting orders? We spoke of it previously.'

'Yes. I'm sorry.'

'Don't apologise. What I want to explain is that it will take time, but that's to be expected. The urgent hearing—which will be much quicker if all goes correctly—is for the location order, do you remember we discussed it? So that we can get information from all available sources. Like Centrelink, where an address for your daughter will certainly be recorded.'

'What if it's the wrong one?'

'We'll deal with that too. This is step one, Mrs Odell.'

She nodded and said she understood, which was partly true.

He told her that he had prepared an affidavit from their first interview. But before she read through it and signed it, he would like her to write a summary for him. Just events that she could remember, concerning her daughter and the children. He could do it from an interview with her, but he wondered if she might be able to think more clearly if she typed it herself. A summary of the last, say, ten years. He pointed her to a second desk with a computer, behind the door of his office, facing into the room. It was his assistant's desk. If Marnie was comfortable there, she could sit for the afternoon. He would not get in her way.

Marnie switched on the old desktop computer, watched it light up and whir pleasantly, restfully, unobtrusively. For the next two hours she typed and thought, while the lawyer sat at his large desk facing the door, working at his own computer. He took two phone calls, his voice quiet enough that she could not follow his conversation. He went out and brought back sandwiches to share. She sent him a copy of what she'd written when it was finished and tried not to watch him reading it. He read it through slowly, then he nodded and thanked her. He asked her to wait while he finalised the affidavit. That took half an hour; Marnie was glad she had a book in her bag.

When the paperwork was finished, the solicitor invited Marnie to read it. Finally, it was signed and she was free to leave.

'It was nice having you here,' he said. 'My assistant and I had larger digs, but we kept our adjoining door open most of the time. I seem to work better with someone around.' He shrugged, then told her that Rhoda was now caravanning around Australia with her husband and a brand-new whizz-bang metal detector. They were living their retirement dream.

'I'm happy for them,' Richard Tregonning said. 'But I'm also quite certain there is nothing I would like to do less.'

She left the solicitor's office in the early evening feeling irrationally heartened, and drove to Maribyrnong. Marko opened the door to her with a cat under his arm.

'Oh, thank Margot,' he said. 'Get in here.'

They drank hot chocolate in the kitchen and she took care to use the coaster. She nursed the cats one at a time and then, when they insisted, both together.

She listened to Marko apologising to her. 'After you left,' he said. 'I felt like excrement.'

'There was no reason to.'

'I beg to differ and so does my shrink. I spent three days mentally self-flagellating about being snooty and offhand and distant and obsessive and then I phoned my shrink and told her how I'd been an arse to the nearest thing to a sister I ever had and she said Well, what is it you want from this relation-ship?—she never gives a straight answer, that's the deal, I'm used to it. So I spent another two days thinking about it and then, just as I work it out, I open the door and there you are. It's either magic, my higher power, or a coincidence.'

'Which?'

'Well *now* I don't care—what am I, Catholic? Crisis over.'

She was laughing but really it was more like trying not to cry. It was his remark about her being the nearest thing to a sister that shook her up. She took a breath and held it. 'Okay, apology accepted. All done.'

'Oh no, no, not so fast. Apology delivered, restitution still required, I know how it goes.'

'Now you're being silly.'

'Silly or rational, sometimes it's hard to tell them apart, am

I right? So show me some pictures of these grandchildren. I want to know what I'm looking for.'

She opened her phone and swiped through a dozen pictures. He asked questions about each of the children, including Michael, found features that reminded him of Marnie. He listened as she described Frankie's pragmatism and Koa's bluster. She pointed out features that he might not otherwise have noticed: Frankie's perfect, square little teeth, the broadness of Koa's hands. Her phone was nearly flat. Marko plugged it in for her next to the kettle.

'Where've you been sleeping?' he said.

'At a backpackers.'

'Marnie, are you going through a midlife crisis?'

'Unexpected compliment. I wasn't expecting to live to one hundred and thirty.'

'Don't be a smartarse. It's tragic. And it reflects very, very badly on me.'

She let Marko bring her bag in from the car and put it in her old office, now a bedroom with immaculate walls, a place for hanging her clothes, a small desk and a TV. There was an indentation on the clotted-cream bedspread where the cats had been sleeping.

'They like this room for morning naps, they follow the sun around the house,' he said. 'You'll need to keep your door closed.'

For dinner they ate soup, followed by fruit. Marko said he had to watch his cholesterol and was trying to wean himself off cheese. She loaded the dishwasher for him, and suspected he was longing to offer advice, but he didn't. When she went to the toilet later, Marnie called out to Marko, 'What did you do with the toilet-roll ballerina?'

'It's in the tip,' he called back. 'I would have kept it for you if I knew you wanted it…No, I wouldn't. There are some things that need to be laid to rest forever.'

In the dark, on a firm mattress with crisp sheets, she remembered Heath coming into that very room more than forty years earlier, holding out papers for her to sign. 'We're organising to adopt Marko,' he said. 'I need you to witness my signature, then we'll go up to Lorna and see how we go there. That could be a problem, I don't think she can hold a pen anymore. But there'll be a way around it. Stat dec or something.'

He was frowning, uncharacteristically. She didn't question him—well, it wasn't her place. She thought, I'll ask Marko about it, because of course she was curious. But she didn't do that, either. She never found the right moment. Marko must have known. He must have agreed to the arrangements, but there were only small differences in how he was acting. If anything, he was quieter. He'd been ensconced in the sewing room for a while. He'd started cooking. The kitchen was tidier. He'd asked for, and received, a new washing machine for the laundry and a new iron and ironing board. Once she overheard Marko reminding Heath about what the doctor had said, he had to cut down on carbs. No, wasn't that earlier? It must have been, because Hollywood was there and overheard. Hollywood smirked at Marko—'Geez, you his old woman now, or what?'—and even in her fevered state of desire for Hollywood she knew he was being malicious. Was it after that when Heath sent Hollywood away?

Anyway, she said nothing. She didn't even tell her mother the news about the adoption, but later she realised Joan already knew. She must have. Joan was a certified JP, because of her job at the pharmacy, and had witnessed the stat dec. So all discussions had taken place, all conclusions had been reached and all solutions put into motion by the time she'd seen the last of Hollywood, had trawled North Melbourne looking for him and finally come to accept that he was out of her life for good.

Now, in the unsettling tranquillity of Heath's house, she felt mystified all over again. Perhaps now she could bring it up in conversation, hear Marko explain how it all came about.

Maybe not. Some things weren't her business. Some things needed to be laid to rest forever.

35

The next morning when she walked out into the kitchen, Marko greeted her with the news that the Queen had died. It had been on the radio overnight. Marko always slept with the radio on, he said, a habit he'd picked up from Heath. He said he wasn't sure what he felt about it. She was old, why wouldn't she die? But he felt something—weird, dislocated, unsettled. 'Feelings, huh?' He went off to the sitting room to switch on the TV, and Marnie's phone started buzzing.

It was seven-thirty. It was a call from Rhiannon.

Marnie thought, now is the time to stop burning bridges. Now is the time to show loyalty to the ones who have remained loyal to you, before it's too late.

She said, 'Rhi.'

'The police are here looking for you.'

This was unexpected. She said, 'How?' Then she remembered she'd given them Rhiannon's address and began a hurried explanation which Rhi continued over the top of.

Rhiannon said, 'You need to speak to them now. It's urgent. I'm putting them on.'

A new voice. 'Mrs Marnie Odell?'

'Yes?'

'The mother of Lenny Odell?'

'Yes.' How was her heart able to suddenly sprint? How was her voice so high and distant?

'We've been trying to call you. We have someone answering your daughter's description at Box Hill.'

'Box Hill?'

'Hospital.'

'Are the children with her?'

Marko was back in the kitchen now, eyebrows raised. She put the phone on speaker for him, and they sat listening to background voices until the first voice came back on. 'Child Protection has been called in, I'm told.'

'Box Hill Hospital. I can go now? Can I get them?'

'We need to establish identity. There's no identification with the person in question and she is currently unconscious.'

'Thank you,' she said. 'Thank you, I'm driving there now.'

Marko said, 'Tell them it'll take you an hour. Traffic.'

'It'll take an hour,' she parroted.

Rhi's voice again: 'Okay?'

'Rhi, I'm so sorry. I have to get to Box Hill Hospital.'

'Stop apologising. It's getting on my tits.'

A sudden panic: 'Are the police still there? I didn't ask about her properly—is she okay?'

'They've gone outside. Just get in the car, I'll see you there.'

301

Marko drove; he said even a crap driver like him would be better than Marnie at the moment. She sat in the car in silence as he navigated his Skoda through snarls of morning traffic, Brunswick, Fitzroy, trams, intersections, until finally they were on a freeway with a clear run to Box Hill.

He dropped her off at Emergency. 'I'll find you,' he said. 'But it's looking like I'll have to park on top of Mount Dandenong, so don't wait. Where's your girlfriend?'

Marnie pointed out Rhiannon who was standing at the entrance. She was in a stretchy green skirt with peacocks on it, black tights and biker boots. Her dreadlocks were spectacular.

'O...kay,' Marko said. 'I'll find you. I'll follow the smell of patchouli. Good luck.'

She didn't see him drive off. She didn't even see Rhiannon, just felt a hand dragging her through the door. 'It's not crowded, this is a good day,' said Rhiannon close to her ear. 'Did you eat breakfast?'

'No.'

'I'll get you a juice, it could be a long wait. Here.' She called out to a hospital worker. 'Marnie Odell—the police rang her to come.'

There was red tape to go through. Rhiannon was not allowed in. Marnie put on a mask, squirted sanitiser on her hands, answered questions, produced ID. Someone came to take her away. She glanced back and saw Rhiannon in the distance. She had the urge to apologise again, but managed to overcome it.

She was ushered along a corridor of curtains. She thought

for the first time, Eleanor is dead, and it stopped her in her tracks, the breath knocked out of her. But curtains were being parted and she was being guided into a green space, the curtains drawn around her again. A female police officer was there. There was a woman with a partly bandaged head lying on a bed, attached to a drip. The face under an oxygen mask was drawn, putty-coloured, dried blood in the hairline; the inside of one arm exposed a Celtic knot from wrist to elbow.

'Is this your daughter?' a voice said. 'Is this Lenny Odell?'

'Eleanor,' she heard herself say.

The story unfolded in fragments, delivered by seemingly random people who came into the cubicle to run obs from time to time. The fragments assembled into a list in her head.

1: Eleanor had collapsed at Box Hill train station.

'Not uncommon,' a nurse said. 'You pull in there on the train most mornings and there's ambos ferrying someone away. Gets like a conveyer belt.'

Another hospital worker, changing the drip, told her the next bit.

2: The stroller had rolled towards the tracks and a PTV officer leapt forward and grabbed it.

She must have reacted to hearing that, because she was pushed backwards into a chair where she sat for some time counting her breaths, one for in, two for out. A bottle of juice appeared in her hand. 'Your friend sent it in,' a voice said. Marnie held the bottle but did not open it.

A police person came in and sat beside her, checking details, giving out a little information.

3: *Eleanor had been in possession of a commercial quantity of methamphetamine.*

Did Marnie know anything about that? She shook her head. The police constable said that it was possible she'd been co-opted to pass the package to someone on the station, which is why she was waiting there. They were studying security footage from the platform. So far, they knew she'd arrived on the station at 6.23 a.m., pushing a stroller. She had waited twenty minutes, gone off to McDonald's, returned with a thickshake, and seven minutes later she collapsed, hitting her head on the edge of a metal seat on the way down.

Marnie received the information in silence. Perhaps taking pity on her, the police officer added that CPS had been notified about Marnie's arrival. They were coming along soon.

'With the children,' said Marnie, finding her voice.

'Not sure. They're running a health check, I think.'

Messages pinged into her phone. Marnie couldn't focus on the screen well enough to read them. What she knew was this: Eleanor was not dead. Child Protection had the children, possibly here in this hospital.

Other details played out in Marnie's imagination while she sat in that muffled cubicle. The one that kept repeating itself was an image of the stroller accelerating towards the platform edge. She fixed her gaze on Eleanor to stop the vision. The dried white stuff around Eleanor's mouth, Marnie realised, was regurgitated thickshake. Her hair on the non-bandaged side of her head was lustreless. The machine by the bed changed numbers from time to time. Someone nearby, in another cubicle, was crying 'Help' over and over.

'BP and pulse are taking a while to come up,' said the first nurse on a later visit. 'We're finding her a bed. She's done a job on herself.'

'Has she been conscious?'

'Not yet. But she's ticking along. It can be like this.'

As if Marnie didn't know.

Before leaving the cubicle, the nurse opened Marnie's drink. 'You're not a good colour yourself,' she advised. 'We don't want two casualties.'

Marnie drank some juice.

Later, a tall woman with creaky shoes came in and said, 'Are you Mrs Odell, Lenny Odell's mother?'

The woman said, 'I've got someone here who'll be relieved to see you.'

Marnie followed the sound of the woman's shoes along a corridor, into a lift, another corridor. Once, the woman said conversationally, 'Did you hear about the Queen?' and she nodded. They eventually came to an office with frosted windows. When they went inside there was another woman there. Koa was on her knee, wearing Frankie's pink and yellow poncho.

He looked at her, pupils enlarged, forehead creased, then his whole face screwed up. He exploded, spitting and choking as he struggled out of the grip of the social worker and lurched towards Marnie, crawling because the poncho kept tripping him up. She dropped to the floor to reach him and he bit her shoulder as he collided with her, grabbing up handfuls of her skin, his chest heaving. He roared at her, one hand digging in at her throat, the other in her hair, yanking and yanking it. She rocked him, her arms folding, unfolding, refolding around him, trying to catch all of him up at once. He was like a boa constrictor. 'It's okay, bubby, it's all right. Ganny's got you.'

She looked up at the social worker and said, 'Where's Frankie?'

The woman frowned slightly. 'There was only one child.'

4: *There was only one child.*

36

Later, she was surprised at how calm she remained. On the
advice of the social worker, she called Rhiannon, who was
in the hospital café with Marko. They both came. Rhiannon
was clear-eyed, at her best in a crisis. Marnie had never
seen Marko's face so serious. The two had been unknown
to each other and now they were working as a team, two
brains to replace hers, which appeared to be in a kind of stasis.
Marko swiped through Marnie's phone and found the photos
of Frankie that she'd shown him the night before, so they
could be uploaded to VicPol; Rhiannon took notes as it was
explained to them what they were going to do from this point.
She also asked questions that were sensible, and seemingly in
tune with the situation.

Who was the child's guardian when the father was
deceased and the mother unconscious? Was it automatically Marnie, or did someone need to be appointed? A police
officer called Bridget received the photos, took more details,

and confirmed that the situation had been escalated. It was a missing child now. It was a priority. If Frankie wasn't found by the end of the afternoon, it would be on the radio and the TV news, she warned Marnie. Be ready for that, Bridget said.

Rhiannon phoned Richard Tregonning because Marnie was still unable to speak. Rhiannon said she needed legal advice; plus, maybe, if he thought it was a good idea, a copy of all the documents to prove that an application for a parenting order had been commenced. Marko phoned Sheenie and got him up to date. Eventually the talking slowed. People moved out of the room.

Marko said, 'First major mistake of the day, I brought my car. We need the kiddie car seats out of yours.'

Rhiannon upended Marnie's bag and found her keys. Marko took them and left the room.

'Where's he going?' said Marnie.

'Getting your car so you can take Koa home. I'll stay here with you. You never told me you had a brother.'

'I don't.'

'Not what he said. I'll get the explanation another time, don't try to speak. Life's like bad macrame sometimes.'

Marnie couldn't make sense of that. She thought it must have something to do with knots.

Rhiannon said, 'Marko's nice. If he was straight, I might have asked him on a date.'

'The solicitor is.'

'Yeah, no, thanks anyway. The lawyers I've rooted were clueless in bed.'

Rhiannon stroked Koa's forehead; he rubbed his face in

Marnie's chest, rejecting the touch. 'He knows where he needs to be,' Rhiannon said.

'Is Eleanor conscious?' Marnie said suddenly, sitting up. 'If they wake her up she can tell them where she was living, that's where Frankie is. Actually, I'd better tell someone—'

'It's okay. They know.'

'But has she woken up yet?'

'Someone's with her.'

'Can't they wake her?'

'She has a head injury, Marnie. It's serious.'

'How do you know?'

'They said so, you heard them.'

Marnie had no recollection. She tried to think back over previous conversations but couldn't get far. 'What time is it?' she said shifting Koa into a more comfortable position. He was nearly asleep, red and sweaty, in need of a wash, one hand inside Marnie's shirt holding tight to her bra strap.

'Two-thirty, just after. Been a long day already. Not over yet.' After a moment of silence, Rhiannon reached across to the desktop in front of her and patted out a rhythm.

'Bongos,' she said. 'It gives you something to do to pass the time.'

Marnie watched Rhiannon's hands. Koa lifted his head and watched too, mesmerised.

Marko's house transformed. It seemed to shrug off Marko's orderliness and revert to Woolley chaos within a day of Marnie bringing Koa into it. It was raining again, so Marko brought in clothes racks to hang things on in front of wall heaters. The cats skulked. A bag of nappies spilled open on an armchair. Rainbow teddies performed ellipses in the dryer.

Marko went out and came back with a portacot and a stroller. Like Heath, he was a keen op-shop user, but said he drew the line at food-encrusted baby gear. He also purchased, new, an expensive night light that projected moving stars onto the ceiling and played ten types of mood music.

'Really?' said Marnie.

'If he doesn't want it, then I do,' Marko said. 'I'm pretty sure this is a game changer for my sleeping habits.'

Koa cried when she left his sight. 'It'll pass,' she said, in case it was getting on Marko's nerves, but he showed no irritation. He went through Marnie's suitcases, pulling out children's clothing which he deemed useful or not, mostly not, then went shopping for more.

'You don't have to do this,' she said.

'I want to,' he said. 'So—is it okay?'

When Bridget, the police officer, came by in the early evening with an offsider, Koa climbed onto the sofa and squeezed himself behind Marnie's back, clutching fistfuls of her shirt.

Bridget reported to her that all surveillance footage had been examined, they were satisfied that Frankie had never accompanied Lenny and Koa to Box Hill. Working backwards, she said there was clear vision of Lenny with the stroller boarding a train at Flinders Street station to get to Box Hill. She had arrived at Flinders Street on a tram from Docklands. There was also footage of her arriving at the Docklands tram stop, having crossed the footbridge. They were checking through locations in Lorimer Street now. There was some evidence of squatters in a disused factory site alongside the freeway.

When the police had gone, Marnie phoned the hospital.

'You okay?' said Marko, passing with an armful of washing. 'Not a good colour.'

She nodded, and waited, bracing herself as she was handballed through departments. What she eventually heard was that the drug screen had confirmed high levels of heroin in Eleanor's system, consistent with a problematic batch that was circulating. Her general bloods showed anaemia, changes in her platelets suggesting malnutrition. Her liver numbers were predictably poor. She currently had scabies, so it was likely the children did too. (Marnie wondered how Marko would react to this news.)

Eleanor was now conscious, her breathing normal, her BP and pulse still low. She was, however, not showing any sign of being aware of her situation. She had been assessed by a neurosurgeon and her brain function was deemed to be within normal range, although they could not yet rule out the possibility of hypoxia. They wanted to know if Lenny had ever had a brain scan, for comparison purposes. Marnie thought it was unlikely.

The voice on the other end of the phone told her it would take a while to build up a profile of Eleanor's intellectual function. The head injury was of concern, and could be responsible for some degree of memory loss that may or may not be permanent, but Eleanor was now considered stable. Marnie was welcome to visit at any time.

'Do you want to go in?' Marko asked, when she relayed the report. He was already stabbing through his phone, trying not to react to the news about the scabies, but she could tell he was having an internal meltdown. He found a graphic photo on Dr Google and held it up to her.

'Does she look like this? Is this going to happen to us?'

'No, and no. Marko, it's not like that, it will be all right.'

'I'm sorry.' He sat on the couch beside her. 'I'll cope better in a minute.'

'You are coping. I don't know how I'd be managing without you.'

'Thank you,' he said, standing abruptly. 'So now I'm off to the chemist for scabies lotion, which is a first for me. I've texted Rhiannon, she's coming over, we've decided you shouldn't be alone.' He pointed to Koa. 'Just keep Typhoid Mary out of my bedroom.'

On the way out the door, he hesitated and turned back to her, slightly guilty. She thought, he will ask me to leave, or at least when am I planning to leave. He's had enough.

Marko said, 'Okay, silly question, but can cats get scabies?'

'I don't know. Maybe ask at the chemist?'

'Right. Good. I'm off.'

37

In the early evening, Marko drove Marnie to the hospital. Rhiannon stayed back to mind Koa, who was asleep with a new dummy in his mouth. A police report on the radio described a missing three-year-old girl, last seen in inner Melbourne. Marko reached over to turn the radio off, but Marnie stopped him.

'They said this would happen,' she said. 'I'm glad they're doing it.'

But it made her feel disconnected, too. Made it difficult to think. She left Marko at the hospital entrance and took herself up to the neuro ward, where she was shown to a hospital bed in a shared room. Eleanor was sleeping.

Marnie sat beside her daughter and watched her. She had Joan Guest's utterly straight nose, and a spot under her right eye that was her own. It had appeared when Eleanor was nearly one, grown a little as she grew, and then stopped. The doctor said it was benign. They used to call them beauty spots, he told her. It really was beautiful, Marnie thought, even now it bestowed something classical on her daughter. She held Eleanor's hand, the nails marked with traces of purple nail polish. Eleanor liked everything purple when she was little. 'Poorpoo,' she would say, pointing out clothing, toys, lollies. 'I want the poorpoo one!'

Now her eyes opened slightly. She heaved herself from her side to her back and said, with a dry mouth, 'Shit.'

'Hey, baby,' Marnie said.

'Mummy?'

'I'm here.'

'Tell Gran...'

'What? Tell her what?'

Eleanor did not reply, she closed her eyes again. Then she said, 'My cigarettes there?'

'They won't let you smoke, honey.'

'Can you just buy me some? I won't say anything.'

'I can't. Sorry.'

'You never...' A moment of stillness and then she roused herself. 'Do anything I want.'

Marnie leaned in and said, 'I've got Koa.'

'Huh?'

Marnie eased her mask down a little way, to speak more clearly. 'Koa's with me, he's safe.'

'...kay.'

'Where's Frankie, honey?'

'Huh?'

'Where's your house?'

'Wha...?'

'Where Frankie is. I want to see Frankie.'

'With my mum,' Eleanor said, as if it should be obvious.

She opened her eyes and looked at her arm. 'Whass sis?' She was trying to see what the tube was attached to but couldn't turn her head. She dragged her hand across the cannula.

'Don't honey, you need it.'

Marnie waved to a nurse outside the door, who came inside and helped her wrest Eleanor's hand away.

'You need it, you have to keep it in,' Marnie said to her.

Eleanor began to cry. She said, 'I want my mum, can you get her?'

'I'm here.'

'No, my mum. I want my mum.'

Outside the hospital, Marnie called Marko and told him she was ready. He was at Shoppingtown, killing time. He said he'd be fifteen minutes. While she waited, Marnie called Gerald and filled him in.

'Jesus,' he said eventually, sounding petulant—unless she was judging him too harshly. 'I'm not sure what I'm supposed to do, Marn.'

'Nothing, it's okay. I thought I should tell you.'

'I spoke with her a few months ago. She told me she was going to live with you.'

'I'm more worried about Frankie. Eleanor's being looked after.'

'How old is the kid? Five?'

How she detested him for that offhand question. The kid.

She said, 'Frankie's three and a half, Koa's one and Michael's eleven now.'

'Jesus,' he said again. 'I barely know them. What's the little one called again?'

'Koa.'

'What's that about?'

'No idea.'

'Anyway, look, this is not my fault. She never wanted to come up here. I can't come down, I've got a knee replacement in three weeks, in a fair bit of pain here, Marnie. We both had Covid at Easter, everything had to be put off because of that.'

'It's okay, I wasn't asking you to come down.'

He was on a run. 'Those people who say it's like the flu are talking crap, it's way worse. Now there's this long Covid. We're both pretty worried about getting that.'

'Hopefully you won't.'

'Jackie still works three days at a linen shop up the road. She doesn't want to have to give it up.'

'I'm sure she'll be okay.'

'We're planning on getting to Bali for my seventieth, we don't want anything getting in the way.'

Why had she phoned him? He was no help, and never would be. She said, 'Well, take care of yourself then, and good luck with the knee.'

There was sudden warmth in his voice. As if, absolved of a need to do anything, he could allow himself to be familial. 'Thanks Marnie. Good to talk to you. Thanks for ringing, listen, she'll be all right. She's tough. So will the kid, if she takes after her mother. It'll be okay, it always is.'

Until it isn't, Marnie thought, ending the call. She texted Rhiannon to find out if Koa was still sleeping. He was. She was glad to see Marko's headlights flash at her from the street.

They took a detour to Docklands on the way home and drove up and down Lorimer Street, because of what the police had said. It was a wide, straight road with a line of young eucalypts up the centre island, flanked on one side by asymmetrical apartment towers, and on the other side by flashy businesses. There was a stifled feeling about the place, no pedestrians. The Bolte Bridge was suspended in air ahead of them, lines of coloured lights moving across it. They passed an unused lot with two brick buildings on it. Old posters flapped raggedly from a temporary fence at the front. Police tape was draped across a drive-through entrance.

On the second pass, Marko pulled up. 'Are we going in?'

'Looks like the police already have. Are we allowed to cross the tape?'

'Not sure.' He added, 'Look at us, all law-abiding.'

They sat in the car for several minutes.

'There's no sign of life,' said Marko eventually. 'I'm not sure we'll see much in the dark.'

But it seemed senseless to drive away without at least trying. Marnie got out of the car and walked the length of the fence. Inside the boundary was a brick building covered in graffiti and scrubby-looking potato vine, all the same dun colour by night. Further in, there was a smaller building that seemed thoroughly sealed. The windows in the larger building were smashed or boarded up. There was a smell of garbage and human waste. She wondered why she was

317

there—did she think she would sense Frankie? Was that even rational? She walked back to the car. They drove home in silence.

Back at Heath and Lorna's house, they drank mint tea with Rhiannon. Marnie was aware of looks being exchanged over her head. Eventually, after talking about the royals for a while, Marko brought in bags from his shopping expedition. He unfurled cot linen and expensive shoes for Koa, a trench coat for Marnie, boots, tights, and a navy dress.

'You can't do this,' she protested.

'Au contraire, it's what I can do,' he said.

'You don't even know my size.'

'Oh, you're kidding me, aren't you? Thirty-five years in wardrobe departments—you think I can't get someone's size in about three seconds? Anyway, it's all end-of-winter-sale stuff.' As if that made a difference to the significance of the purchases.

Rhiannon said, 'Not me, but this stuff is definitely what you need for court. And, face it, there'll be a court appearance somewhere down the track. Actually, I'd probably wear the coat.' She stood up and put it on, making too much effort to be congenial.

Marko jerked a thumb at Rhiannon. 'What she said.'

'Okay, but no more.'

'Well, one thing more—'

'No, Marko!'

'You've got a haircut tomorrow up the road. She owes me. I made Snugglepot and Cuddlepie costumes for her twins. They won a prize—naturally—now she wants to do my hair free for the rest of my life, but this will discharge the debt, I told her. Nine-thirty.'

Rhiannon said, 'Just say yes, you don't have to think about it. And he won't do this again, am I right?' She looked at Marko, who shrugged.

Marnie knew she should thank him. Why was she angry? With both of them? She felt ganged-up on, powerless.

'I like my hair short!'

'She's not going to make it long, is she? Just shape it up.'

'I like the person who cut it for me.'

'It's not about loyalty, it's about…I don't know…Doing something for yourself.'

Or for you, Marko, she thought. She wondered if he was embarrassed by her appearance, if that was at the bottom of all this. She wondered if she even liked him.

'How important is it, Marnie?' said Rhiannon quietly. Marnie simmered. From the TV came the sound of sombre voices singing God save our gracious queen. Behind that, the creak and wail of Koa waking.

38

The next morning, there she was, wearing her new trench coat over old trackpants, with Koa on her knee—which annoyed the hairdresser and gave Marnie a futile sense of revenge—having herself 'shaped up'. She could not engage in hairdresser chat. The only feelings she could summon up were resentment and desolation. Koa cried for the last five minutes and she didn't apologise for it to anyone in the salon.

Outside again, she pushed Koa to the car. He wanted to be held, so she nursed him while he ate yoghurt. She phoned her police contact, Bridget. She liked the name, and she liked Bridget's reassuring, matter-of-fact voice. Bridget looked at you directly, the way Mr Tregonning did. She did not look at other people and say things with her eyes. Bridget told her they had found evidence of children living in the Lorimer Street squat quite recently, but it looked like the place had been vacated in a hurry.

They had picked up a backpack. Bridget texted through a

photo while she was speaking, but Marnie did not recognise it. There were tissues in it, a comb, a drink straw, anonymous empty pill packages, tampons—everything about it said it was owned by a female, at any rate. Bridget said she would bring it over to Marnie later in the day: 3-D was better than 2-D, she said. Marnie phoned the hospital next. Eleanor had eaten breakfast. She was talking about someone called TJ.

TJ—why would Lenny mention TJ all of a sudden? Marnie wondered if she should phone TJ herself. Would he need to know what was happening? Did Michael ever ask about his mother? She drove aimlessly around and found herself in Niddrie, parking her car opposite Treen's and staring at a window display less dazzling than she remembered. It was mostly blue. Plastic tubs, baskets, linen, a shelf of glittering tiaras. A large beach towel with an image depicting Queen Elizabeth's head on a postage stamp was taped to the window, dead centre.

As she watched, Trinh came outside with an armful of miniature Union Jacks. She was thinner, but it was definitely Trinh. Marnie was out of the car without thinking about it, extricating Koa and darting with him in her arms across the road.

'I thought I wouldn't see you again,' Trinh said, and hugged her.

There was a new girl behind the counter. 'Accountancy student,' Trinh said. 'Good worker.' She offloaded the Union Jacks into the girl's hands while ushering Marnie down the back, adding in less than a whisper, 'But still a bit scared of customers. Patsy—too friendly. This one—not friendly enough.' She shrugged, pulled a plastic truck off a shelf as she passed it and put it in Koa's hands.

They sat in the back room among cardboard boxes full of stock, knees almost touching in the muffled space. There was green tea and caramel snows. Koa lay against Marnie, turning his truck over and over in his hands.

'I thought you were sick,' Marnie said.

Trinh flapped her hand. She had a hysterectomy, she explained, fibroids. She took a long time recovering. It was all right now, or getting that way, at least. She had had time to think, and she'd laid down the law to her grand-daughter. Now she was seventy-one, she would not be working full time, she would not be picking up the children after school, they would have to do before- and after-school program like other kids. 'I'm having time for me. Just a little bit,' she said. 'Maybe a holiday. Maybe see some of the country—I've never been out of this city. That's crazy! Maybe I'll go home to Vietnam for a visit to my sisters. You come with me,' she said. 'Your company I can put up with. Tom will do us a deal on tickets.'

The surge of happiness, illogical and unexpected, that rushed through Marnie, all the flooding warmth of anticipation. They talked about the world they had not seen. 'Even Sydney,' Trinh said. 'I haven't even seen the Opera House! What's the matter with me?'

'You've been looking after too many people.'

'Once you start they won't let you stop, that's the thing we have to remember.' Trinh nodded to her, as to a compatriot.

When Trinh started asking questions about Marnie's life, she feigned an appointment and got ready to leave. She said

322

her daughter was in hospital, that was all she could manage. She promised to come by again. After that, she drove to a park and watched Koa sift through damp tanbark and push at swings until he was cranky. Then she drove back to Marko's.

'I'm all right,' she said, throwing her bag on the couch and passing him with Koa asleep in her arms. 'I'm sorry, Marko, I just need to lie down.'

He said nothing. She went into the little room that had once been her office and lay with Koa on the bed for the rest of the afternoon. She could hear Marko, his footsteps on the floorboards, backwards and forwards going room to room, speaking to the cats, sometimes in German and sometimes in English. She heard him make a phone call, his voice restrained. At some point she must have fallen asleep, because after a while she experienced the strangest sensation of being kissed on the side of her face. She felt that she was awake but couldn't seem to open her eyes. She tried to speak. 'Mum? Is it you?' She knew that was what she wanted to say but it wasn't coming out. She said, 'Where are you?' and then she was driving the big removal truck. They were all there, all the boys. Bomba—didn't he die?—Iceberg, Marko, Sheenie. Hollywood was there, only he was hiding They were on a hill. Below them the road narrowed to a creek and beyond the creek it was too dark to see. Marko said from the back, 'It's your turn, kiddo, we've all had a go, just hold the wheel steady.'

She did, but then the entire steering wheel lifted out in her hands and the truck gathered speed. 'Woo-hoo!' Bomba said.

'It's not funny! It's not a joke!' she shouted as the Bedford careered towards the bushes, and she woke abruptly just before impact.

Koa was no longer in the bed with her. She ran out into the living room; looked up the hallway. From the mat inside the front door, two cats looked back at her, startled.

Koa was in the kitchen, on a towel on the floor with a tea towel tied around his neck, being fed macaroni cheese by Marko, who was also on the floor.

'We need a highchair,' he said, seeing Marnie in the doorway. 'This system sucks.'

'How long have I been asleep?'

'Long time, a couple of hours. Your phone just buzzed, it's on the couch I think. Sorry, getting down here was hard enough. My foot's gone to sleep. Are you okay?'

'I woke up too fast.' She went back to the living room. 'Was it a call or a message?'

'Message, I'm guessing.'

Marnie found her phone but couldn't find her glasses. She went into her bedroom and rummaged around under the bed, brought them out and looked at a message from Vincent Russo.

> *Can you come here please. Grandchild dropped off.*
> *Sylvana*

Her fingers fumbled over the keypad prompting Autocorrect to go into nonsensical overdrive. *Comingling wait ea der cling*

She took a breath and corrected it. *Coming wait please I'm coming.*

'Marko!' She was in the kitchen. He looked at her and said, 'Just go. He's all right here, I'll call Rhiannon.'

He shouted after her as she headed for the door. 'Where do you have to be?'

'Niddrie,' she said, and heard him repeat the word with wonder.

A few hours earlier she had been here, two streets away, drinking tea with Trinh. When Marnie pulled up outside Vincent's place, the street was as anodyne as she remembered. Vincent's house with its sloping driveway, the neat front lawn, low brick fence, bland letterbox.

But Vincent was at his door, waving to her. Then his sister was pushing past him. 'Here! Here!' Marnie ran up the path to the door and followed them down the passage to the wide family room with the kitchen that looked out at the granny flat, the plum tree, the Hills hoist.

There on the couch, white-faced, with a man's dressing-gown around her, was Frankie.

Sylvie had already called the police, the police had called an ambulance. She tried to explain it all to Marnie in the several minutes before the house filled up with people in uniforms. Two people had arrived, Vincent had told his sister: a man and a woman. They came to the door with the address on a post-it note that they'd got from a wallet.

It was Eleanor's wallet. There was her licence, coffee cards, Medicare card, a dog-eared pension card, an ATM card, an assortment of rubbish. The skinny woman was carrying Frankie, Vincent said. She put her down on the floor and

Frankie just lay there. They put the wallet on the kitchen counter; kept saying they didn't want trouble. Frankie had been left at their place because she was sick, they said. They hadn't taken her, they didn't want the police to think that's what happened, they'd just been there, all in the same house, and Lenny never came back.

The post-it was decorated with Easter eggs, and the writing on it was Marnie's. She remembered scribbling her address down that first day, when Eleanor had shown up at Treen's.

Vincent was animated, more than usual. He said, 'I knew who it was because she saw the cat and started meowing. Just lying there, trying to touch the cat, but she didn't look right. I'm thinking: that's Marnie's little grandkid, the little girl, I'm thinking: I better not let them take her away, they didn't look all right, no offence, but they ponged. They go: can you call us an Uber? I go: I'm phoning my sister, so wait a second, and they just went. They ran.'

'Because they thought you were phoning the police,' Sylvie said. She added, 'He hasn't done anything wrong, Marnie.' She lowered her voice slightly. 'Okay, he's a bit on the spectrum, but he's not—he wouldn't do anything bad, I promise you. I promise!' Sylvie's face was red, her prominent eyes hot and tearful.

Marnie nodded. She held Frankie tightly. The child turned her face into Marnie's front.

'That's why I called the police,' Sylvie added. 'When he phoned me I came over straight away. I thought we should try to get hold of you first, but then I thought waiting would look bad. I had no idea she was connected with you, it was

Vinny who said it.' She looked desperate. 'I wish I'd seen those people, I wish I could have made them stay because... oh God, how will the police believe us?'

'They're here,' said Vincent, lifting up the front-room curtain and calling back through the house. 'Police and ambulance.' He came down the hall to the family room. 'It'll be all right, Sylv. It's okay.' He turned his face to his sister. His kind face. He said, 'Looks like the latest model Ford Ranger.'

Sylvie nodded, already on the phone to another brother, telling him the story. She said, 'Sorry I gotta go, come over home, bring Tony. Right now.' Assembling the troops in case they were needed, Marnie thought. And yes, the troops would come. When Sylvie ran to the front door, Marnie watched her smoothing her hair back over her ears, heard her clear her throat. Her voice, when she opened the door was low and grave. Marnie thought, Marko is right, you need to look okay to talk to people. Too late for her, unfortunately, she had slept in her clothes. She didn't even have the smart trench coat to pull across her shirt. Her newly neatened hair was flat on one side.

Bridget came into the room wearing a mask, straight over to Marnie. 'All good?' she said. Marnie nodded. Then there were masked ambulance officers kneeling on the floor in front of her and a whimper of alarm from Frankie. Soothing voices, no one trying to take Frankie from her. Marnie thought, I have to phone Rhi and tell her. But at that moment she couldn't move.

She phoned Rhi and Marko from the Royal Children's. Frankie was dehydrated and was put on a drip. She had a

327

temperature so they took blood and a urine sample, and a suspected wrist fracture for which they gave her pain-killers that made her sleepy, and wheeled her down to X-ray. Marnie walked with her, talking to her. Bridget walked beside Marnie. People stared at them because of the police uniform. The two women sat together in their masks watching Frankie's wrist being plastered. Bridget left after that and Marnie sat on for what seemed hours. Then they came to get Frankie and she followed the gurney up to a ward and watched them move Frankie onto a bed, still asleep.

Marnie thought, now while nothing is happening she should text people, let them know, Sheenie and Colleen at least. She could phone through to Box Hill and leave a message for Eleanor. *Both children well*, her message would be. *All okay, all safe*. Then she remembered Eleanor didn't even know there was a problem. Eleanor could wait.

In the evening, Rhiannon and Marko arrived with Koa. Koa was dressed in rust-coloured overalls and a navy shirt, with clean white socks and leather shoes—the expensive ones that Marko had brought home from his shopping spree. Koa looked utterly not himself, Marnie thought, but beautiful, too. He climbed onto the hospital bed saying 'Ak-ak-ak,' and hit Frankie on the head. When she started to cry, so did he. For a while the room vibrated with rage and outrage. Marko was baffled by it. Marnie saw his face and felt a bubble of laughter rising in her. Rhiannon whistled and clicked her fingers at the children to distract them. Two unflustered nurses appeared at the door. 'Everything okay?' said one of them.

Rhiannon looked at Marnie, who couldn't speak, she was laughing too much. Rhiannon said: 'Yeah, it's cool. We've got this.'

39

Richard Tregonning came to Marko's house a couple of days later. Marko took his coat and offered refreshments, tea, coffee, Scotch with ice. He was playing a deferential role for Marnie's sake: touching, but a bit obvious.

The solicitor accepted tea and sat down with Marnie while the children played on the floor in front of them. The application for a location order was now not needed, but he had proceeded with the interim application for a recovery order so that the children would be put officially into Marnie's care. She told him Eleanor had been moved to a neurological rehab. Her memory loss was not significantly improved. It would be a long time before they would know if it was permanent.

'How does it seem to you?' he asked.

'She knows names, but she doesn't know what happened.'

'Asking for the children?'

'Not yet.'

'What if she does?' said Marko. 'Will they give them back to her?'

Richard Tregonning wasn't sure about answering, you could see it. He looked from Marko to Marnie.

'It's all right,' she said.

'Your daughter can make an application for a parenting order, just as we're doing. There'll be the usual requirements,' he said.

Marnie told him her plans. She was going back to the country, as soon as Frankie had her follow-up cast check. She would come back whenever he needed her to, of course. She would come back regularly to check on Eleanor. It's just that there was a house for her up there, from a friend.

'Another brother,' said Marko, sitting down on a nearby chair. Deferential or not, he had no qualms about invading her personal space. He said to Richard, conversationally, 'Has Marnie told you about her brothers?'

Richard Tregonning looked at her and she said, 'I'm actually an only child. But my first job was with a man who employed boys who were at risk—that's the way they used to put it, there's probably a new term for them now. Anyway, it was a special program. Some of the boys were straight out of detention.'

'His name was Heath Woolley. We were his juvie boys,' said Marko. 'And Miss Marnie—or Caroline, Heath called you that sometimes, just to confuse everyone. Helluva joker, Heath. She did the paperwork and most of the legwork— inductions, invoicing, kept tabs on us, took us shopping for toothbrushes and work boots, got us our tetanus shots. Some of us became model citizens.'

'Not all?'

'Well, that'd be unrealistic, wouldn't it?'

'Are you enjoying this?' said Marnie. She turned to Marko. 'I really don't think he wants to hear it.'

'I don't mind,' Richard said.

'Thank you.' Marko made a told-you-so face at Marnie and said, 'She's a good person, she helped a lot of people when she was young, what goes around, comes around, right? That's why there's a house for her up there, from Sheenie, and why there's a house for her here, with me. Of course I'm a complete headcase to live with, there's always a price.'

Richard Tregonning looked at Marnie with interest. She said, 'Okay, shut up, Marko. And I didn't do anything, I was employed, I did what Heath told me, it was my job.'

'Too late,' he said. 'I'm on a roll.' To Richard: 'Marnie and me used to visit my adoptive mother together. She spent her last years up the road in a nursing home with Parkinson's. Marnie read to her.'

'And Marko was the comic relief,' said Marnie, repeating his words. 'He wasn't, though. He was brilliant. The way her eyes lit up when he came in the room, that was amazing, you should have seen it.'

Richard said, 'What did you read?'

Marko answered promptly: '*The Hound of Heaven.* You know it? It's a poem by some English dude with repressed sexual problems like you would not believe—do your head in.'

'We read heaps of stuff,' Marnie said. 'It changed my life, actually.'

'Dombey-whats-it,' Marko said.

'Dickens, yes, Eliot. Thomas Hardy—'

Jonathan Livingston Seagull.

Marnie looked at him askance. He was defensive. 'I bought it for her from a book exchange, the lady told me it was famous. *I* read it to her, not you. That's why you don't remember, it was when you were off bonking Voldemort.'

Could he get more embarrassing? But what was the point in being shocked. Richard wasn't. He seemed entertained.

Marko added, 'And Lorna told me she loved it, so sucks to you.'

'Captive audience,' she reminded him.

'It was poetic! I was dead proud of myself, reading that.'

'What else did you read to her?' Richard Tregonning asked Marnie.

'Oh, I don't know.'

'She does,' said Marko.

'Books from the forties, right up through the sixties. All Lorna's books, not mine. We read a Patrick White.'

'Did we?' said Marko, seeming impressed.

'My first one. *Riders in the Chariot.*'

'Zero recollection.'

'It's up there.' Marnie stood and pointed out the book on the shelf. She turned back to Marko and Richard Tregonning with triumph, and saw the whole house differently.

The children on the floor were part of it, Frankie with her plaster cast decorated with glitter, rainbow teddies, the new clean walls were part of it. Behind them, old walls covered in stained wallpaper were still there: dim photographic negatives,

333

the way they used to come jumbled in a tracing-paper sleeve so that you could look right through the layers. Life upon life was there—Lorna at her sewing machine, brides with bare feet wearing shiny frocks turning this way, that way, boys lolling in doorways trying to be cool, Bomba doing a handstand on the living-room carpet because being cool didn't matter to him, smoke spiralling from ashtrays, Heath young, ageing, old, foxtrotting Lorna in the kitchen, throwing Eleanor in the air and catching her—negative upon negative, a palimpsest into which Marnie herself was inscribed. The vision was overwhelming.

40

That evening Rhiannon came around, as she'd done most evenings. She was in her uniform with its council logo on it—cargo pants, polo shirt, sensible shoes. Before Josh, she had been an optometrist, now she did home help. The children ran to her and she swung them around, kissed them and put handwoven bracelets on their hands. She had a bracelet for Marnie and one for Marko. Marnie was sure that Marko would dislike his, but he put it on and examined it. His only comment: 'Are we all in a club now?'

'I did a workshop,' Rhi said. 'Weaving's good for you.'

Marnie left them and went to visit Eleanor.

Eleanor's neuro-rehabilitation hospital was in the outer east, a fair way out. The drive made Marnie anxious. She thought of the random roads she'd taken with the children all those months ago, the way fears played out in her head while she drove and magnified into behemoths during the nights.

Richard Tregonning was confident that there would be a parenting order in Marnie's favour. Where would that leave Eleanor?

The hospital was old-style with fawn-coloured walls, a wooden rail along the length of every corridor on both sides, wheelchairs outside the doors. The staff checked Marnie's ID. She was given a mask and directed to a room where Eleanor was sitting in a chair wearing trackpants and fluffy mauve bedsocks, and watching *Married at First Sight*.

'Can I turn it down?' Marnie said. 'I brought you some things.'

Eleanor whined a protest, so the sound remained up.

Marnie put down her bag of gifts—washbag and pyjamas, a new hoodie with a fox on the front—then sat and watched the television with her daughter. Mostly, she watched Eleanor watching it. Eleanor had begun to fill out—puffy cheeks instead of hollows—and her hair was chopped short, probably to match it up better with the part of her head that had been shaved and stitched. There were shadows like bruises under her eyes. Her fingers and wrists looked doughy, her bitten fingernails were painted dark green. At this moment, she was completely engrossed.

Marnie opened a bag of jelly babies and offered it. Eleanor took a handful without looking away from the program. 'You're gunna get dumped,' she growled in a warning voice, startling Marnie, until she realised Eleanor was talking to the TV. Another time, Eleanor said to someone on the screen, 'Face it, she's just a cunt.'

'Hey, don't say that,' Marnie said.

Eleanor grunted but did not look around. Marnie had bought a picture frame at Treen's with three spaces in it. She had printed out pictures of the children on Marko's printer and put them in the frame, which was decorated with stars. When the program finished, she gave the frame to Eleanor, who stared at it for a moment, then pointed. 'Who's that?'

'Mikey, honey.'

Eleanor frowned at the image.

Marnie said, 'He's eleven now.' She took a breath. 'I texted TJ and told him you were in hospital, and he sent it through for you.'

In the past there would have been a reaction. Eleanor said, 'He looks weird.'

'Oh, no, he's just older. Still cute. You can see he's yours, Koa's got the same mouth, and his eyes are like Frankie and you. Gran said your eyes were like the ocean, remember?'

'Fucking awful teeth.' The photo showed Michael in school uniform with large front teeth, crossed over in the middle.

'Well, he might get braces. TJ said he's good at music, remember he told you Michael's learning piano? He helps out on the farm. They live on a farm, remember?'

Eleanor tossed the picture frame onto her bed. 'Yeah, nice,' she said. 'Hey, can you take me out in the courtyard? I can smoke there, but I gotta have someone with me.' She stood up, reaching for a walking frame that Marnie had not noticed. She saw that Eleanor's hands had a tremor, that she rose to her feet awkwardly, leaning on the handles of the walker, that her trackpants had been pulled up crookedly and the seam was skewed to one side. She wanted to straighten it, to make her daughter neat, to comb her hair. Should she have got that new hoodie in a larger size? She didn't want her daughter to stress about her body, of course she would probably gain weight, with three meals a day and not much to do.

'Bring the lollies,' Eleanor said. 'My smokes are over there,' pointing to the bed stand. They walked along the corridor to a courtyard and stood in cold night air while Eleanor smoked. The whole area reeked of butts. After a while, Marnie said, 'Did you hear the Queen died?'

'Uh—yeah.' Sarcastic.

'I guess they'll put the funeral on TV,' Marnie said. 'I'll probably watch it. It's weird, the end of something big. It feels sad.'

'It's all going to shit, you watch.' Out of nowhere, Eleanor was animated. 'The knives'll come out now, Meghan Markle wants to bring them all down.' She shot Marnie a look for emphasis and said, 'I'm pissed off for those little kids. Prince Louis's the best one, I love him. He's all, Don't tell me what to do! I hope he gives them shit. Harry's no good, I feel sorry for his brother. Him and Kate want to be friends, but they're doing it in a respectful way, and the other two just want everything their way. She does, anyway, and she's poisoned Harry. He used to be my favourite but he's a loser.' She pushed her walker over to a terracotta plant pot filled with sand and drove her cigarette butt into it. 'It's the kids that suffer,' she continued. 'They're the meat in the sandwich, it really breaks your heart.' She was moving to the door now, heading back inside. Marnie watched her daughter for a few moments before following her, getting ahead, holding the door open. Eleanor passed her without comment. She called out to someone at the end of the corridor. 'Hey, Dickhead!'

A staff member wearing blue scrubs raised his hand to her. 'Hi, Lenny, how's it going?'

'Same shit, different day.' She gave a short, fruity laugh—a smoker's laugh, keeping up her slow pace back to her room. Marnie walked behind her. She felt hardness inside her. A stone turning in her chest. Would that be the thing in the end—this sneering, feeble distaste? Would that become the full-stop and underline that meant 'finished'?

Still. On the way home in the car she found herself making a list.

a) *Slippers*
b) *Dressing-gown*
c) *Hair products*
d) *New jeans*
e) *Earrings/bangles*
f) *DIY hair colour—purple*

She'd try to get at least some of them before the next visit.

41

Marnie dressed up for her next meeting with Mr Tregonning. Dress, boots, trench coat. Marko approved, she could tell. He stood at the door with the children, and they all waved her away.

At the solicitor's office she drank coffee and told him that the children had a new caseworker, a person she felt she could work with. Mr Tregonning told her he had applied for a hearing seeking parenting orders, and a court date had been set for eight months' time.

'That long,' said Marnie.

'Earlier than some. It's not a bad thing.'

Marnie could see that, and it made her feel guilty. Lenny was still in rehab, but she would be assessed soon for assisted living. Probably a shared facility. Down the track she might be sufficiently recovered to live alone. 'What happens then, though?' Marnie said. 'I don't really understand the process yet.'

'If she's well enough, she'll be served with court documents,' he said. 'Unfortunately, and it's significant, she'll also be charged with drug offences.'

He seemed to be saying that, either way, Eleanor's failures were too significant to be ignored. Marnie wasn't sure if she was relieved or not. She told him she would be looking for accommodation for Eleanor, close to her. 'I know there are places,' she said. 'I think it'll be better for Eleanor to be away from the city. I can visit, and she can stay with us on weekends.' She hesitated. 'Some weekends.'

At the end of the meeting they shook hands and Mr Tregonning walked Marnie to her car. He said, 'We seem to be navigating our way through the labyrinth.'

She said, 'The thing about labyrinths is you don't know until you actually reach the exit.'

He laughed, but Marnie didn't.

Then he said, 'I need to say this. I hope you don't mind. You're not under any obligation to have your daughter live with you, I want to be clear about that.' He added, 'Your daughter doesn't need to have accommodation near you, either. There'll be nothing in Pimpinio. Horsham's a possibility but, I'm sorry to repeat myself, you are under no obligation.'

He pronounced perfectly the name of the place she was going to. Colleen had told her no one except locals ever said it right, with the emphasis on the unexpected syllable. Marnie knew she had never mentioned the name to him, she'd only sent him the information in an email. That meant he'd done some research.

341

She said, 'Thanks for everything. I'm sorry, it doesn't seem enough—just saying thanks.'

He said, 'It's not over yet. As you say. But you can be optimistic, you can allow yourself that.' Then he handed her a book. 'Bought this on impulse.' It was *David Copperfield*, second-hand, bound in leather with original copperplate illustrations.

'My first Dickens,' Richard Tregonning said. 'You always love your first best.'

Marnie drove home thinking about what the solicitor had said about obligation and what Rhiannon had said about solicitors. It was easier to believe Rhiannon.

42

Rhi opened champagne and Marko assembled dip and biscuits. Marnie nursed Frankie while Koa pursued cats from room to room, wearing only a pyjama top and nappy, along with his good shoes.

'To us, I guess,' said Marko.

'To whatever comes next,' said Rhiannon. They both held out their glasses to Marnie and she saw their faces sag slightly.

'Sorry,' she said. 'Don't worry, I'm completely fine.' This was probably not true, but it felt close enough. She was neither jubilant nor dismal, simply crying.

Frankie looked up at her then turned her head away. Marnie kissed the top of Frankie's head quickly. 'I'm okay, honey-kitten, we're all okay.'

'When in doubt, eat,' said Marko, and they all took something off the platter and washed it down with the champagne, which was dry and apple-y.

'You too,' said Marko to Frankie, handing her a cube of

cheese. She took it from him and held it.

'I don't know when I'm going to feel normal again,' said Marnie. 'Do I just drive away now? Don't I have to wait to find out if she's going to be all right?'

'You do what you want to do, you know that,' said Rhi.

'And if I don't know what I want?'

'Wait. Think. When you can't think, just wait.' Rhi shrugged.

'You make it sound easy.'

'It is easy, just not fun. Clutching at straws is fun, by which I mean it gives you a good feeling—like you're doing something, even when you're not. It's also not real.'

Marko put a box of tissues on the table. 'Listen to her,' he advised. 'I pay my shrink a shitload of money to tell me stuff like that.'

Marnie said, 'I owe my daughter something, not to walk away from her in a crisis.' There was no response. Marnie said, 'I took the kids off her. Whatever she did after that, whatever choices she made, I started it off when I took the kids away.'

'She asked you to,' said Rhiannon.

Marnie took a breath. 'I've been saying that, but it's bullshit. I just took them. I did that thing, oh God, Rhi, I did that thing you said. Grabbed at a straw. I took them away because I didn't want to look at them anymore, Lenny and Bray, lying there all over my bed with their crap all over my flat. Off their faces, useless— the kids on the floor, on a doona, both wet right up their T-shirts to their necks, sucking on an empty bottle, both sucking on the same bottle because there wasn't anything else. Maybe I should give my daughter credit, she gave them something, she didn't want them to starve, she put them on the floor so they wouldn't fall off the bed. They weren't even crying—' She stopped abruptly. 'Sorry.'

She thought she should wash down her disquiet, but when she lifted her champagne she couldn't drink. 'I wanted her to be...' She didn't say it, because of Frankie being there. She said, 'I wanted her gone. I need to tell you. I need to tell someone. I wanted it to happen so it would stop going on and on and on. I mean, none of that stuff was new to me, it was the feeling that was new, it was so strong. *No more.* It wasn't even words, it was the feeling of the words. So I took them. And I hoped Lenny and Bray would be too bombed to remember, and if I kept up the lie about them asking me they'd accept it as well as everyone else. Which is the way it happened, exactly like that. I get believed, not her, because I'm ordinary, still got all my teeth, not covered in tatts, middling in everything—education, work, tastes—just Mrs Average Don't-rock-the-boat. I knew, I absolutely knew it would be like that and I exploited it. What does that make me?'

She stopped speaking. It was said.

Marko and Rhiannon looked at each other, then back to her. Rhiannon gave the slightest shrug.

Frankie reached up and patted Marnie. 'Oorwite,' she said. 'It's oorwite, bubby.'

43

Something made her sit up in bed during the night. Frankie was asleep beside her, Koa rustling in the portacot beside her bed. Her phone had woken her. She switched on the bed lamp and found her glasses. It was midnight. There was a message from TJ. The second in as many days after a year of silence.

Against her better judgment, Marnie had stopped all contact with TJ after Koa was born, after Lenny had a meltdown in the hospital about Marnie texting him with the news.

Eleanor had baby boy today. Hope all well with you and Mikey. Just wanted you to know. Best love, M

'Why would you even tell him about me?' Eleanor yelled at her. TJ had sent a text to Lenny, it turned out—congratulations from himself and from Michael with emojis of balloons and a teddy bear. It enraged her.

'He doesn't get to know about my life, Mum! He abandoned me!'

'It was good news,' Marnie protested. 'I wanted to include Michael—he has a little brother now, as well as a sister—'

'Can't you just be on my side once? Just once?' Eleanor sobbed and sobbed, putting out her arms to Brayden, the interloper, who was slouched on a hospital chair, smirking. Just looking at him, Marnie was baffled that the hospital staff had allowed him in. He was frightful. Frankie, strapped in her stroller, two years old, began crying. She was saying, 'Ganny! Ganny!' Brayden, ignoring Frankie, got up and went to Eleanor, swaggering in the role of hero.

'Just tell her to get out. Tell her she has to go,' Eleanor raged.

Marnie didn't wait for him to tell her, she exited the room, humiliated. She didn't even kiss Frankie goodbye, and next day Eleanor and Brayden left the hospital and drove to South Australia. The borders were closed, but they got through somehow. Rules didn't apply to them. They would always do as they wanted.

So now, looking at the text from TJ, Marnie felt crippled with old guilt. TJ wrote:

Hope this plays. 4 U & Lenny. Michael on piano.

There was a heart emoji, followed by musical notes and clapping hands—TJ still liked emojis, apparently—and a video attachment. Marnie clicked on it and there was Michael, gangly, sitting at a piano, playing. Another text pinged in:

Called Tiggy Touchwood. Can play harder ones but wanted this to send you becus knew he cud do it no mistakes. Hes relly good! TJ

347

She watched it twice. Then she got out of bed and went to the kitchen to make tea. Marko, hearing her, came into the kitchen and accepted a cup. They sat at the table together. She said, 'When Frankie and Koa reach twenty-one, I'll be in my eighties.'

'Yep.'

'How is that good for them? I might not even make it that far.'

'Yep.'

'Whatever I did to screw up Eleanor, I don't know what, probably a million things, how will I stop it happening again with them? I can't.'

Marko fetched the biscuit tin.

'Michael is the lucky one,' she said, waving away a biscuit. 'I know that now, he got away from Lenny and he got away from me. He's got the best chance.'

'Yep.'

'Please, Marko, you have to do better than yep.'

Marko told her she didn't have to leave the city. 'I'm getting used to you being here,' he said. 'It was easier than I thought.'

'Easier.'

'Having people around. I always felt after I finished renovating, the house kind of lost something. And bingo, you come along and here it is, back.'

'Chaos?'

'No, life.'

It sounded like romanticising. She reminded him of the nicotine-stained walls, the grimy cobwebbed corners, unwashed sheets, smelly toilet, the kitchen sink filled with dishes. He laughed. 'Heath was a freaking grot, wasn't he? Why did you even take a job with him?'

She couldn't at that moment remember. She said, 'My mother wanted me to do teaching.'

'Why didn't you?'

Possibilities flooded her head. How would her life have run if she'd taken her mother's advice? No Gerald, no Eleanor, no damaged boys. No dead-end job, let's face it. There would have been a teaching degree that might have given her joy, might have led to other things. Would she still have washed up at this spot? Not possible. But there was no guarantee of happiness down that other path either. Perhaps marriage, a child, more than one...

She said out of the blue, 'Why did they adopt you?'

He gave her a swift, hawkish look that made her regret her impulse. 'Got a theory?' he asked.

'No.'

'Most people did at the time.'

'You were nearly eighteen. It just seemed—'

'Unnecessary, I know. Some would say suspicious, even creepy?'

'No!' She wanted to backtrack. She said, 'Look, I asked Eleanor once if Heath ever...She spent a fair bit of time here, with me, when she was little. She went out in the truck with Heath heaps of times, I never thought a thing about it.'

He waited for her to continue speaking, his expression inviting her to continue. It made her wary. She said, 'Why are you looking at me like that?'

'Just interested to hear what she said. I know the answer,

by the way, I just want to hear you say it.'

'She said nothing happened—no, she didn't say it outright, she dismissed it.'

'Is that why you're asking me?'

'I'm sorry, Marko. I didn't mean to imply that there was anything weird going on.'

'It's okay. There wasn't. I know how it looked, but it was simple. They had no family, they both loved me.' He hesitated, then added, 'I didn't believe it either. It was all through my childhood—abuse, bad stuff, I'm not going into it—I started running away at seven, succeeded at ten, lived on the streets, spent time in detention, got released to some crappy share-house for kids no one wanted to foster, the kind of place where all the really broken kids end up, where every pissy thing I owned got pinched or wrecked, and my teeth got knocked out. When Heath gave me a job I was waiting for it to all start up, more of the same, and it never did. I kept waiting. Worst thing that happened was the dentist. You took me along I don't know how many times.'

'I'd forgotten all that. Anyway, it was Heath's idea, not mine, don't blame me.'

'I know who paid the bills, but you sat there in the waiting room every time while they tightened my braces and checked my caps. With your nose in a book.'

'You're welcome.'

'How many visits?'

'I didn't count.'

'On the way home you'd tell me about the book, and I'd make fun of you. What was that weird one?'

'*The Sea, The Sea*. I loved it. You said it sounded like boring shit, and the main character was a stalker.'

'So—you don't remember going to the dentist but you remember the book? How does that work?'

'I remember you making me laugh so much I nearly ran off the road.' It was so clear in her head now, the laughing. The feeling of laughing.

'We went up to Lorna together how many times?'

'I didn't count, Marko!'

'If you'd been the homeless one, I wouldn't have stood a chance. They loved you, too. And your mother—Heath was crazy about her.'

'Huh? My mother worked full time.'

'At the chemist, I know.'

'She was older than him.'

'So was Lorna.'

'What are you saying?'

He could see it in her eyes, her sudden panic, and said, 'Oh, get over yourself. Heath and Lorna loved each other. They loved me. They loved you. They loved your mother. Well, Heath sort of idolised her really, but it wasn't sordid. It wasn't even seedy. It was just life the way normal people live it.'

Marnie thought about watching Heath and Joan through the window of the office, the way they sat together, the way she patted his back, his head on Joan's shoulder in the weeks after Lorna died.

Marko went on, 'And yes, they could have just left everything to me, just put it in a will, no adoption needed. But they wanted me to see it as a commitment, not an impulse.

The big Dean Martin philosophy,' said Marko. 'That's Amore.'

'Do *not* break into song!' She was laughing now. 'And don't wake the children.' After a while she said, 'Why did he call me Caroline? I could never work it out.'

'Derr. Because your mother was Princess Grace, doofus.'

Holy cow. Had she always been this blind to subtext? There was too much that she should ask him. But the conversation was over. And for some reason her impulse to know more was waning as quickly as it had risen.

Marko stood up. 'You can't go back to bed now. Stuff my cholesterol, I'm making cheese on toast, and I'm blaming Heath for my terrible diet. I have to find something bad to say about him.'

Heathcliff Woolley, rescuer of the lost and betrayed, stalwart of the underdog, faithful, dutiful, steadfast, inspiring.

Marnie said, 'He ate like a labrador.'

'Yep, the bastard. He really did eat like a labrador.'

She drove north with the children a few days later. The car was clean and serviced, packed full of things from Rhiannon and Marko, who stood in the street and waved them off, promising visits. Marnie allowed herself to believe them.

She drove through city outskirts, outer suburbs, industrial wastelands, then north over folded green hills with forested gullies that gave way, in turn, to paddocks glittering under the spring sky. The children made animal sounds. She told them it would take a few hours before they got there. They were on their way to an all-right house, Colleen had called it, in an all-right town.

Eleanor complained once that Marnie always settled for second best. But face it, what would she do with best? Squander it, probably. Maybe she'd already had it and failed to recognise it. Best made her think of big emotions that she would never be able to manage. Joy would be a waste of energy. Triumph would be fraudulent. All-right was enough, and there it was ahead of them, as good as a promise. She just needed to grab it and hang on.

The children slept. Marnie watched the road, waiting for the first sight of the mountain range that she would follow to its northernmost tip, and then west. Directly ahead of her a pair of eagles rose, languorous, on flattened wings so straight and so perfect they could have been made of steel.

ACKNOWLEDGMENTS

I wish to thank the following people for advice and information: Patrick Howman, Greta Prozesky, Emrys Le Nay Black, Heather Dunne, Simone Jones, Michelle Hallam.

Thanks also to my husband Daryl Black and his weather-eye over my grammar, and to Katrina Foster, whose observations and insights were always correct and whose faith in my work was a game changer. And to my brother-in-law, Richard Turnbull, who decided that what I needed most in the world was a new laptop, then just bought it for me.

Thanks to Clare Ryan who drove with me around the Wimmera on many weekend outings, awed, like me, by the landscape.

My thanks to Mandy Brett at Text for her warmth as well as her sensitive and skilful editing; to Lyn Tranter and Karen Colston at ALM for their unstinting support.

A special thanks to Danny Watt of Tralee, who took me around the ewes and lambs.

To my children, Victoria and Emrys, their partners and my six grandchildren, who brought the children in my story to life. I appropriated Victoria's dry sense of humour for Lenny.

Finally, I would like to sincerely thank Gwenda and Mal who are always there, along with all the friends of Bill and Lois. You know who you are.

Louise Le Nay